PRAISE FOR
HELEN HARDT

"I'm dead from the strongest book hangover ever. Helen exceeded every expectation I had for this book. It was heart pounding, heartbreaking, intense, full throttle genius."
~ Tina at Bookalicious Babes Blog

"Proving the masterful writer she is, Ms. Hardt continues to weave her beautifully constructed web of deceit, terror, disappointment, passion, love, and hope as if there was never a pause between releases. A true artist never reveals their secrets, and Ms. Hardt is definitely a true artist."
~ Bare Naked Words

"The love scenes are beautifully written and so scorching hot I'm fanning my face just thinking about them."
~ The Book Sirens

Unraveled

**STEEL BROTHERS SAGA
BOOK NINE**

Unraveled

STEEL BROTHERS SAGA
BOOK NINE

WATERHOUSE PRESS

To my brilliant editors—Celina, Michele, and Scott—who made the Steel Brothers Saga better than I ever could have alone. And to all the fans who stuck with me through nine books and believed in the story I was telling. Thank you all so much!

WARNING

This book contains adult language and scenes, including flashbacks of child physical and sexual abuse, which may cause trigger reactions. This story is meant only for adults as defined by the laws of the country where you made your purchase. Store your books and e-books carefully where they cannot be accessed by younger readers.

PROLOGUE

Ruby

"How did you get in here?"

"The same way I got in the other night."

"So you left the book."

"I did."

"You should know. I'm armed."

He smiled, and a spooky recognition oozed through me. His smile resembled mine, right down to the slightly lower gumline on the left side of his mouth. I'd never noticed that before.

"I am no threat to you. I never was."

"Oh...except for the time you tried to rape me."

"That was unfortunate. I was a different person then. I regret it."

"Well, you won't get the chance to try it again." I pointed my gun at him.

"Kill me, Ruby, and you'll never find what you're looking for."

"Maybe all I'm looking for is to send you to hell."

He smiled again, and I gulped back nausea at the resemblance.

"Then do it, Ruby. Pull that trigger. Murder me in cold blood."

I laughed. Actually laughed! "Cold blood? Are you kidding me? This would be the most hot-blooded murder ever committed. But I assure you, I'd get away with it. You broke into my house. Pure self-defense."

"Then what are you waiting for?"

What was I waiting for? I aimed the gun right between his eyes.

"Kill me, though," he said, "and you'll never discover the truth."

"I know all the truth I need. You raped Gina. You tortured and raped Talon Steel. You tried to rape me. You had something to do with the disappearance of those girls I met in Jamaica. You tried to have Brooke Bailey killed for insurance money. And God himself only knows what other heinous acts you've committed or had a part in."

"I had reasons for everything I did, including letting you live all these years."

"I've often wondered about that," I said. "Why didn't you have me taken care of long ago?"

He smiled. "A father's pride."

I scoffed, even though I knew he could have killed me at any time. Still, his statement rang with morsels of truth. "Please."

"It's true. You're strong and determined. I've watched you since you left. I helped keep you safe."

"I kept myself safe, you shithead."

"Did you never wonder why, as a fifteen-year-old girl, you were never caught? Never arrested? Never violated?"

"I stayed under the radar."

"Yes, you did. With a lot of help from me."

That was bullshit. He was playing mind games. I had taken

care of myself all those years. So I changed the subject on him.

"I'm not interested in your reasons for anything you did." I cocked the gun. "Say goodbye, Daddy."

CHAPTER ONE

Ryan

"Mr. Wade was murdered last night."

My veins turned to ice. Not that I gave a shit that the motherfucker was dead, but now another source of information had dried up.

Talon looked visibly relieved. He hadn't wanted to face Larry again. He'd had issues the first time he'd tried it, but my brother was nothing if not strong, and he would have done it. Now he didn't have to.

"Murdered?" Joe asked.

"Yes. And it appears to have been an inside job."

"Another inmate, you mean?" I said.

The warden cleared his throat. "No. Not another inmate. Mr. Wade was in a solitary cell...on suicide watch."

I widened my eyes, and Talon's looked like they were going to pop out of his head.

"Suicide watch?" Joe said.

"Yes. Our psychologist had determined Mr. Wade was a suicide risk. Plus, he'd been routinely attacked by other prisoners. He was fading fast and succumbing to severe depression. So he was put in solitary on suicide watch."

Joe scoffed. "Putting prisoners on suicide watch. Give me a break."

"They're still people, Mr. Steel."

"If you knew what this so-called person—"

Talon gripped Joe's arm. "It's okay, Joe. We don't need to go there."

"We're well aware of what Mr. Wade was accused of. However, he was still innocent until proven guilty in a court of law. He hadn't gone to trial yet."

Joe stood. "I guess our business is done here. We won't be getting any more information out of our dear old uncle."

"Please have a seat, Mr. Steel," the warden said. "I'm afraid our business is far from done here."

"Look. If you think I'm going to shed tears over the loss of that piece of shit, think again." Joe motioned to Talon and me. "Let's go, guys."

I stood as Joe headed toward the door, but a large guard blocked his exit.

"What the hell is going on here?" Joe demanded.

"Have a seat, like the warden said," the guard said.

"Are you fucking kidding me? Get the hell out of my way."

"Joe," Talon said. "Let's just see what the guy has to say."

Joe rolled his eyes. "Fine." He plunked back into his chair. "What is it?"

"Like I told you," the warden said. "It was an inside job. But not by another inmate. A prison guard killed Mr. Wade."

"And we should care because...?" Joe said.

"You should care, Mr. Steel, because I have sworn testimony from two of my guards that you paid them off to rough Mr. Wade up."

Joe's eyes widened. "That's bullshit."

"That's not for you or for me to say. Now, that said, normally we look the other way when this happens. A few beatings don't concern us. But a murder? We have to investigate that."

"I can assure you that my brothers and I had nothing to do with Larry's murder," I interjected.

"Maybe not. But one of my guards murdered Larry Wade. It couldn't have been anyone else because no one else had access. And oddly, one of my guards has since disappeared into thin air."

"So what?" Joe said.

"So this," the warden countered. "It seems pretty plausible that this guard might have been given a sum of money to do Mr. Wade in. A large sum of money. And you three certainly could have come up with a large sum of money."

Joe stood again, raising a fist. "Don't you dare try to hang this on us."

"We already have evidence that you paid a couple of guards to rough him up," the warden said.

"So? That's their word against mine. And that doesn't mean I had him murdered."

"No, it doesn't. But it does mean I can have you questioned, and I will."

"We don't have time for this," I said. "We're going on a trip. A very important trip. You can't hold us here."

"You're right. I can't. But the police want to question all three of you. Don't leave the state until they do."

Joe rubbed his stubbled chin. "Christ."

"It's not your fault, Joe," I said.

Talon punched some numbers into his phone. "I'm calling Jade. We need an attorney."

"The police expect you sometime today," the warden said.

"My girlfriend is a detective on the force," I said. "I can assure you this will all come to nothing."

"For all of your sakes, I hope you're right," the warden said. "But we have to investigate. Good day."

We all stood, and the guard moved from the doorway, letting us pass.

"I'm sorry," Joe said, once we were alone. "This is on me. I did slip a guard a benji. On two separate occasions."

"Don't blame yourself," I said. "We all wanted to see him get the shit kicked out of him."

"You were just taking care of things," Talon said. "Just like you always have, big brother."

"I wanted him to suffer for what he did to you," Joe said.

"We understand that," I said.

Joe rubbed his forehead. "Shit. I swear to God I never paid anyone off to kill him."

"We know, Joe," Talon said. "He's no use to us dead."

"Look," I said. "We'll talk to the cops, assure them we had nothing to do with Larry's murder, and then we'll get out of town."

Talon eyed his phone screen. "Jade just texted me. She's getting an attorney at the top criminal defense firm in the city to meet us at the station. Everything will be fine."

I sighed. "All right, then. Let's get this over with."

★ ★ ★

Talon and I sat, rigid, waiting for Joe's interrogation to end. The attorney Jade had hired, Catherine Fox, was in the room with him. I cracked the knuckles of my left hand and inhaled. Pine cleaner. An antiseptic smell, kind of like an office basement. I arched my back. The plastic chairs were uncomfortable.

"What's taking so long?" Tal asked, wringing his hands.

"Hell if I know." I leaned my head against the wall and closed my eyes. "Just when we were getting so close, too."

"You can't think Joe had anything to do with this," Talon said.

I opened my eyes. "No, I don't. I just hope he can convince the cops he didn't. Him palming some Franklins to the guards to rough up Larry doesn't look good."

Talon sighed. "It doesn't. But it's circumstantial at this point."

"Jade's legalese is rubbing off on you."

"A little." He looked toward the door. "How long are they going to keep him in there?"

As if on cue, the door opened, and Joe stepped out, his dark hair more unruly than usual. "Tal, they want to talk to you now."

Talon stood, nodded, and walked into the interrogation room.

Joe sat down next to me, his face pale.

"Should I ask how it went?"

"They grilled me pretty good. I was glad to have the lawyer there. But they have nothing to hold me on. The guard who they think killed Larry has disappeared, and he wasn't one of the two I gave money to."

"Did you tell them about that?"

"Yeah. The attorney advised me to tell the truth."

"Are you going to get in trouble for bribing a guard?"

"No. They're not interested in that, thank God. Last time I'll ever throw money around like that. Though I can't say I regret it."

"It's okay. Let's just get this shit over with so we can get the hell out of town and deal with Mathias once and for all."

Joe rubbed his hands together, looking down at his lap. "I can't, Ry. They want me to stay in town because they might have more questions."

"Shit." I didn't blame my brother for bribing the guards, but this definitely hurled a wrench in our plans.

We didn't talk anymore, and a few minutes later, Talon emerged from the room.

"Wow," Joe said. "They kept me in there a lot longer."

"I only saw Larry once while he was in prison, and I freaked and didn't stay long. There wasn't much they could ask me."

Surprising that they hadn't asked him about what Larry had done to him—or allegedly done to him. Seemed like Talon had just as much of a motive—or more so—than Joe to do Larry in. But I wasn't going to bring that up.

"Ryan?" The attorney stuck her head out of the room. "They're ready for you."

I inhaled. "All right." I walked in the door. The walls were a sterile white, and a large mirror hung on one side. A two-way mirror? Most likely. I resisted the urge to make a face. Even the smell in the room was sterile, as if it had just been doused in alcohol.

A man in plain clothes sat behind a table. He stood. "Mr. Steel, I'm Detective Andrew Benjamin. Please, have a seat."

I sat down, and Catherine sat next to me.

"This is just routine questioning. No need to be nervous."

I wasn't—not for myself, anyway—though my fidgeting need to get out of town might have looked like nerves to the detective.

"Please just answer all of my questions honestly, unless your attorney instructs you not to respond. Do you understand?"

Yes, I'm not an idiot. "Yes."

"All right. I have here the visitors log from the prison." He went on to list the few times I'd been to the prison to see Larry Wade. He asked me about the visits, and I answered as best I could remember.

The detective was a middle-aged man who was graying and balding. He most likely knew Ruby, though I wasn't going to bring her up.

He, however, did. "The last time you saw Mr. Wade you were accompanied by Detective Ruby Lee."

"I was."

"Why did Detective Lee accompany you? This isn't her case."

"She's my"—I cleared my throat—"fiancée."

"Oh? That's news to us."

"It just happened." And she hadn't yet said yes, but that was a minor detail I planned to fix as soon as possible.

"Congratulations."

"Thank you." I wasn't going to tell him that Ruby had a personal interest in the case. He probably already knew anyway.

"Mr. Steel, I don't think I have any more questions. Thank you for your honesty. You're free to go."

I stood. He hadn't said anything about not leaving town. I turned to Catherine. "We need to go on a trip. Soon."

She addressed Detective Benjamin. "I assume you're fine with Ryan and Talon Steel leaving town?"

He nodded. "That's fine. Only Jonah Steel needs to remain available. I don't anticipate having any more questions for either Ryan or Talon."

I let out a sigh of relief. Joe might be stuck here—and with Melanie pregnant, that wasn't necessarily a bad thing—but Talon and I could get moving.

Together, we'd find our father and bring Theodore Mathias down.

CHAPTER TWO

Ruby

"Don't pull that trigger, Ruby," he said, a bead of sweat dripping from his hairline. "If you do, you'll never find Brad Steel. You'll never find Gina."

"They could be dead for all I know."

"They aren't. They're both alive, and I can take you to them."

"I don't believe anything you say. You're history." I steadied my hand, itching to turn my head and survey my surroundings. I didn't think my father was working with anyone—Simpson was dead and Wade was incarcerated, after all—but something niggled at the back of my neck. I began moving slowly backward toward the nearest wall.

"You won't kill me," he said, "because you need me. Now that Larry Wade is dead, I'm the only—"

"What? Wade is dead?" I tightened my hold on my weapon to keep my hand from shaking. If Larry was dead, Ryan and his brothers would never get the information they needed. My father was their only chance.

"That's right. So you need me alive. We're leaving here together. Right now."

"Like hell we are. I'm not going anywhere with y—"

A moist handkerchief covered my mouth and nose, and

I inhaled instinctively. Red wine, rum, and chemicals. Sweet and rotten at the same time.

Chloroform.

If only I'd turned my head when I'd had the urge.

I dropped my gun and grabbed at the person—who was it?—behind me.

In front of me, my father's image blurred.

Don't breathe in. Don't breathe in.

The sickly sweet aroma permeated the cotton fabric.

Don't breathe in. Don't breathe—

But I had to. I inhaled, and my feet fell from under me. I crumpled onto the floor. My father and another fuzzy figure—I squinted but couldn't make out any features—loomed over me.

Then, blackness.

★ ★ ★

Ryan was thrusting into me in a primitive rhythm. "I love you, Ruby. I love you, baby." His words beat in time with his thrusts.

I love you. I love you.

Then—

A pounding headache, like a bass drum with each beat of my pulse. Something cold and hard pressed against my cheek. My eyes were open in slits, but I couldn't see anything but gray. My tongue was pasted to the roof of my mouth. I tried to move but couldn't. Slowly I detached my tongue, feeling like I'd torn off a layer of skin along with it.

Water. Needed water.

I opened my eyes wider. Still gray, but something sat a few feet in front of me. A white blob. A scent of decay hung in the air, as if we were next to a compost pile.

I closed my eyes, trying to orient myself. Where was I? I'd been making love with Ryan...

No. That had been a dream. The last thing I remembered was—

"Hey," a soft voice said. "Are you awake?"

The voice was female. I tried to reach forward to the white thing... I squinted. It was a...pitcher. Yes! Maybe it held water! My dry mouth rejoiced. I reached again—why was it sideways?—but my arm didn't want to work. Signals weren't getting from my brain to my limb. Then my hand twitched, and my arm moved an inch. Then another.

"I'd help if I could," the voice said.

I didn't need help. I just needed everything to be right side up. What was happening?

My body hurt. Not a bruising, achy hurt but an allover malaise—like I was getting over the flu. Something wasn't right.

"It'll be all right." The voice again. "I'm so glad you're here, Ruby."

Ruby? That was me. Ruby. This person knew me?

As my eyes adjusted to the dark grayness, I noticed a figure, also sitting sideways. Why was everything all convoluted? I tried again to move, and something scratched my cheek. I tried to swat it away, but my other arm wouldn't move. In fact, I couldn't even feel my other arm.

What the—

Then it dawned on me. I was lying down. On gray concrete. My cheek was scratching against the roughness of the concrete floor, and my other arm was trapped under my body. That's why everything was sideways.

"Go slowly. You'll be all right. The drugs are wearing off."

Drugs?

Right. The chloroform. Fragmented images rushed into my mind. My father had drugged me and brought me here. Wherever here was.

I should have killed the motherfucker when I had the chance. Should have pulled that trigger. Should have...

"Where are we?" I asked. At least that was what I asked in my head. What came out of my mouth sounded more like "wheee awww weee?"

But the voice seemed to understand. "In the dorms. That's what they call them, anyway. They're actually more like prison cells."

Prison cells? That got me moving. I forced my muscles out of rigidity and scraped myself off the floor and into a slumped-over sitting position.

"You're lucky," the voice said. "You aren't chained up. Yet."

I squinted at her form, my eyes still adjusting to the darkness. She was dressed in a ragged T-shirt and sweatpants. One of her hands appeared to be cuffed, attached to a chain that ended somewhere I couldn't see.

I looked down at my own hands and then at my feet. She had spoken the truth. I wasn't bound. I was still wearing my work clothes, and my hair was a tangled mass around my head and shoulders.

My brain still wasn't functioning quite right, but my physical body took over. I reached for the pitcher. Thank God! It was filled with water. Could be laced with more drugs, but at the moment, I didn't care. My thirst ruled me.

I gulped down the liquid, letting it dribble down my chin and onto my shirt. I forced myself to stop after a few seconds. I didn't want to make myself sick. I wasn't sure when I had last eaten.

I wiped my chin on my sleeve and looked around the dark room. A toilet and sink sat in one corner along with a few tattered blankets. The walls were concrete blocks painted gray. The ground underneath me was hard and gray, like an unfinished basement floor. Along one wall was a door, and on another, a small window with bars over it.

No light streamed in. It must be nighttime.

"Where are we?" I asked again.

"I told you. The dorms."

I shook my head, and the drum pounding inside my skull grew louder. "No. I mean where. Am I still in Colorado?"

She scoffed. "Colorado? Ruby, you're far away from Colorado. I'm not exactly sure where we are, but it's somewhere in the Caribbean."

The Caribbean? What the—? No. Not possible. I hadn't been gone that long. I must have misheard her.

She was still talking, but I couldn't make out her words. The sound of her voice nagged at me. I'd heard it before somewhere. Which made sense since she had called me by name.

I rubbed my temples, trying to soothe the pounding bass. My vision still wasn't very clear. The woman appeared to be blond. Her hair was pulled back from her face, but I couldn't make out her features. "How do you know me?"

"We met in Jamaica, remember? I'm Juliet."

CHAPTER THREE

R y a n

"Ruby? Ruby!" The door to her apartment was unlocked, and I shoved it open, Talon behind me. "Where are you?"

It was nearly five p.m., and I hadn't heard from her all day despite texting her every half hour.

She wasn't at work. I'd called there and was told she'd quit that morning over a squabble about vacation time. Her superiors must not have wanted her to leave again so soon. Nothing except the possibility of bringing her father to justice would have convinced Ruby to quit the police force. It was a huge part of her life and her identity.

I frantically searched the small abode. "Damn it, where is she?" My nerves jumped under my skin as fear catapulted through me.

"Calm down, Ry." Talon walked through the kitchen. "I'm sure everything is fine."

"Everything is not fine, Tal. She would've texted me. For God's sake, I proposed to her last night!"

Talon jerked around, his eyes boring into mine. "You what?"

"I proposed to her."

"Are you serious? That's great."

"Well, not so great. She hasn't exactly said yes yet." I

ransacked her living room, much like I had when I found the feminist book under her couch.

"Hell, Ryan. Don't trash the place. You're not a professional. You don't want to destroy any clues the cops might be able to dig up."

My mind was whirling with possibilities, none of them good. The best alternative traveling through my head at light speed was that Ruby had freaked out about my proposal and flown the coop.

On any other day, I'd be devastated if that was true. Today? It was the best option. Which meant I knew it wasn't what had happened.

"Look for anything," I said. "Mathias must have been here. He must have taken her."

"I'm going to call the PD. Maybe they can trace her cell phone."

"That will only help if she has it with her." I balled my hands into fists. "She wouldn't go anywhere without her phone or gun, but what if…" I couldn't bring myself to finish the sentence. What if, indeed? What if so many things? Her father was a lunatic. He'd most likely just had Larry Wade taken out. He was truly on his own now, and if Ruby was correct in her assumption, he was also running out of money.

Talon ended his call. "The department is going to do what they can."

I was sure they would. I was also sure it wouldn't be enough.

"Damn." I plunked my ass on her couch, looking down. The cushions separated under my weight, and something shiny peeked up at me. Something gold.

I reached down and grabbed the object. My heart sped up

like a jet taking off. "Look what I found."

He sat down next to me. "What is it?"

I handed it to him. "See for yourself."

He examined the heavy eighteen-karat-gold ring. "I'll be damned."

"Her father was here. He took her. I know it. Let me have a look at that thing."

Talon handed the ring back to me. It was identical to Tom Simpson's ring. I looked at the inside of the band. The same etchings that I couldn't make out were there, but also something else—something absent on Tom's ring.

My blood ran cold.

A name was engraved in elegant script.

Bradford Steel.

★ ★ ★

Twenty-four hours later, Talon and I arrived in Kingston, Jamaica.

I inhaled the moist tropical air laced with the sweet fragrance of jasmine and mango, and an overwhelming calmness enveloped me.

I was frantic about Ruby. She hadn't left my thoughts in the last day and a half, but something peaceful flowed through me.

It was truth. I wasn't sure how I knew, but I knew.

We'd find the truth here.

Two men met us—a limo driver, who took our luggage, and the private investigator we had hired.

The investigator was a large man with dark-brown skin and a wide smile. He stuck out his hand. "Mr. Steel times two.

I'm Rajae Williams."

Talon took his hand. "I'm Talon Steel. Thank you for meeting us, Mr. Williams. We hear you're the best."

"Call me Raj," he said in his Jamaican accent. "And you hear correctly. From what I understand, we have a lot of work ahead of us, but if money is no issue—"

"It's not," I interjected.

"Good," Raj said. "I've booked a cruising yacht for the next two weeks. The captain is notoriously discreet. We leave tonight. You'll just be two American tourists and real estate developers visiting the smaller islands of the Caribbean, and I'll be your Jamaican guide."

"Have you done anything like this before?" I asked.

"Yes, of course. Though not with this much style. I was instrumental in bringing down a couple of smaller trafficking rings. From what you've described though, we're looking for something bigger. I heard about the two girls who went missing from the Destination Desire resort when you two were here a few weeks ago. Since then, four other young women have disappeared from three other resorts. These things tend to happen in waves."

"The other two rings you brought down," I said. "Were they on a separate island?"

Raj shook his head. "One was here in Jamaica, and the other had its headquarters in the Dominican Republic. They're everywhere. Even in your own country."

I swallowed. Even though I knew what he said was true, the thought of humans being bought and sold in the US made my flesh crawl. But it had been happening under our noses.

Raj continued, "Because you've assured me that money is not an issue, we'll have access to more information. I have informants who aren't above taking bribes."

"Let's see what they'll tell us before we start handing out cash," I said.

"We will," Raj said. "But it's amazing how the sight of American green stuff makes people start remembering. The people we'll be dealing with aren't the best of society."

Really? Of course anyone who knew about this wasn't the best of society. This was no surprise. And damn it, it would be worth every penny we had if we could ferret out Theodore Mathias and get rid of him for good. Now that Tom Simpson and Larry Wade had both met their maker, once Mathias was behind bars, Talon could truly heal.

We all could.

Including Ruby.

Where the hell was she? I closed my eyes for a split second. Her beautiful face appeared, her eyes sparkling...but then they morphed into something else. Cold blue. Fear. Ruby was frightened. I'll find you, baby. I'll find you and bring you home.

As I suspected, the PD hadn't been able to uncover anything on Ruby's phone. I was tempted to have Raj try to find her, but she could be anywhere. Wouldn't hurt to ask though.

I quickly filled Raj in on Ruby's disappearance, and he began punching stuff into his phone. "I'll do what I can, mon. Let's get you two to the yacht and get settled in. We'll be cruising all night."

CHAPTER FOUR

Ruby

"Juliet?" I tried to stand but stumbled onto my hands and knees. "Fuck!" The concrete scraped against my palms, shooting pain into them.

"Easy," she said. Her voice was gravelly, as if she'd been screaming a lot. Maybe not getting enough to drink.

My vision was still a little fuzzy, but I could see that her baggy T-shirt and sweats were grayish and soiled. I squinted again, and this time her face became clearer. Her cheeks had hollowed out in the few weeks since I'd seen her, and lacerations were scabbing on her chin and forehead. The skin around her right eye was tinged yellow, as if a black eye was healing.

"It takes a while for the drugs to completely leave your system."

"Drugs? It was just chloro— Oh, shit."

I crawled as quickly as I could to the toilet in the corner and heaved. Nothing but stomach acid. It coated my tongue with bitterness and made me gag again.

When had I last eaten? I'd scrambled some eggs at Ryan's house—God, I wanted Ryan—and drunk a cup of coffee. Right? I willed my mind to churn. Yes, and then I had gone to work. I hadn't been able to get the vacation time I requested, so I had quit. I went home to pack and—

My father.

My father had brought me here.

He intended to sell me into human slavery after all.

I couldn't say I was surprised.

An image crept into my mind—of two blurry figures standing over me.

Someone else... Someone had helped my father drug and take me.

"Juliet..." My voice was nearly as gravelly as hers.

"The drugs make you sick. Coming out of it really sucks. I'm afraid you'll have another couple hours of it."

"Great." I spewed into the toilet again.

"I wish I could help you. But I can't move to where you are."

I didn't really need any help vomiting, but the thought was nice. I retched once more and then leaned back, gravity taking over until I was flat on my back. Sweat poured from my forehead. I tried to lift my arm to wipe it off on my sleeve, but I couldn't find the strength.

"How long have I—"

The door opening interrupted me. Someone entered. I was still lying supine, so I couldn't see.

"Ready for some fun?" A man's voice. A masked face looked down at me. "She's a mess, but that's a tight little body she's got."

"She's off-limits, remember?" another voice said.

I forced my eyes to stay open.

"Why should she be?" the man staring at me said. "No one's off-limits around here."

"She is. Boss's orders."

"Can't even knock her around a little?" His eyes were brown. Brown and laced with evil.

"Only if you make sure you don't leave a mark. And Bud, you always leave a mark."

So I was hands off. Not a bad thing. But what did that mean for—

I dragged myself into a sitting position. Another man turned Juliet around and pushed her sweats down her legs.

"Hey!" I pushed myself to my feet. "Get the fuck off of her!"

"It's all right, Ruby." Juliet sniffled. "Just let them get it over with."

"The hell I will." I ran—more like stumbled like a drunk—toward the man who was now unbuckling his jeans.

The other one grabbed my arm and wrenched it until I shouted in pain.

"Let go of me, you fucking brute!"

Try as I might, though, I couldn't get free. My mind was still muddled, and he was twice my size. My body wouldn't form any self-defense moves. It wasn't cooperating.

"I can't just stand here and let him rape you!"

"It's okay," she said again.

No. This was so far from okay.

She wasn't crying. Wasn't even whimpering. In fact, she didn't even flinch when he shoved himself into her.

A vile scent hung around the dank room—a putrid aroma of soiled bodies laced with corruption and misery. All I could do was watch the fat hairy ass pumping as the man forced himself inside Juliet.

All I could do was watch.

★ ★ ★

They'd both taken a turn.

I'd tried to close my eyes, to close my ears to the grunting, the painful silence of Juliet's resignation to her fate.

But after fighting so hard to open them, two invisible toothpicks had propped them wide apart like two separated curtains. I couldn't look away from the train wreck, and I couldn't do anything to stop it. Instead, I'd held back the nausea that threatened to consume me and let the horrid scene imprint itself on my brain.

Juliet was slumped in the corner, and I crawled over to her, guilt overwhelming me. They hadn't touched me. Why?

"Can I do anything for you?"

She sighed softly. "I wish you could. I wish I could go back to that day on the beach and listen to you. I should have never gotten on that Jet Ski."

True, but now wasn't the time to press the point. "No matter what you did, what mistakes you made, you didn't deserve this. No one deserves this." I helped her pull her sweats back up to cover herself.

"It's okay," she said. "Sometimes they keep us naked. I'm used to it."

I cringed at her words. No one should ever be "used to" this.

"Juliet, you need to help me. You need to tell me everything you know. I'm going to get us out of here."

She turned toward me and laughed—actually laughed, though it was still entwined with stoicism. "How? How the hell are you going to get us out of here? It's not possible. Believe me, I've tried everything. I tried sucking up to them. That just made them beat me harder. I tried starving myself. They didn't care. I tried yelling and screaming until my voice was nothing but a rasp. I tried stealing a cell phone, and I got caught. There's nothing in here. Nothing to use as a tool or weapon. Just a toilet and sink, which I can't even get to until they come and unchain me. I've learned to hold everything in until they let me go."

Damn! If only my mind were working better. I had to figure this out. "Who brought you here?"

"Those three guys." Then she shook her head. "No, that's not right. They put us on a boat. We never saw them again. I'm not sure who brought me here. This is the second place I've been. They..." She choked out a sob.

It was the most emotion I'd seen from her yet.

"What?"

"They killed Lisa. She fought back hard. Bit them a few times. They decided she was too much trouble, and they killed her."

I hadn't thought I could be more sickened than when I'd witnessed Juliet's rape. I was wrong. "How do you know? Maybe they just moved her."

"Because they made me watch! They beat her until she was unconscious."

I managed to swallow the bile erupting in my throat. Fucking bastards. And my father was a part of this.

The acid overtook me then, and I barely made it to the toilet. The taste was putrid on my tongue and left vile stickiness around my gums.

I didn't ask Juliet any more details about what happened to Lisa, even though I was morbidly curious. I needed to know as much about my captors as I could if I was going to get us out of here. Later. After she'd settled down a bit. The woman had just been raped.

"Juliet, you said you stole a cell phone. How did you do that?"

"One time when one of them was in here, you know, raping me, his phone fell out of his pocket. I slid it under my foot before he noticed."

"Did you text anyone?"

"I texted my mother. And Shayna. Those were the only two numbers I could remember." She laughed sarcastically. "I had everything on speed dial. No need to remember anything. God, first world problems! If only I could go back."

"How many times did you text Shayna?"

"Once. Just once. I typed 'help' and sent it, and I texted 'help' to my mother, but they caught me with the phone before I could hit send." She pointed to her healing black eye. "I got this for that stunt. It was worth it though."

Hmm. Shayna had gotten two texts saying "help" from a private number.

"You only texted Shayna once?"

"Yeah."

I had no explanation. Unless the sadistic bastard whose phone she'd stolen had sent the text again. Why would he do that? Why would any of these monsters do anything like this?

I didn't want to get into that now. I simply walked slowly to Juliet and held on to her, trying to soothe her.

Oddly, after tearing up over Lisa, she became apathetic again. Though she didn't turn me away.

"It's going to be okay," I said again. "I'm going to get us out of here."

She laid her head on my shoulder. "You won't. I've

accepted it. This is my life now."

I grabbed her by the shoulders and forced her head up so she was looking at me. "Don't ever let me hear you say that again. This is not your life. You don't deserve this."

"But it was my f—"

"Stop it!" I had to refrain from shaking her. I didn't have the strength anyway. "We're going to get out of here. I haven't been gone very long. There are people who will look for me. And they'll find me. When they find me, they'll find you."

"If they haven't found us by now, they'll never find us."

"Bullshit. My boyfriend and his brothers will have the cavalry looking. Besides, I haven't been gone long."

She remained stoic. "Ruby, they put you in this room over a day ago."

CHAPTER FIVE

Ryan

The yacht was first class all the way. Two master suites for Talon and me and another queen suite for Raj. A crew of four, including a chef, were there to cater to all our needs. Raj had given them the story that we were two American brothers looking to buy real estate in the Caribbean, possibly a private island.

We were treated like royalty when we boarded, and a bottle of Dom Pérignon was waiting for us to toast our adventure. Though neither Talon nor I felt up to celebrating, we kept up the act and each took a champagne flute.

Once we were seaborne, the chef prepared a Jamaican meal of brown stewed chicken with cabbage and okra. I couldn't help thinking how well my seasoned Cab would go with the dish—if I actually felt like eating. For dessert we had banana fritters.

Talon and I both cleaned our plates to keep up the show, though neither of us was hungry. The meal, which normally I'd have enjoyed, had tasted like mud.

After dinner, while the crew was cleaning up, Talon and I went out on the deck with Raj to discuss plans. The air smelled of sand and salt, and the water was blue as Ruby's eyes.

Ruby. My baby. How I wished we were sharing the beauty

of the ocean together. Without her, and not knowing her fate, I couldn't enjoy anything.

"We'll be traveling at night to avoid suspicion," Raj said, "but it's important to stay aware. One of us must be awake at all times. I'll do it as much as I can, since I know what clues to look for, but even I have to sleep sometime."

"Understood," Talon said.

"Not a problem. I volunteer." I pushed my hair out of my eyes. "I won't be able to sleep anyway. Not until I know Ruby is safe."

"You sure?" Raj said.

"Yeah. I'm sure. You guys get some shut-eye. I'll be fine out here on the deck."

"I don't want to leave you alone," Talon said. "Let's have a nightcap, bro."

"Tal, I'll be fine."

"Look," Raj said. "It doesn't make any sense for both of you to stay awake. We all have to take turns. That's the only way this will work."

"I just want to join my brother for a nightcap. No harm, no foul. I'll hit the sheets after, okay?"

"You two are the bosses," Raj said. "Just trying to make this as easy as possible on you."

"I understand," I said. "I'll make sure he goes to bed."

"How much you sleep is totally up to the two of you. Just know this isn't going to be easy, and we all need our rest."

"We get it," Talon said. "But Raj, this isn't going to be easy on us whether we sleep or not."

"No shit," I said under my breath as Raj nodded and left the deck.

"You want a drink?" Talon asked me.

I shook my head. "I want to stay awake."

"Yeah, I don't want one either. I just said that to give Raj a reason why I'm staying with you for a few."

"Do you trust him?" I asked.

"He comes highly recommended. Of course, we only had a day to get him hired, and the fact that he was available at the last minute makes me wonder. He seems okay to me, but I'm going to keep one eye on him."

"Me too," I said. "And on this crew. We only have Raj's word that they're discreet."

Talon nodded, stroking his stubbled chin. Then he turned to me. "Thanks for doing this, Ry. Thanks for helping me put this to rest."

"Hey, it stopped being just about you a long time ago, but even if it were, you know I'd be here for you, bro. You're still my hero."

Although I'd found out recently that Talon probably hadn't saved me from his horrible fate that day—in all likelihood my mother had—I still felt beholden to my big brother. He'd tried to help me get away, and had I been bigger and stronger, I'd have done the same for him.

That's what brothers do.

Talon had said those words to Joe and me after telling us he'd have gladly gone through his hell just to spare the two of us the same.

Even though he was only my half brother, we were bonded by more than blood. All three of us were.

The Steel brotherhood.

That was us.

There was a time when I thought my father would have been a part of any brotherhood among us Steel men.

I pulled the future lawmakers ring that bore his name out of my pocket.

No longer.

He'd banded together with a group of sociopaths before any of us were even born.

Talon didn't speak. He'd always been a little uncomfortable with my hero worship, though he was better now that he'd been healing with the help of his wife, Jade, and Joe's wife, Melanie, who was his therapist.

Finally, he said, "Dad's ring?"

"Yeah. I don't know why I'm carrying it with me. Tom's is down in my cabin in the safe. But this one..." I tossed it in the air and caught it. Its weight was heavy in my palm.

"Yeah, I get it. Weird to think you're holding something that belonged—or belongs, for all we know—to Dad. Something we never saw him wear. Something we never imagined he'd wear in a million years."

"He wasn't the man we always thought he was," I said. "Not if he was involved with the other people who wore this ring."

"How do you think it got in Ruby's place?"

"Mathias, no doubt. Somehow he got his hands on it and planted it there. It proves he was there when she disappeared. I turned the place upside down before, when I found the Wollstonecraft book, and this ring never turned up."

"How could Mathias have gotten hold of Dad's ring, though?"

I blew out a breath of air. "Hell if I know. But we do know this. None of us ever remember Dad wearing a ring like this, but clearly he had one, because he's wearing it in the yearbook photo of the club. Maybe Mathias has had it since high school.

Since Dad bowed out of their business."

"If Dad bowed out of their business." Talon cocked his head. "I'm not sure what I believe anymore. This thing with him and Wendy..."

Wendy. My psycho mother, Wendy Madigan. Crazy as a loon but brilliant as Einstein. A lethal combination. She'd been the mastermind behind this whole thing, and according to clues we'd found, the symbol on the ring represented her—an evil female.

I rubbed the ring between my fingers. It was identical to Tom's except for the name engraved on the inside. I slid my fingers over the black onyx stone, the twisted female symbol on the side, and then to the band at the back—

What?

My fingers hit something raised. I turned the ring in my hand. The back of the band had some engraving on it.

In the darkness, I couldn't see what it was, and I doubted even with natural light I'd be able to see the tiny figures.

"Tal, check this out."

"What?"

I handed him the ring. "There's something engraved on the back of the band, on the outside. I don't recall anything like that on Tom's ring."

"One way to find out," Talon said. "Let's go get Tom's ring and compare the two."

"I'm supposed to stay outside and keep watch. It's in the safe in my cabin." I handed him the key to my room. "The combination is Marj's birthday."

"Got it. I'll be right back."

Talon returned ten minutes later with the ring.

"I'm not seeing anything on the outside of the band on this

one."

I took the ring and inspected it. He was right. Nothing.

"I need to get a good look at these markings," he said. "We need light...and probably a magnifying glass."

"They'll have magnifiers on the bridge for looking at maps and stuff. Maybe a flashlight too. I'll go check."

Again, he was gone only about ten minutes. He came back with a small Maglite and several magnifying glasses.

"This one's the strongest." He handed it to me with the ring. "Check it out. I'll hold the light."

I stopped for a few seconds to wonder how conspicuous we might be, shining a flashlight in the dark in the middle of the Caribbean, but my curiosity won out. I held the magnifier in front of me and moved it back and forth until the image of the etching became clear. A series of numbers stood out.

My heart nearly stopped. "I'll be goddamned."

CHAPTER SIX

Ruby

They put you in this room over a day ago.

I couldn't wrap my still-hazy mind around Juliet's words. Over a day ago?

How long had I been out from that chloroform? No wonder I was so sick.

"Do you remember them bringing me in here?"

"No. When they moved me in, you were already here, asleep with your cheek embedded in the floor. I can tell when a day passes because of the window. They brought me here about this time yesterday. I'm just assuming you got here right before then, but honestly, I don't know. You could have been here longer than that."

I shook my head, willing my brain cells to start firing correctly. I was dehydrated. That explained my unquenchable thirst and also part of my fogginess. But there was no way they'd used chloroform to put me under for that long. A dose like that would have killed me. I'd been drugged with something else. I touched my upper arm, searching for a lump or sensitive area where they might have injected me. Nothing.

God, what had they put inside my body?

What had my father put inside my body?

I fought back another wave of queasiness and reached for

the pitcher of water. It was nearly empty. I drained it.

"They'll bring food soon."

Ugh. Food. But I'd eat. I had to eat. I needed to regain my strength. If it had been close to twenty-four hours, I needed sustenance.

I backed away from Juliet. It was time to get serious. "I need you to be straight with me. Tell me exactly what has happened since you got here."

Her eyes dimmed. "Did Shayna make it?"

Did she not know? Juliet had texted her friend, but she hadn't had the phone long enough to know if Shayna had responded, which she hadn't.

I tried to smile, though I wasn't sure my facial muscles were cooperating. "Yes. She made it."

"Thank God! I always held out hope, even though they told us she'd drowned. They didn't know what an awesome swimmer she is."

"She nearly did drown. Luckily some locals spotted her and pulled her onto their boat. They took her back to the resort."

Juliet's eyes misted. "She's so brave. So much braver than I ever could be."

"Listen to me." I choked out the words, my mouth still dry and tight from dehydration and stomach acid. "You're brave. You hear me? Look at what you've been through."

She leaned back, closed her eyes, and sighed. "I'm not brave. Lisa was brave. She refused to give in."

"Lisa's dead," I said, my headache returning with a vengeance. "I'm sorry to say it so harshly, but dying is not an option. You do what you need to do to survive."

"Easy for you to say."

"It is easy for me to say." Juliet might not be ready to hear the truth, but she needed to if I was going to convince her she had a chance of getting out of this hellish situation. "I've been on my own since I was fifteen because my father tried to rape me. Luckily, I got away, but let me tell you, life isn't easy for a fifteen-year-old on the streets."

"I'm sorry," Juliet said. "I had no idea. You seem so together."

I doubted I seemed all that together at the moment. "We've all been through our hardships. I could tell you stories about what others have been through that would make you think you're living in luxury right now. Don't take that the wrong way. You don't deserve this, and we're going to get you out of here." I touched her forearm. It was cold and clammy. "Don't give up. Do what you need to do to stay alive, because as long as you're alive, you have a chance."

"I know that. But Lisa seemed so brave."

"Lisa was brave. But she's also not here anymore. The last memory she'll ever have is of this horrible place. I promise you. Your last memory will be a lot nicer."

Juliet didn't know how serious I was. Since she and Lisa had been taken from the resort, I'd felt responsible. I'd tried to get them to listen to me, to see that they were being naïve and downright stupid. They'd gone anyway. Then I'd found out my father had been involved in taking them, and I'd talked to Melanie pretty extensively about why I felt responsible for everything my father did.

"You can't make that promise."

"I can." If my father had seriously told them—whoever they were—that I was off-limits, I could use that to help protect Juliet. My mind was becoming less fuzzy by the minute. Once

I had some food—

The door opened, and one of the masked men—was it one of the two who'd raped Juliet? I couldn't tell—entered with a tray.

"Eat up, ladies," he said. Then, to Juliet, "I'll be back in half an hour to unchain you so you can use the john." He left the room.

I scrambled to the tray.

"A gourmet feast, huh?" Juliet said with no emotion.

"Whatever it is, you need to eat it. We both need to keep up our strength." I lifted the foil from the tray. Two sandwiches, two bottles of water, and a baguette. I picked up one of the sandwiches to examine it. Peanut butter and jelly. Not my favorite and not overly filling. Mostly carbs, with the baguette. Good for short-term energy, but not much protein other than the peanut butter for long term.

But I found, suddenly, that I was famished. I carried the tray over to Juliet and handed her one of the sandwiches. I picked up the other and touched it to hers. "Cheers."

"Eat slowly," she advised. "They only feed us twice a day, and it's never much. And that's more than what some girls get. Lisa only got food once a day once they labeled her a troublemaker."

I took her advice to heart and sank my teeth into the sandwich. The jelly was sweet and had no discernible flavor. The color was purplish red. Could have been anything.

I'd have to get us better food. I'd demand to see my father. Maybe that would make them sweat a little.

A plan began to take shape inside my head. When they came to unchain Juliet so she could use the toilet, I'd—

I looked swiftly around the room for hidden mics or

cameras. Although the force could never afford the best, I kept myself well-versed in top surveillance technology. I might not be able to see anything with my naked eye. Still, I squinted and surveyed every inch of the walls and ceiling, paying special attention to the window frame.

Nothing, but I knew my father. He was watching and listening from somewhere. I couldn't take the chance of telling Juliet my plan.

"It's usually peanut butter and jelly," Juliet went on. "On stale bread. This is fresher than normal. I wonder if it's because you're here."

"Why would that matter?"

"Obviously they're not allowed to touch you. How'd you manage that?"

I opened my mouth to tell her about my father but shut it before the words emerged. If he was listening, I didn't want him to know she knew. "I have no idea. I'm sure my turn will come soon."

"I don't know," she said. "They raped Lisa and me on the boat before we even got here. Seems you're getting special treatment." Despite her words, her tone was still devoid of emotion.

"If I am, I have no idea why."

I hated lying to her, but I had to watch what I said until I knew for sure whether anyone was listening to us. I longed to ask Juliet if they were, but she might not know, and if they were, I didn't want to alert them that I was suspicious.

"How many girls were on the boat with you?" I asked.

She swallowed the bite of bread she'd been chewing. "Quite a few. I don't know the exact number. But that wasn't the worst part."

"What was the worst part?" I asked, wishing I didn't already know what she was going to say.

"There were kids. Little boys and little girls. We could hear their screams..." She put down her sandwich. "I can't eat this right now."

"I know this is hard for you to talk about. Believe me, I get that." And she'd just confirmed what I already knew. The human trafficking my father was involved in wasn't limited to adults.

"I can't, Ruby. I can't talk about it."

"If you want to get out of here, you have to. I need to know everything you know."

She sighed. "I'll try."

"Good girl. Go as slowly as you need to. What happened to the guys on the Jet Skis?"

"They drove us up to the boat, and several men came out and grabbed us off the Jet Skis."

"All right. What did the men look like?"

"Most of them were black with Caribbean accents. I think two were white, or maybe light Hispanic. It's hard to remember."

"They didn't wear masks?"

"No. But once we got to the compound—that's what they called it—everyone did. Black masks, like the guys who were here earlier."

"Do you remember anything else about the men on the boat?"

"Only their skin colors. I just... I didn't think to remember. Lisa and I were both so scared. I do remember one thing. When we got to the boat, one of the men asked why there were only two. I guess they were expecting Shayna."

"Which means the men on the Jet Skis had contacted them ahead of time."

"Yeah. Probably."

"Any names?"

"Only the men on the Jet Skis. Mark, Rashaun, and J.J. I never heard any other names once we got on the boat."

"So then what happened?"

"The guys on the Jet Skis left. Lisa and I were screaming at them to come back, but they jetted off like we were nothing."

"Did you see any money exchange hands? When they brought you to the guys on the boat?"

She shook her head. "But I wasn't looking either. I was so surprised that this had happened, and I felt like such an idiot for going with them. And I was scared, Ruby. So scared."

Her eyes glazed over. Maybe this was enough interrogation for now. The man would be back to unchain her soon. I had plans to figure out. I handed her sandwich back to her. "Please. I know it's difficult, but you need to eat. You need your strength. I need you to be strong, okay? I need you to help me get us out of here."

She nodded slightly and took a bite of the sandwich, chewing slowly.

The man who entered after a few minutes, though, was not the one who'd brought the food. He was masked, but I recognized his odd blue eyes.

I stood. "Hello, Theo."

CHAPTER SEVEN

Ryan

"What is it?" Talon asked.

"These are GPS coordinates. Here. Take a look." I handed him the ring and the magnifier while taking the flashlight. I held it up so the light shined where he needed it.

"Wow. They sure are." He studied them. "I don't know what the hell they mean, but whoever is navigating this tub will. Let's go wake up the captain."

★ ★ ★

"What the hell do you want? It's the middle of the night." The captain, Leroy Faucett, stood in nothing but black, yellow, and green—the colors of the Jamaican flag—boxers. "My man's on the bridge. Bother him."

"For what you're getting paid, we can bother you anytime we want." Talon handed him a slip of paper upon which he'd written the GPS coordinates from our father's ring. "We want you to take us here. And we leave now."

He eyed the paper, squinting. "That's about a day's journey."

"Get there faster."

"This yacht can go about thirty knots, but it won't keep it up for long."

"How soon can we get there if we go that speed?" I asked.

"About twelve hours."

Talon and I looked at each other. "Do it," we said in unison.

"You're crazy," Faucett said. "Going thirty for twelve hours straight isn't doable."

"Make it happen," I said. "We'll make it worth your while."

"I'm not sacrificing this boat for any more cash. Cruising speed is about six knots per hour. I can push her to twelve, but that's it. I won't do thirty for any amount. I'm sorry."

I had to admire his lack of greed. We Steels weren't used to that.

"Twelve it is, then," I said. "We should make it in twenty-four hours, right?"

Faucett rolled his eyes. "More or less. Probably more."

"Do your best. There'll be a nice bonus in it for you," Talon said.

"Fine. For Christ's sake. Let me get dressed. I'll be sleeping for thirty hours straight once I get you there." He slammed the door in our faces.

"That wasn't pleasant," I said.

"At least he's doing what he can," Talon replied. "I'm going to give Joe a call and fill him in."

"Sounds good. I guess I'm still on watch duty." I headed back up to the deck.

Ruby never left my mind. I pulled my father's ring out of my pocket and fingered it once more. He—or at least someone who had his ring—had been in her apartment. My best guess was Mathias. But Mathias wasn't stupid. He never did anything without a reason, which meant he'd left the ring on purpose for someone to find.

For me to find.

He knew I'd go looking for Ruby, and when I did, I'd find my father's ring.

Until I'd found the GPS coordinates, I wasn't sure why he'd left the ring. I still wasn't completely sure. For all I knew, we could be embarking on a wild-goose chase. It wouldn't be the first wild-goose chase we'd been on since we'd been pursuing this phantom of my father's doing.

My father. Somehow, in the end, it was all leading back to him. Ever since Joe had found his photo with the other future lawmakers in that yearbook from Tejon Prep School, we'd known he wasn't the honorable man we remembered.

I thought back, shaking my head.

We'd always known, in a subconscious way. We'd always wondered why he wouldn't let our family deal with the horror that Talon had been through. Why he'd swept it all under the rug. Why he hadn't let us see our mother's body.

Why?

I'd been over and over the facts and theories in my mind, and only one answer made sense.

He had something to hide. Something sinister. Something he probably hoped we'd never know. Never uncover.

My father was alive. I was sure of it.

He'd stayed until the last of us, Marjorie, had reached adulthood. I had to at least respect that.

Then he had died.

Except he hadn't died. He'd faked his own death, with the help of my mother, according to her.

Still so many questions were unanswered, the biggest of which was how I'd come to be in the first place. What was the reason behind my parents' coupling? Had my father truly loved Wendy, as she claimed? Or had he just slept with her, producing me? Had she seduced him when she knew she was fertile? I'd toyed with the idea of her inseminating herself with his sperm, but then I'd rejected that theory. My father wouldn't have given her access to his sperm.

At least I didn't think so.

I knew very little about my own father. That was becoming increasingly clear. I longed to know the whole story, but something else was far more important at the moment.

Ruby.

I had to find her. Failure was not an option. She had come to mean everything to me. Finally I understood what my brothers felt for their wives—that soul-wrenching love and need for another person.

My father's ring was a clue. It had to be.

Mathias had planted it. He must have, because no one else could have.

Except my father himself.

For that to be true, my father would have had to have been in Ruby's apartment, and that couldn't have happened. Wendy had said he was being held captive somewhere.

But Wendy could have been lying. And if she was lying, she had a good—good in her twisted mind, anyway—reason for it.

I shook my head to clear it. The only thing that mattered right now was finding Ruby. That and bringing an end to this for Talon's sake, so he could put it behind him and truly finish healing. I couldn't let my emotions get the best of me. As much as I feared for Ruby, I had to keep my sanity and my logic.

But God...I missed her. I loved her so fucking much. Wherever she was, she had taken my heart with her.

I'd find her, and when I did, she and I would put an end to all of this once and for all.

CHAPTER EIGHT

Ruby

Juliet gasped. "You know this guy?"

I stood my ground. I'd called him Theo on purpose. I didn't want to alert Juliet to the fact that he was my father. "We've met."

"Then you should have put him away. He's a rapist and a murderer!" Juliet then cowered in a corner, bracing herself to be hit.

"Don't touch her," I warned my father.

"I don't have any intention to," he said. "I came for you."

"Are you crazy? I'm not going anywhere with you."

He stalked forward.

"Don't lay one slimy finger on me," I said, resisting the urge to back away and hoping my still shaky legs would hold me. "I swear to God you'll be sorry."

"Stop the melodramatics." He grabbed my shoulder. "I could have had you locked in chains, starved, and beaten. Or worse. You should be thanking me."

"For drugging me? Bringing me here against my will? You've got to be kidding."

"I couldn't help the accommodations," he said. "This was the best we had on short notice. I moved your friend in here as a gesture of good faith. This is a better room than she's seen."

"Was it also a gesture of good faith when two goons came in and raped her?"

Juliet gasped in the corner.

"Excuse me?" he said.

"You heard me. Two of your masked monsters raped her while I was forced to watch."

My father's strange blue eyes closed for a few seconds and then opened. "That wasn't supposed to happen. They will be... dealt with."

"Unless you're going to chain them up, starve them, and then shove fat cucumbers up their asses, however you plan to deal with them won't be sufficient."

Another gasp from Juliet at my graphic words.

"Enough of your mouth, girl." He forced me toward the door.

As much as I wanted to fight back, my body still wasn't working quite right. I looked back at Juliet. "They didn't use condoms. She could be pregnant!"

"Condoms aren't necessary. We keep all women of childbearing age on birth control. We also test them all, and all our trainers are tested as well. Every month. We can't deliver diseased goods to buyers."

"Trainers? Is that another word for rapists? Goods? They're people, Theo! People!"

He pushed me out the door.

"I'll be back for you," I said to Juliet. "I promise."

Her eyes were sunken, and her countenance resolved to her fate. She didn't believe me. I didn't blame her.

But I would be back.

My father dragged me down a dimly lit hallway, past about five other doors identical to the one to the room where I had been. I kept my lips sealed, even though I wanted to scream for help. I knew better. No help would come here.

Finally, he pushed me up a flight of stairs and into a small office. It was sparsely decorated with a metal desk, a computer, a couple chairs, and an old sofa.

"Have a seat." He indicated the sofa.

"I'll stand."

"Have it your own way. You won't be standing for long."

"You going to push me down?"

"No. But you're still coming out of a drug-induced state. Your legs won't hold you for long."

I gave in and sat on the couch. It was worn green velour, and it smelled like fake banana flavoring. Yuck. "Fine."

He sat behind the desk and began tapping on the keyboard. "Your Steel boyfriend will be here soon. Probably about a day, I'd say."

"Don't you dare drag him into this."

"Why not? Don't you want to be the damsel in distress? Don't you want to be rescued? I've laid out the breadcrumbs so well that he won't be able to resist them."

My father didn't know me at all. I'd spent the better part of my life rescuing myself. I didn't need Ryan or anyone else to rescue me. In fact, I didn't want him anywhere near this place, but he'd come. I knew he'd come for me. "If you hurt him, I sw—"

"I have no intention of hurting him."

"Then why are you bringing him here? I don't understand." The thought of Ryan walking into danger speared me in the heart. I had to make sure he wasn't in any peril. Had to keep him safe. Had to get back to him—to the man I loved. "Hasn't he been through enough? Hasn't his brother been through enough? His whole damned family? Can't this all just end?"

My father regarded me. Something in his eyes changed. At least I think it did. His eyes weren't actually his eyes. They were that eerie blue fakeness.

But I couldn't deny I'd seen something. A...softening? I blinked. Then again. Theodore Mathias could never soften. I'd imagined it.

"Unfortunately, some things never end, daughter. Even when you want them to."

It had been a softening. My father was showing a rare morsel of remorse. I hadn't known he had it in him.

"You're wrong. This can end."

"Not well."

I wasn't going to lie to him. "Not without you spending the rest of your life in prison. That's true."

His eyes went icy. "I assure you I'll never go to prison. I'm a hell of a lot smarter than Larry Wade."

I didn't doubt it.

"Speaking of Wade, why did you have him knocked off? He never rolled over on you. Not once. The Steels and I offered him everything."

"What makes you think I had anything to do with his death?"

"Just a hunch, Theo."

"I don't expect you to believe anything I say, Ruby, but I didn't have Larry Wade killed. And I didn't have Tom Simpson killed."

"I know that. Tom Simpson committed suicide."

"Without any help from me."

"Without any help from anyone." I rubbed my tight temples. "You know damned well Simpson killed himself.

Jonah witnessed it and saw the coroner take the body. This one was identified, and he's actually dead."

"Simpson may have pulled the trigger that put the bullet in his own brain, but someone else was behind it. Someone else wanted him dead, and it wasn't me. It doesn't matter. You'll believe what you want to believe, no matter what I tell you."

"True. Because you're a lying psychopath. That's why I don't believe you."

He sighed. Or at least I thought it was a sigh. Hard to tell with him. "Would you believe I never meant for anything to go as far as it did?"

I rubbed my eyes. They wanted to close so badly. "No, I wouldn't. Because if you'd never meant for it to go so far, you wouldn't have raped Gina. Or Talon. Or Colin Morse."

"Not that this will change your mind about me, but I never touched Colin Morse. He was Tom's bitch. I was against that one. Not only is Morse's father a loose cannon, but we have no market for adult men. Tom had acquired the taste over the years and couldn't help himself."

I rubbed my forehead, trying to ease the invisible rubber band around it. "Oh my God. Couldn't help himself? Do you ever actually listen to the words that come out of your mouth?"

"Tom was worse that way than I was. It was an urge with him. A compulsion. I told you once he was an amateur and I meant it. He had no control. Murdering his nephew and then slicing him up in front of the Steel boy was Tom's idea, not mine. He was the true monster of the three of us, no matter what you might have heard."

"Sure, blame the dead guy." I scoffed.

"I'm not blaming anyone. But Tom was what he was. He was convinced he was immortal, could do whatever he pleased and get away with it, all while keeping up his beautiful family life as mayor of Snow Creek. He was devoid of emotion. He was truly cold-hearted."

Cold-hearted. Ryan and his brothers had referred to Tom as an ice man. Apparently they hadn't been far off. I resisted the urge to shudder. I'd never meet the man, and I was damned glad of it.

"And what... Colin Morse just stumbled into his path one day?"

"Essentially, yes. Morse was in Snow Creek, trying to bait the Steel brothers one evening before Talon was due in court. Tom witnessed the exchange and followed him. He took him later that night. He figured the Steels would be blamed for the disappearance. He kept him holed up for a few weeks until Jonah Steel found him." My father shook his head. "The man never learned. I was pissed off. I should have let Jonah Steel beat the shit out of Simpson, maybe even kill him, but I felt guilty and went back for him. I got him out of there before the cops came."

"I have a hard time believing you've ever felt anything slightly akin to guilt."

He removed his mask, and his unruly black hair fell around his olive-skinned face. "Tom was a friend. A brother. I couldn't let him go down. Not like that. Not for something as stupid as kidnapping Colin Morse."

"You couldn't let him go down for torturing and raping an innocent man? That was big of you."

"I don't expect you to understand about our brotherhood. That's what the future lawmakers really were. A brotherhood."

"A brotherhood? What about Wendy Madigan?"

"She's a different story."

"Meaning?"

"She was brilliant, in a way. Actually, in many ways. She had a way of getting us caught up in things that we had no business being caught up in. Tom was the first to succumb."

"Please." I rolled my eyes.

"I'm serious. Tom was greedy. That greed was what did him in at the end. Like I said, he thought he was immortal. He'd gotten away with literally everything for so long he figured he'd never get caught. I was never that naïve. I never stayed anywhere long enough to get caught, and I used a lot of names."

Nothing I didn't already know. "So you were careful. And you stayed away from adult men because they weren't part of your market. Am I really hearing this? It's all about the market?"

"Well, there is a market for adult men. But the company we provide for isn't interested in that particular commodity."

"Commodity? These are fucking people, Theo! God, what made you so sick in the head?"

"Everyone needs to make a living."

"Seriously? Making a living is one thing. Why the torture? Why the rape? Why not leave that to someone else?"

He had no answer for me. Or if he did, he kept it to himself. I eyed him. His features went slightly rigid.

"You know what it is? You fucking enjoy it. You enjoy exerting power and control over those weaker than you are. That's why the women, the little kids. It's not sexual at all for you, is it?"

He didn't answer again, and I was just as glad. I didn't want to know why he did it. I didn't want to get any more inside his twisted head than I already was.

"There are things you don't understand."

"These are things I don't want to understand."

"None of this was ever planned."

"I don't believe you."

"We were forced into a lot of it."

"Still don't believe you."

"At times, we were stuck between a rock and a hard place."

This was going nowhere fast, and my eyelids were drooping. The old velour couch was beginning to feel soft under me. God, what I'd do for a bed. "Just tell me why you brought me here."

"I already did. You will lure the Steels here, right into my trap."

"Damn it! You said you wouldn't hurt them."

"I won't. Not if they play their cards right. Their father owes me something. And I intend to collect."

CHAPTER NINE

R y a n

Raj showed up around four a.m. to relieve me, but I had no intention of going anywhere. I filled him in on the GPS coordinates and our new route.

"If there's land there, it's probably privately owned," he said. "Have you looked at a map? If the island's a decent size, it will show up on a map of the area."

"We haven't looked at a map. But whether anything shows up or not, we're going." I scratched the back of my neck. "There's land there. Owned by Mathias or some other degenerate, no doubt."

"How can you be so sure?"

"It's a clue. Left by my father. It has to be."

He shook his head. "Don't get your hopes up until we get there."

I wouldn't budge. Those coordinates had been planted in Ruby's apartment for a reason. They would lead me to her... and to something more. I was sure of it.

"You need to get some sleep, mon," Raj said, interrupting my thoughts. "You won't be any good without it."

"I can't."

"Listen to me. Go to your cabin. Try. You won't be any good to anyone if you're not well rested."

As he finished his sentence, a great yawn split my face.

"See what I mean?" Raj said.

"Fine. I'll go. But I won't sleep." I headed down to my cabin and slid the key card through the slot.

I collapsed on my bed and closed my eyes.

Ruby, I said in my mind. Ruby, please be there when I get there. Please help me find you. I love you. I need you.

I'm here. I'm right here, Ryan.

I jerked my eyes open.

I'd actually heard her voice!

I stood abruptly and started pacing around the cabin. Of course it hadn't been her. I was just exhausted, overwhelmed with fatigue. I lay down again and closed my eyes. I had to get some rest. Raj was right about one thing. I'd be no good to Ruby without some sleep.

★ ★ ★

"He's beautiful, Brad."

I was lying in bed. I shared a room with Talon. Our house was big. Bigger than any of my friends' homes. But I liked sharing a room with Talon. I liked hearing him breathe.

I opened my eyes and found a woman staring down at me. I'd seen her before. She was a friend of the family. She did stories on TV. I couldn't remember her name, but she was pretty. She had brown hair—lighter than my mother's—and blue eyes.

"Go back to sleep, buddy."

My father's voice. Deep and stern. That was Daddy. I always obeyed him. So I shut my eyes.

"I want so much to hold him," the woman said in a whisper.

"You can't," my father whispered back.

"Please, Brad. Just once. I haven't held him since—"

The whispers stopped suddenly, and footsteps faded away until I heard my door close quietly.

I opened my eyes and sat up in bed. Then I got up and walked to my door, placing my ear against the wood.

Nothing.

Then, "I'm his mother!"

Weeping. My mother cried a lot. But not like this. My mother's sobs were big and bountiful. These sobs were soft and weak.

More whispers...my father's stern whispers. I pushed my ear into the door, but I couldn't understand his words. I heard only hissing, like two snakes talking. Then one word.

Bigger sobs. "You promised!"

"She's my wife, Wendy."

Wendy. Yes, that was her name. The lady who did stories on TV and newspapers.

"Never. I'll never believe that. You'll pay for this, Brad. I swear to God you'll pay."

★ ★ ★

I jerked up in bed. Damn! I'd fallen asleep. And I'd been dreaming. It had the feeling of a long-lost memory. Had my mother come to see me when I was a little boy? Just that time, or were there others? As much as I never wanted to see the bitch again, I had so many unanswered questions. I also had no way of guaranteeing she would be truthful with me.

I closed my eyes and concentrated, and the vision came back to me in muted colors. It had been dark in my room, and

I hadn't opened my eyes until they'd left. I'd looked toward Talon and found him sleeping soundly. Then I'd gotten up, gone to the door, and listened.

Remember, Ryan. Remember.

The whispers. One word. One word...

Then it whooshed into my head as if it had always been there. Pregnant.

That was when my father had told Wendy that my other mother, Daphne Steel, was pregnant. Pregnant with what would become our baby sister, Marjorie.

Chills coursed through me. Daphne's pregnancy had been the reason Wendy had Talon abducted and tortured. Starved and beaten. Raped.

To punish my father for sleeping with his wife and getting her pregnant.

She'd admitted it to me the last time I saw her.

Repugnance swept up my throat. This wasn't new information, but every time it crossed my mind, it was still just as difficult to digest.

How could I come to terms with this? Having a mother who was such a cold-hearted bitch?

I pulled on a T-shirt and jeans and went up on deck.

"You're supposed to be sleeping," Talon said when he saw me.

"I thought Raj was keeping watch."

"He was, but I couldn't sleep. I told him to get lost."

"You did?"

"Not in those exact words. But I wanted to be alone."

"Oh. Sorry."

"No, you're fine. I just didn't want to be with him, and I didn't want to sleep, so I told him to go to bed for a few hours.

What are you doing up?"

"I had a weird dream. Or rather, a flashback. I think."

"I'm the king of flashbacks. You want to tell me about it?"

I quickly explained, stumbling over some of the words. Though Talon swore he didn't blame me for my mother's part in his horror, I still felt terrible about all of it. But it wouldn't do either of us any good for me to continue apologizing. He'd just have to continue saying it was okay.

"I feel like there's something I'm missing," I said. "Like there's more to the memory, but I can't quite access it."

"You were a kid. It's funny. We keep some memories and can recall them in living color like it was yesterday, and others..." Talon sighed.

I knew what he was thinking. He'd worked hard for many hours with Melanie to recall some of the things he'd forced far into his subconscious.

"Is it painful?" I asked. "I mean...you know. Remembering."

"I doubt you have anything too painful to remember."

A knife cut into my heart. "I didn't mean—"

"I know you didn't, and I shouldn't have said that," Talon said. "I'm sorry. I know you're battling your own demons. I don't mean to minimize them."

"They're nothing compared to yours." I meant those words with all my heart.

"So you want to know if you can access the rest of that memory. I get it. Melanie can help you."

"Melanie's not here. I need you to help me."

Talon twisted his lips. "Are you crazy? I'm not qualified to do that."

"Just do what Melanie did with you."

He shook his head. "It's not that simple. She has training

in guided hypnosis. She knew how to bring me out if it got too tough. I wouldn't be able to do any of that."

"Please, Tal."

He shook his head again. "I won't. I won't risk hurting you. Not ever." The look in his eyes was pained.

It was enough for me to stop this inquiry. "All right. I understand."

"When we get back, talk to Melanie. She'll be able to help you."

I had no doubt he was right. Problem was, Melanie wasn't here, and I had the distinct feeling that I needed to access this memory now.

Before we got where we were going.

CHAPTER TEN

Ruby

I'd heard that song before. Simpson and my father had said something similar to Jonah when Wendy Madigan had kidnapped him. That his father owed them something. Then it had been my uncle, Rodney Cates, who had told us that Brad Steel had been the future lawmakers club's financial backer.

Interestingly, the last time I'd talked to him, Rodney had also told me that Brad Steel was the one person my father had trusted.

I doubted Theodore Mathias felt that way now.

"What exactly does Brad Steel owe you?" I asked.

"None of your business. The less you know the better. Trust me."

"Trust you?" I shook my head vehemently. "Not going to happen in this lifetime, Pops."

A knock sounded on the door.

"Come in," my father said.

Another black-masked goon entered with a covered tray. "Best I could come up with on short notice." He set the tray on the desk.

"Thank you. Now leave," my father said.

The man walked out, shutting the door behind him.

I inhaled. Smelled like chicken. Not roasted chicken or

anything, but the fake kind that came with ramen noodles. My stomach gurgled.

My father uncovered the tray. "I thought you might like some better food."

The platter held a bowl of some kind of soup and a plate containing what might be a brownie. Or a slab of shit. I couldn't tell.

"I'm fine." My stomach again betrayed me.

"Eat, Ruby. I know you're hungry."

I sighed and pulled the tray toward me. I took a spoonful of the soup. Yup, ramen. Still, I hated to admit it, but it tasted good, and the warm broth was heaven on my dry throat.

"I don't usually eat here."

"Why am I not surprised?" I said, my mouth full of noodles. "But don't change the subject. What do you think Brad Steel owes you?"

"I said I'm not going to talk about that."

"Then maybe you'll talk about this," I said, swallowing. "Rodney Cates told me that Brad Steel was one of the only men you ever trusted."

He said nothing, his features betraying nothing.

"When exactly did that change?"

"Believe it or not," he said, "Brad Steel is actually one of the most trustworthy people on the planet."

Though it went against every instinct I possessed, I truly felt he was telling me the truth. Everything that Ryan had told me about his father indicated that he was a good man with good ethics.

Then my father's words from moments before rammed into my mind.

None of this was ever planned. We were forced into a lot

of it.

I didn't believe for a second that my father had been forced into any of this. But what about Brad Steel? Maybe he was the good man his children remembered. The circumstances surrounding Ryan's birth contradicted that, but shouldn't every man be allowed one mistake?

That was one big mistake, though.

Still, I couldn't begrudge Brad Steel that error in judgment. If he hadn't strayed, Ryan Steel wouldn't exist.

The man I loved wouldn't exist.

"Look," I said. "Let me help you. If you want to get out, I'll help you get out." I was lying through my teeth, but I had to try.

"You were a cop. An officer of the law. You won't help me. I'm in too deep to get out anyway."

"No, you're not. There are ways. Are we being monitored?" I looked around the room cautiously.

"No. I'm the boss here. No one monitors me."

"Good. You can turn state's evidence. I can get you out. I'll do what I can."

"It's too late. And I don't believe you anyway."

I couldn't fault his observation.

Time to change tactics. "Where's Brad Steel?"

"He's here."

I widened my eyes. No song and dance? I'd expected a little side step. "Where?"

"He's here. Close, anyway. On an adjacent island."

"Is he being kept in captivity?"

"What would ever give you that idea?"

"Wendy Madigan."

My father chuckled. Actually chuckled! "And you believed her?"

"Who am I supposed to believe, Theo? All of you have lied to me. Wendy, Larry Wade. Everyone. Now where's Brad Steel?"

"I wasn't lying. He's here. And he's not in captivity."

"Why would Wendy say he was?"

"I don't have the vaguest clue," my father said. "But if she did, she had a reason. That woman has a reason for everything she does. She goes crazy when it's convenient."

"I've already figured that out. That doesn't explain why she abducted Jonah Steel, though."

"She's obsessed with Brad. Jonah's a dead ringer for him."

"If she's so obsessed with him, why take his son? Why not just come here and be with him?"

"Because," my father said, "Brad doesn't want her here. He's gone to great effort to keep certain things from her."

I jolted in my chair. "But Wendy said—"

"Ruby, it doesn't matter what Wendy said. She's been running Brad Steel's life since we were kids. She's been running all our lives, actually, but Brad's most of all."

"What does she have on you?" I asked.

"What doesn't she have on me?"

Good point. "Hey, I know you're no paragon of society—no one knows that better than I do—but you've eluded capture this far. You've never even been arrested. Surely Wendy can't hurt you."

He sighed and pushed his chair back from the desk and leaned backward, his head hitting the wall. "Wendy Madigan can hurt everyone. And I'm going to make sure she doesn't hurt you."

CHAPTER ELEVEN

Ryan

"Either of you guys done any scuba diving before?" Raj had joined us on the deck once the sun rose.

"No," I said.

"Well, it's time to learn a thing or two."

"What?" Talon said. "That was never part of this deal."

"You're both in good shape. You'll be fine. You can swim, can't you?"

"Of course," Talon and I said together.

"Good. Lesson number one—"

"Hold on right there," I said. "Why do we need to learn scuba? We're not stopping the boat for anything."

"Well, when we get to those coordinates you gave me, you don't really think it's a good idea to just sail up and dock this floating luxury home, do you?"

I hadn't thought of that. From the look on Talon's face, neither had he. We had no idea who or what we would encounter once we got there. We couldn't just waltz right in and announce our presence.

"I'll take your silence as your agreement. We'll anchor far enough away that anyone who sees the yacht won't see a threat. The rich and famous cruise the Caribbean frequently."

"Got it," I said.

"Once I give you the basics, we'll stop the boat for—"

"Wait," Talon interjected. "Why can't we use one of those underwater dive propulsion things, like in the movies?"

"Uh...because you're not James Bond, mon. And this isn't a movie."

I couldn't help a chuckle.

"The yacht has top-notch equipment, but they don't stock dive scooters," Raj said. He added a sarcastic, "Sorry."

"Fine," Talon said. "Sorry I asked."

"As I was saying...we'll stop and I'll give you the quick open-water dive lesson. Then, when we reach the coordinates, we'll anchor somewhere out of sight and swim underwater to the island. It's daylight now, and we'll reach the coordinates after dark. That gives us the day to learn the basics, and we'll have Faucett stop for an hour for open-water practice. Follow me."

He led us to the stern of the ship and opened a cabinet. He pulled out masks, tanks, fins, and a bunch of other stuff I didn't recognize.

"First rule," Raj said. "Breathing out of a tank feels different. You need to stay calm, or you'll use up your oxygen. But you don't need to worry too much about that. We won't be underwater for very long."

"Wait a minute," I said, interrupting. "What is all this shit?"

He pulled out each item and named it—a regulator, an extra alternate regulator that Raj called an octopus, a snorkel, a buoyancy control device, a dive computer. I felt like I was back in school.

"Don't we need wet suits?" I asked.

"The water is warm here. That's just something else to

hold you back. We'll be wearing dive shorts."

"What are dive shorts?" Talon asked.

Raj pulled out a garment made of black Lycra. A Speedo with legs.

No fucking way. "Uh-uh." I shook my head.

"You guys are in good shape. I'm the one who should be embarrassed," Raj said.

Actually, Raj looked like he was in fine shape.

"How about we just wear our regular trunks?" Talon said.

"Because regular trunks bunch up and impede your movement."

"We can move just fine," I said.

"Give me much more of this shit, and I'll be making you shave your legs and head for ultimate movement. This is what you'll be wearing, mon. Best get used to it."

Talon and I both sighed. No way was I shaving my legs. Or my head. Ruby loved my hair.

Ruby.

Fuck. Where the hell was she?

If I had to wear tight Lycra shorts and haul my ass through water to find her, I'd do it.

I'd do anything.

★ ★ ★

"Land ho," Raj said sarcastically. "You two knew there'd be an island here all along, didn't you?"

"We had our suspicions," I said. "Didn't Faucett tell you there was land there? I assume he charted the course."

"I haven't talked to him. Where'd you get those coordinates, anyway?"

"We told you," Talon said. "They were a clue. They were kind of dropped in our lap."

"Whatever, mon. I don't ask questions unless I'm paid to." He looked up. "The sun's almost down. Once it's dark, we head out. Let's get something to eat in the meantime."

I didn't think I could eat. I'd done okay during our practice runs during the day, but I'd had to talk Talon down. He'd freaked at first about breathing underwater. Said it reminded him of being in that dark basement.

That had been hard for him to admit, but I'd talked to him gently and he'd been okay. The second trial run had gone smoothly.

Still, as I looked at my brother, I could see something dark in his eyes. This bothered him.

"It'll be okay, Tal," I said. "Come on. Let's eat something."

"Not hungry."

"Neither am I, but you know as well as I do we can't do this without sustenance." I nudged his arm. "Come on."

"I need to call Jade."

"Okay. There's time for that. Give her a call."

I wanted desperately to call Ruby, but I couldn't. I didn't need to remind Talon of that though. Right now, just as the yacht was anchored, Talon was looking for his anchor. His anchor was Jade.

I didn't have my anchor, but that wouldn't stop me.

I would go forward and find her.

If it was the last thing I did.

CHAPTER TWELVE

Ruby

"Since when do you care who hurts me?" I asked. "You tried to rape me. Or have you conveniently forgotten that?"

"Believe it or not, Ruby, I haven't raped anyone in the last decade."

I didn't believe it. "Maybe you have and maybe you haven't. That still doesn't excuse the damage you inflicted before then. On Gina. On Talon Steel. Even on me. And on myriad others."

He sighed. "I understand that. All I can say is that I have my regrets."

"What about murder? Are you going to try to tell me you had nothing to do with the murder of Jordan Hayes? The receptionist at your old high school?"

"I did not. Tom did that."

"And the business card that was planted in her apartment? Joe's business card?"

"Again, Tom. After Joe was beginning to prove that Tom wasn't the upstanding mayor everyone thought he was, Tom went insane."

"Because he wasn't insane before that?" I said sarcastically.

"He wanted to pin Jordan's murder on Joe."

"What about the business card left at Talon's house by the housekeeper? The same MO. Are you telling me that was Tom as well? Because Felicia told the Steels that the masked man who threatened her into doing it had strange icy-blue eyes. And Melanie said the same thing about the man who abducted her from her loft and pushed her into that garage and left her to die."

"My eyes are brown, Ruby."

I couldn't help but laugh. "You're wearing the freaky lenses right now, Theo."

"And that makes me the only suspect?" He lifted his brow. "Have you forgotten what color of eyes Simpson had?"

My veins froze. I had never met Tom Simpson, but Joe said that Bryce looked a lot like his father. Bryce's eyes were blue, but they were a warm blue. A gentle blue. Yet that same color in the eyes of an ice man...

Had we been wrong all this time?

"Tom was determined to bring the Steels down. He found out Jade had been digging, and he sent the rose as a warning, trying to frame Larry at the same time. He went so far as to have Larry's fingerprints changed in the database to match the set on her ex's business card. And then Joe... Tom thought Joe was a hothead, and when he and Melanie got more involved, Tom was determined to take them both out."

"Joe is his son's best friend."

"Do you think he cared about that?"

I let out a huff. "No, I don't. I don't think any of you have ever cared about anything other than money and saving your own sorry asses."

"That was Tom to the very end."

"And Larry?"

"Larry was trying to get everything out in the open without having Wendy come down on him. Why do you think

79

he asked Jade to research the Steels? He was leading her to clues. That's how his mind worked. Rather than squeal, he set people up to figure things out for themselves. He was brilliant in his own way. The problem with Larry was that he had no common sense, so Tom and I didn't always trust him."

"Yeah. You had him beaten to within an inch of his life for letting Talon Steel go, didn't you?"

"Actually, we didn't. That was all Wendy."

Wendy. That name again. Ryan's biological mother. We'd already figured out that she had been the true mastermind behind Talon's abduction, and she claimed to be the true mastermind behind everything. I'd spoken to Melanie about it on more than one occasion. Melanie was convinced that Wendy was the ultimate id with narcissistic personality disorder and delusions of grandeur.

Melanie was no doubt right. But one thing she hadn't factored in was Wendy's creative brilliance.

I didn't bother asking my father whether he was telling the truth. I already knew he was. The very marrow of my bones knew. Wendy had arranged Talon's abduction to punish his father for getting his mother pregnant with Marjorie. It only made sense that she was the one who punished Larry for letting him go.

"Larry seemed convinced that you and Tom were the ones who had him beaten."

"Larry wasn't aware of the ultimate power Wendy had over the rest of us."

"You mean over Brad Steel."

"No, Ruby. I mean over the rest of us."

"Then by all means, Father, enlighten me."

He sighed and pushed up the sleeves of his black shirt. The

phoenix on his left forearm was still as bright as I remembered. "I don't expect you to understand any of this."

"I'm pretty sure I won't. I still want to hear it. How did a little cheerleader like Wendy have power over any of you? She moved after her sophomore year. Plus, you claim Larry didn't know how dangerous she was. Larry already told the Steels that you weren't the most dangerous, which would indicate that Wendy was. Who else could he have been talking about?"

"I didn't say Larry didn't know how dangerous she was. I only said he didn't understand the power she had."

"Semantics, Theo. Let's skip over the bullshit and get down to one thing. The goddamned truth."

"You trust me to tell you the truth?"

I had to laugh. "No, not really, but at the moment, you're all I've got. So spill it."

He opened his mouth to speak when the door to his office burst open. "Boss, we've got a problem."

"I'm in a meeting, as you can see," my father said.

"Sorry, but you're needed elsewhere."

"Handle it, please."

"Some new ones have gone rogue. We need your help."

"You don't need my help. Show them who's boss."

I looked at the masked man's eyes. They were a familiar brown. This was one of the men who had raped Juliet.

And new ones? Were they bringing new women to the compound? I stood. "Take me to the 'new ones.'"

My father shook his head. "No."

"I demand it, damn it. In fact, I demand that you let them go. And not just them. All of them. Juliet. And where the hell is Gina?"

"Ruby." My father gritted his teeth. "Not now."

"Look," the other guy said, "our contract is coming due, and—"

I jerked my head back to him. "Contract? What you people are doing here is illegal, not to mention immoral. The laws don't exist. Who the hell cares about a contract?"

"Ruby," my father said calmly, "you don't understand. This business has its own laws, and we can't default on a contract."

"Why not?"

"Do I have to spell it out for you? They'll kill us."

"Hopefully not before they torture and rape you," I couldn't help saying.

Something in my father's fake eyes changed, but I couldn't pinpoint what it was.

"Who the fuck is this woman, boss?" the man asked.

"She's not your concern."

He eyed me, his tongue slithering along his lower lip. "Let me take a stab at her. Please. God, that body..."

Disgust crept up my throat. "You're not getting near me, you psycho."

"She's off-limits," my father said. "That's all you need to know."

My father's words didn't make me feel any better. I already harbored so much guilt for what he had done to so many, and now I was being spared what Juliet had been forced to endure because I was his daughter? Not that I wanted to be beaten and raped, but my God. When had my father grown scruples? This was the same man who'd attempted to rape me seventeen years earlier. Who'd raped Gina. Who'd raped and tortured Talon.

Talon. Oh my God.

My mind whirled. I knew now how Ryan felt. He'd been

spared Talon's fate because he was Wendy's son, just as I was now being spared Juliet's fate because I was my father's daughter.

A mixture of nauseous gratitude and disgust swirled through my mind and body. How could I be even the littlest bit thankful that I was the spawn of this monster?

I didn't deserve to be handled with kid gloves. And I hadn't been. He'd stuck me in that concrete cell with Juliet. Yet I had been spared the worst of it—what I'd been forced to witness happen to her.

Ryan and I had more in common than I'd ever imagined.

The thought of him warmed me. I hoped with everything in me that he hadn't found the bread crumbs my father claimed he'd left. I couldn't bear the thought of him wandering into a trap. I'll find you, Ryan. I'll do anything to get back to you.

My father eyed me, as if looking for me to say something.

"Am I supposed to thank you?" I said.

"You don't owe me anything," he said.

"You got that right."

"She's got a mouth on her, boss," the other guy said. "And when I say mouth, I mean I'd love to shove my cock into it."

My father stood and advanced on his goon, grabbing him at the neck. "You touch one hair on her head, and I'll choke the life out of you." He squeezed the man's throat. "Do you understand me?"

"Sure," the man rasped. "I get it, boss."

"Now get the fuck out of here." My father loosened his hold. "Take care of things yourself."

"If you say so." He rubbed his neck and left.

I suppressed a shiver. Theo's fake blue eyes had held the look of an insane killer. He'd meant every word he said. I cleared my throat, determined not to give him the "thank you" he no doubt expected.

"So you're bringing in new blood, huh?"

"Business doesn't stop just because you're here, Ruby."

"Where'd you get this batch? Another raid on a resort? Or did you pick up some homeless people?"

He didn't respond. Not that I expected him to.

"You do understand that I'm going to do everything within my power to free these innocent people and bring you and the rest of your goons down."

"I'd expect nothing less," he said, his voice resigned.

"Take me to them. The new ones."

"No."

"I'll follow you when you leave here, then."

"If I have to, I'll chain you down. Do you understand me?"

I understood perfectly.

"Where's Gina?"

He cleared his throat but again didn't answer.

"Is she here?"

He let out a sigh. "If you must know, no, she's not here."

"Where is she, then?"

"She's been sold."

My gut nearly exploded as I swallowed back brine. Sold. I couldn't wrap my head around it. I fought back the need to vomit. "To whom?"

"I don't have those records. We just provide the merchandise. We don't deliver it."

This time I couldn't hold back. Though I tried choking it down, I threw up all over my father's desk. The ramen I'd eaten made a second appearance.

"Now look what you've done," he said.

"What I've done? My beautiful cousin, who you set up to look like she'd killed herself, is now someone's property? I'm going to get her back, Theo, if it's the last thing I do."

"It may very well be. If she went where I think she did, her master is a powerful man."

"He doesn't scare me."

"He should."

Yes, he probably should. But right now my anger was taking over.

"Those other kids who were taken around the same time that Talon was... Where are they?"

"I don't know."

"You're lying."

"Ruby, that was twenty-five years ago. Kids are sold, but they eventually grow up. I don't know what's done with them after that. It's not my business."

"Not your business? These are human beings!" I stood and threw the tray still holding ramen onto the ground. I fought back more retching. "How did you get like this? How, for all of these years, have you been able to treat people like things to be bought and sold? Used and abused? How?"

He sighed, his countenance resigned. "It's a long story."

CHAPTER THIRTEEN

R y a n

Raj went down first, and then Talon. Because Talon had freaked a bit during practice, we'd decided to let him go in the middle. Finally, I dropped into the dark water. We were using lights since we'd otherwise be basically blind. I'd been prepared for the noise. Breathing through a regulator was loud, and it had startled me during our practice runs. Inhale, and then exhale fully. I'd done okay during practice, but now my nerves were frazzled. I had to stay calm, or I'd hyperventilate. I turned my head to look to each side. My mask cut off part of my peripheral vision, and I was surprised at how much I missed it. Raj had taught us some hand signals to communicate with each other underwater, but vision would be limited because it was nighttime. He was taking us toward the island. I tried to control the urge to continuously adjust. He'd told us to relax and let the water take us where we needed to go.

Talon swam ahead, between Raj and me. I kept my eyes on his fins and followed.

I tried to calm my rattling nerves by making Talon my anchor. Keep your eyes on Talon.

He seemed to slow down. When my mask bumped his fins, though, I knew something was amiss.

I stared at him, looking for hand signals. I gave him the

okay sign, questioning him.

He didn't "okay" back. Was he even looking at me?

One of his arms flailed out suddenly. I went closer, and when I saw his eyes through the glass of his mask, sheer panic looked back at me.

What was wrong?

Raj was ahead of us, but if something was going wrong with Talon, I couldn't afford to take the time to alert Raj. I tried the okay signal once again, and again Talon offered no response. Bubbles rose from his mouth in a constant stream instead of shutting off between breaths.

When his arms started flailing, I knew I had to act.

Was he breathing? I couldn't tell. He hadn't used the "out of air" signal, but then he hadn't used any signals at all. I ripped my octopus out of its holder and offered it to him.

Talon spat out his regulator and grabbed the octopus, inserting it into his mouth. He took what looked to be two long breaths.

I gave him the okay sign again, and this time he returned it. I pointed upward, indicating that we should rise to the surface.

His tank must have malfunctioned. When we reached the surface of the water, I pulled the regulator out of my mouth. "What the hell happened?"

Talon removed my extra regulator and took a long, deep breath. "I don't know," he said, still breathless. "My air started coming really fast. Like a fire hose. I didn't know what to do."

Raj rose to the surface and swam back toward us. "Everything okay?"

Everything was not okay, or we wouldn't have come up. But I didn't say that. Talon was still a little breathless, so I spoke. "He had a problem with his tank and regulator. The air started coming really fast."

"Free flowing. Shit," Raj said. "We're close enough that we can swim from here."

About ten minutes later, we reached a point where we could stand on the ground and get our shoulders out of the water. Although we removed our fins, walking with all the equipment was arduous, but we soon reached the sandy shore.

Talon was still visibly shaken up, his body rigid and tense.

"Why didn't you signal?" Raj asked him.

"He was frantic. He forgot. We only just learned this shit a few hours ago," I said. "Leave him alone."

"Hey, mon, I didn't mean anything. I admit I went through everything quicker than a dive instructor would. Don't you remember what I said about a free-flow malfunction?"

"I said he was frantic. You don't know his past." No way was I going to let him give Talon a hard time.

"Ry," Talon said, his eyes pleading with me.

I said no more about his past. "What do you suppose happened?" I asked Raj.

"Could have been a simple malfunction," he said. "It's certainly not unheard of. Or...someone could have tampered with it."

I didn't want to think about the latter option. Only four others on the yacht besides the three of us. Did one of them want to keep us from reaching this island?

Talon was still shuddering. I touched his shoulder.

"Hey. It's okay. We're okay." I looked ahead. "We're going to make it."

"I'm never doing that again," Talon said.

I clutched at the waterproof container strapped to my hip. It contained a change of clothes and some supplies. It also contained a loaded gun and as much extra ammo as would fit—not much. Raj and Talon each had one as well. We'd be safe. And I wasn't leaving Talon's side.

We trudged along the deserted beach. The moon and stars in the clear night sky gave adequate guidance. My nerves were a mess, and I didn't take my eyes off my brother. He'd been my hero for so long. My anchor. Now I needed to be his.

Someone on that boat might have just tried to kill him.

I didn't take that lightly.

We pulled off our fins and changed clothes quickly.

"We need to find a place to stash our tanks and snorkels," Raj said.

I looked around and squinted. Trees blanketed the land, surprisingly.

"Before settlement, the Caribbean islands were a diverse forested ecosystem," Raj said when I asked about the foliage.

I looked around the coastline. It was dark, but I sure couldn't see any ending. This wasn't a small island. A faint light shone in the distance through the trees. "Do you see that?" I asked, pointing.

"Yah, mon," Raj said. "Go toward the light, as they say. But first let's hide our stuff somewhere out here where no one will look."

"Why not bury it in the sand?" Talon said.

"Good idea," Raj said. "But we have to be able to find it again if we need it. I'll be in touch with the captain on the boat, but we need to be cautious. Someone may have tampered with your tank. We don't know who we can trust now." He looked around. "I don't see a cell phone tower anywhere around, but I do seem to have service." He fidgeted with his phone. "So there's something around here somewhere. There are Wi-Fi networks too."

I turned to regard my brother. He was still pale.

"Hey." I grabbed his forearm. "You okay?"

He nodded.

"You sure? You don't have to do this. We can leave right now." Though I wasn't sure how, since someone on the boat possibly wanted us dead.

"We have to do this. I have to do this. I have to put an end to this once and for all." He stiffened and inhaled. "Let's do it."

I nodded, sending up a message of thanks to whoever was listening. I didn't want to leave Talon in Raj's care, but that's what I would have done.

Whether Talon went forward or not, I had to.

I had to find Ruby.

CHAPTER FOURTEEN

Ruby

"Seems we've got time," I said, looking out the window. "It's dark now, and I have no desire to go back to that cell you had me in. So tell me the long story."

He opened his mouth to speak when his phone buzzed on the desk. He glanced at it. "They're here."

"Who?"

"Who do you think? Three men have been spotted on the outskirts of the island."

Three men. The Steel brothers.

A lump formed in my throat. "Don't you dare hurt them."

"I told you they'd follow the bread crumbs. That they'd come for you. Didn't you believe me?"

I tried swallowing the lump, to no avail. I hadn't doubted him. Ryan would have come for me through a blinding snowstorm. Nothing would stop him, even though I'd wished so hard for him not to follow me. I couldn't bear the thought of him being in harm's way.

"Haven't the Steels been through enough?" I said.

"Not nearly," he said.

"What do you have against them, anyway?"

"My beef is with Brad, not his sons."

"Then why bring them here? I don't understand."

"I have my reasons."

"You have Brad Steel. He's somewhere here. You've obviously been keeping him here for seven years, letting his children think he's dead. Why not just let the family be?"

"I don't exactly have Brad Steel."

I was sick of him pussyfooting around. "He's here. You've said so yourself. So let his sons go." I swallowed, about to do something that already had me gagging. "Please...Dad. If you ever cared for me at all, please let them go." Yuck. I needed some mouthwash after that. But it was worth it. I'd do anything for Ryan.

He shook his head. "I've told you before that I have no intention of hurting them."

"Then why did you lure them here?"

He sighed. "I want out, Ruby."

"Out of what?"

"What do you think? Out of this! I'm old. I'm tired. I'm going broke. It's taken me most of my savings to deal with the fallout of the Steels' interference. Once Talon Steel got into therapy and Larry hired Jade to be his assistant city attorney, everything started crumbling. I want out."

"So you want out because you're getting close to getting caught. That's nice."

"No, I want out because I'm tired. Believe it or not, I'm not proud of everything I've done."

I rolled my eyes and let out an indignant huff.

"Scoff if you want. I'm nearly out of funds. You were right."

"It's a shame Brooke Bailey didn't die in that accident you staged."

"That was a million-dollar policy, Ruby. It would have bought me a little time, but not much. A million dollars isn't a lot in this business. Besides, I don't expect you to believe this, but I actually cared for Brooke."

"No, I don't believe it."

"Suit yourself. But I'm glad she's not dead."

"You got in touch with her. Wanted her to go away with you somewhere."

"I did."

"Jade told her everything. She wants nothing to do with you." I didn't know if that was true, but I did know Jade had talked to her mother.

"So be it." He rubbed the back of his neck until it popped.

Time to change tactics. "I want to know about Wendy. I want to know about the symbol on those rings. I want to know what Wendy has on all of you to make you get into this horrible business. According to her, you guys simply got greedy and found out how lucrative the business of selling human beings is."

"I won't deny being greedy. I also won't deny having some odd...tendencies."

"Odd tendencies? Is that what you call pedophilia? Rape? Odd?"

He closed his eyes. "So much you don't know. You'll never understand."

"How the hell did you find two other guys—Larry and Tom—who shared your sickness? The three of you were on some kind of macho power trip induced by greed and a psychopathy you all shared."

"It's not that simple."

"You're right about that. It isn't simple at all."

"Doing heinous things becomes easier after a while."

"It shouldn't."

"Maybe not. But it does. The first time you break a rule, you're filled with remorse, but when you don't get caught, it's easier to break it the second time. And it gets easier each time afterward, until it's the norm." He closed his eyes again, leaning his head back. "Things get twisted after a while. After you..." He opened his eyes and stared at me with those eerie blue eyes. "Never mind."

"We're not talking about jaywalking here, Theo. We're talking about abusing women and kids. People, Theo. They're fucking people!"

"It was Wendy—"

"Spare me. Three big tough guys were outsmarted and manipulated by one teenage girl? I'm not buying it."

"You don't know her."

He was wrong about that. I did know her. She was evil. As evil as they were. But I couldn't believe that she had been able to manipulate three strong men. Four, including Ryan's father. Five, including my Uncle Rodney. All the while having a successful career as a TV and newspaper journalist.

Unbelievable.

Something sinister was lurking here. Something I couldn't even begin to comprehend. Something no one in his right mind could begin to comprehend.

My father had said it was a long story. My patience was growing thin.

"I need to see Ryan," I said.

"That's not possible."

"He's here. He's come for me. If he finds me, he'll leave."

"No, he won't. He's with his brothers."

"You asked me to guarantee you safe travel out of the country when you met me at the hotel," I said. "You managed to get out without my help, because here you are. You're not as helpless as you'd like me to believe, Theo. Not at all."

He didn't deny my words. Not that I expected him to.

"Now that it's dark again," he said, "I'm taking you to more suitable accommodations."

CHAPTER FIFTEEN

Ryan

I reached for my phone to text Joe that we'd made it to the island where the compound supposedly was. It was a pretty long text, because we hadn't had decent service for over twenty-four hours. I had to tell him that we'd found the coordinates on our father's ring.

He texted me back within seconds.

*Good. Be careful. When you can get away, we
need to talk.*

I looked around. In the darkness I couldn't see any wiring. It was probably all buried anyway. This island had killer cell service.

What's up?

*I met with Dad's attorney. Finally. Got some
information out of him.*

I didn't want to think about what Joe had done to get any information out of anyone. My oldest brother had both a hot temper and a dark side—a lethal combination when he unleashed them together.

We're hiding our stuff.

Then what?

Hell, then what? I had no idea. We didn't have a plan per se because we hadn't known what we'd find when we got here. Only the coordinates. The basic plan was to stay out of sight until we figured out where we were and who else was here.

We already had a pretty good idea of who we'd find here. Where? That was the question.

I texted Joe back.

We'll need to find somewhere to spend the night.

Okay. When you get settled in, like I said, I need to talk to you both. Get me on speakerphone.

I didn't like the idea of talking in front of Raj. He hadn't given me any reason not to trust him, but the thing with Talon's tank had me shaken up more than a bit.

Start a group text. Let's do it that way for now. Don't want to talk out loud.

Understood. Will add Tal into the text. Just let me know when you're both available.

I sent him the thumbs-up icon and continued on my way. I'd fallen behind a bit.

Raj had stopped about a hundred or so feet ahead where the trees made a small clearing. I jogged to reach him and

Talon.

"This looks like a good place to rest," Raj said.

Not that I would be able to sleep, but he and Talon should get some. "I'll keep the first watch," I said.

"Sounds good to me," Raj said. "I'm beat." He sat down on the dirt. "Not the most comfortable bed, but it's a beautiful night, mon. Nothing like sleeping under the stars."

"I'll stay with you until I start to nod off," Talon said, arching one eyebrow. He'd obviously gotten the group text from Joe.

"Works for me. Just remember, you won't be at your best without sleep." Raj lay down on his back and closed his eyes.

I signaled to Talon. We stood until Raj's breathing had gotten less shallow and steady, a snore after every few breaths, and then we moved away from him.

We each took a seat on the dirt, our backs against what I thought was a banyan tree. Not that I'd had a chance to familiarize myself with the local flora. I kicked off our group text conversation.

We're here.

Joe: *Good. I've got a lot to tell you.*

Talon: *Go ahead.*

We waited. Joe was obviously writing a long text. The tiny ellipsis was moving. Finally, after what seemed like hours, his text appeared.

Joe: *I finally got in to see Dad's attorney. The one who read his will when he supposedly died.*

I demanded to see the will. He was squirrely at first, said I had no right to see it. I got in his face and said as his oldest child and one of his heirs, who the hell had more right? He saw it my way when fists got involved.

Talon: *Jesus, Joe. You've got the cops questioning you about Larry's death, and you decide to pick a fight with Dad's attorney?*

Simultaneously, I texted: *For God's sake.*

Joe: *He had it coming. He finally got the document out of a locked safe behind a portrait in his office. Can you believe it? He kept Dad's will in a locked safe.*

Me: *Is that normal?*

Joe: *No. I called Jade. Attorneys don't normally lock up their client's files. At least not in a hidden safe. They might lock their filing cabinets. Anyway, I grabbed it out of his hands. I read through it, and it turns out it was a decoy.*

Me: *What?*

Joe: *It wasn't his real will. Well, it was, but a page was missing. Dad's attorney had been an idiot and hadn't bothered renumbering the pages of the will, and I noticed right off that a page was missing.*

Talon: *Did he have the other page?*

Joe: *Yeah. After I threatened him with more violence and showed him Rosie strapped to my ankle.*

I smiled. Rosie was Joe's Glock 23. He was a master marksman.

Joe: *He got the missing page out of yet another safe. And you won't believe what it says.*

Talon: *What?*

My skin chilled around me as I waited for Joe's text. Seconds turned into minutes.

Joe: *What he read to us after Dad's death was all there. All of his property, real and personal, went into the Steel Trust for the benefit of the four of us equally. But there was a sentence on that missing page. Except as detailed in section four. Then, also on that page, was section four.*

Neither Talon nor I texted him. We waited for the next text to show up.

Joe: *In section four, Dad specifically bequeathed fifty million dollars to the Fleming*

Corporation.

A brick lodged in my gut. I'd heard that name before.

Joe: *In case you don't remember, the Fleming Corporation is the dummy corp that owns the house where Melanie was kept and also the house where I found Tom Simpson. The house where they kept you, Tal.*

I chilled, shivering.
The Fleming Corporation...
Damn.
Talon must be freaking, but when I looked over at him, he was frantically typing.
His text came up a few seconds later.

Talon: *What about the Steel Family Trust? Anything about that?*

Talon was holding it together better than I was. Good for him. I hadn't even thought about the Steel Family Trust. It was a separate trust that none of us had known existed. My father had used it to convey by quitclaim the Shane ranch.

Joe: *I asked about it. And I'll get to that. But first, the Fleming Corp. The attorney had nothing to say about it. Said he didn't know anything about it. He'd only written the will. He was an estate attorney, so I took him at his word. I'm going to go see the registered agent for the corporation tomorrow. Remember Melanie and I went to see him? Frederick*

Jolley? Anyway, that's on the agenda for tomorrow or the next day.

A pause. Then,

Joe: *Now, back to the Steel Family Trust. He admitted setting up the trust before Dad "died."*

Me: *Wait. Does this attorney know that Dad isn't dead?*

Joe: *We didn't get into that. He ushered me out. Said he had an appointment that couldn't be rescheduled, and he'd call the cops if I didn't leave. Said he'd cry assault and battery because of my gun. I told him I had a concealed carry and had every right to have the gun. But then I figured, since the cops were already questioning me about Larry, I'd better leave for now.*

Talon: *Good call.*

Me: *I agree with Tal.*

Joe: *I'm not done with him yet, though. Not by a long shot.*

Talon: *Be careful.*

Joe: *I'm always careful.*

I wasn't sure I agreed with that, but I didn't say anything.

Joe: *So tomorrow I'm going to try to see Jolley about the Fleming Corp, and then I'm going back to see this joker. He's going to answer to me.*

Talon: *Joe, Jade explained to me how trusts work. An attorney sets it up, but after that, it's just a matter of transferring things into the trust. Dad probably did that himself.*

Joe: *Maybe. But I'm pretty sure there's still stuff this guy isn't telling me. He's going to talk.*

Me: *Be careful, brother. What we don't need is—*

My phone fell into the soft dirt when a meaty hand gripped my shoulder.

CHAPTER SIXTEEN

Ruby

My father ushered me out of the small office, down a dark hallway, and out a doorway into an unlit alley.

I weighed my options. I could run from him, but where would I go? I had no idea where I was, and my eyes hadn't yet adjusted to the darkness. I could try to take my father down, though he was probably armed. Again, though, where would I go?

I could go back inside and find Juliet, but if they had her chained up, I had no way of releasing her. I had no way of releasing anyone.

Though guilt permeated me for leaving her and what I assumed were many others as prisoners in that abominable place, I had no choice but to go with Theo. The more I learned about wherever I was, the more I'd have in my arsenal of knowledge.

He led me to a black SUV and opened the door for me. Could have knocked me over with a feather with that one. He got into the driver's seat while I secured my seat belt.

"Can I have a cell phone?" I asked.

"Your cell phone is at home. In your apartment."

"I didn't ask if I could have my cell phone. I asked if I could have a cell phone."

"Eventually. Maybe."

"Where are we?"

"On the island. In the Caribbean. The one I told you about."

"How did you get me all the way out here while I was passed out?"

"You didn't pass out. You were drugged. A drug that induces amnesia and makes you extremely...pliable."

"You fucking roofied me? Jesus Christ."

"It's an extremely safe medication, Ruby."

"Medication? It's not even legal in the US."

"We're not in the US."

"You must have given it to me before—" I shook my head. "Since when do you care what's legal?"

"I administered it myself in the correct dose. You will have no lasting effects."

"Yeah? When did you get your medical degree?"

He ignored my snide comment. "I've decided to give you a gift," he said. "It should be here soon."

"The only gift I want is the Steel brothers' safety. After that, to go home."

"I've told you the Steels won't be harmed. Nevertheless, I think you'll like what's coming." He looked out his window. "Ah, here it is now."

A man dressed all in black walked toward the SUV, dragging a woman with a fabric bag over her head. He opened the back door and shoved her inside. "Get in, bitch."

"Hey!" I shouted. "Don't call her that." I turned around and ripped the fabric off her head. "Juliet!"

She squinted. "Where am I?"

Her hands were cuffed. I bounded into the back seat and

started working on them. "Uncuff her," I demanded to my father.

"Later."

"No. Now. You said she was my gift. I want her comfortable."

"For Christ's sake." He turned to the masked man. "Release her."

"She'll run."

"Then you'll catch her, or you'll wish you had."

"You're the boss." He quickly pulled out a chain of keys and, finding one, unlocked the cuffs.

"Get up here, Ruby," my father said. "We need to get moving."

"No way. I'm riding back here with her."

"You're riding up here, or we're not going," he said.

"It's all right," Juliet said, her voice raspy. "I'll be okay. Do what he says."

"I don't follow his orders," I said.

"You should. He'll..." She closed her eyes and sighed, not finishing her thought.

"Get the fuck up here, or we're not going," Theo said.

Juliet nodded to me and mouthed, "I'll be okay."

My father had said he was taking me to better accommodations. Almost anything would be better than where we'd been, and I wasn't going to screw this up for Juliet.

Of course, my father could very well be lying.

I had to take the chance. If I could get Juliet away from the other goons—and it appeared I might be able to—I had to go for it. Maybe I could figure out a way for the two of us to escape. Then I'd have a better chance of helping all the others trapped at the "dorms."

The others... I didn't want to leave them to their fate, but I had to let them go for now. I could only do so much.

The story of my life.

I moved back up to the front seat and yawned despite trying to stay awake.

"Sleep if you want to," he said. "We'll be on the road for a few hours."

I yawned again and then looked back at Juliet. She had put the seat back into a reclining position and closed her eyes. This was probably the most comfort she'd had in almost a month.

The lights on the dashboard were on, but other than that, all I could see was what the headlights illuminated. A yawn split my jaw again, but no way was I falling asleep.

★ ★ ★

"Undress."

I always did what he told me, even though I didn't understand why. I fingered the sheer silky fabric of the gossamer aqua gown I wore. Where I'd gotten it, I didn't know. But the softness was heaven against my skin.

Within seconds, it lay on the floor. Because I'd do anything he asked.

Absolutely anything.

He walked toward me then, slowly, stalking me. My nipples hardened, straining forward. I found myself stepping toward him, as if being led by the throbbing in my breasts.

He grabbed one and squeezed it. I gasped without meaning to. It hadn't hurt, but still I was surprised. Then he tugged on the nipple.

Hard.

Lightning bolted through me, landing between my thighs.

"You're mine," he growled. "Mine to do with as I please." He grabbed my hair, yanking on my ponytail. It was uncomfortable...yet oh, so comfortable.

I wouldn't stop him.

He could do anything to me.

Anything.

He pulled me toward him, not gently, and bit on my earlobe hard enough to draw blood. "Tell me you know you're mine, Ruby. Tell me."

"I...know I'm yours," I whimpered, my whole body reaching for something... Something...

He took my lips with the force of an angry wolf. He devoured me, stole from me with that kiss.

And I willingly surrendered.

When we were both breathless, he ripped his mouth from mine and turned me around, forcing me facedown onto a bed covered in blue silk, my feet still on the floor.

He thrust inside me hard.

So very fucking hard.

So very fucking good.

Then, a slap to my ass. Another. And another.

The sharp pain morphed to heat and then to pleasure.

"Such a firm, red ass," he said through a groan. "And it's mine. It's all fucking mine."

I grabbed the bedcovers, each thrust of his pushing me farther into the mattress. Drowning. I was drowning in Ryan Steel.

He slapped me again. Again. Again.

So quickly I hardly knew what was happening, he turned me around and pushed back inside me. His handsome face glistened with sweat, his dark hair sticking to his forehead and cheeks.

"Mine," he said again. "Mine to do with what I want."

"Yours," I repeated. "Yours to do with what you want." I closed my eyes.

He pushed harder, harder...until—

I sucked in a breath. The sweet plunging of his cock...had turned to...

Sharpness. Stabbing. A knife.

Then the smell...coppery and metallic.

Blood.

Pain.

God, the pain! I shuddered as my body rebelled.

A dark voice. "Mine. Mine. Mine. Mine to hurt. Mine to punish."

I opened my eyes.

A scream tore from my throat.

It was no longer Ryan forcing himself into me...

★ ★ ★

My eyes shot open. I jerked my head to one side and then the other. Where was I?

My father. Yes, he was driving. Juliet lay in the back seat. I rubbed my eyes. How had I fallen asleep? I'd been so determined not to.

The dream pervaded my mind. Ryan had been there... and then not there. Everything had changed. The feelings, the desire...had morphed into pain and fear. My skin prickled, and I rubbed my arms.

My father turned the car onto a desolate road. "We're

here."

Dawn was breaking, and before us stood a concrete wall with a wrought iron gate in the middle. The thing had to be twenty feet high at least. I looked back at Juliet, who was still sleeping soundly. I hated to wake her, so I didn't.

"I need to call and get the gate opened," Theo said.

I yawned. "Who lives here?"

"Several people."

"We are on the same island, aren't we? How long were we driving?" I wished I'd stayed awake. I had no phone and no watch, so no way to know what time it was.

This time, Theo yawned. "We're on an adjacent island. We took a small ferry. You slept through it all."

The gate opened, and we drove in to what appeared to be a country estate. On an island in the Caribbean. I had to blink a few times to be sure I wasn't seeing things. "What the hell?"

"You'll see soon enough," he said. "It's just a few more miles from here."

"Lower your voice. She's still asleep." I turned to see Juliet moving a little. "Never mind. You woke her up."

I tumbled over into the back seat once more. Screw what my father wanted. I touched her arm gently. "How are you?"

"I don't know," she said. "I think I slept."

"You did."

"That's the best sleep I've had in a while."

In the back of an SUV. I didn't like it, but I felt a sliver of gratitude toward my father for letting her have this rest. I'd heard that babies found the movement of a car soothing. Apparently, so did abused women.

"Are you hungry?" I asked.

She shook her head. "I stopped being hungry a while ago.

Do you know where we're going?"

"I don't have a clue, but you're safe with me, okay? I'm going to protect you."

They were empty words, I knew. I hadn't been able to protect her from being raped in front of my eyes. But I'd do my damndest to make sure that never happened again. I'd take the punishment for her if I had to.

Just the thought made me want to retch.

But I would. I owed her that much.

Melanie would say I didn't owe Juliet anything, that it wasn't my fault she was here. Melanie would be right, but that couldn't negate the guilt that permeated my soul.

Melanie. Just thinking of one member of the Steel family brought Ryan crashing to the forefront of my mind.

Not that he was ever out of my mind.

According to my father, he was here. Near.

My father wasn't known for his truthfulness, but for some reason, I didn't think he was lying to me. I didn't think he'd lied to me at all since he'd made contact with me recently. I had no reason for this—just a gut feeling. Something in him had changed. Whether it was good or bad, I didn't know.

For a split second, I almost wished my father hadn't brought Juliet along. I had to keep her safe, and she would take my focus off Ryan. I hated myself for even having the thought. Besides, Ryan and his brothers could take care of themselves, right?

I kept repeating that to myself. Over and over, until—

I inhaled a sharp breath.

We arrived at a sprawling ranch house.

My father stopped the car and looked into the back seat I was sharing with Juliet. "Look familiar?"

CHAPTER SEVENTEEN

R y a n

"Get the fuck up," a low voice said.

My heart pumped wildly. A man in black, including a mask, stood above me. Another was gripping Talon.

Talon easily dislodged the grip. "Get your filthy hands off me." Rage glared in his dark eyes, the moonlight accentuating it. He looked like a wolf gone mad under the full moon.

"Easy, Tal," I said.

I understood. He'd been grabbed once before, and it had led to the most horrible time in his life.

Several yards away, another man was rustling Raj out of his deep sleep.

"You're coming with us," the man holding me said.

"The hell we are." I broke his grip. Now if only I could reach my gun.

Talon shoved his fist under his attacker's chin in a perfect uppercut. The attacker let out an oof but managed to grab my brother again. Talon easily broke the grip once more and pounded the guy's face into the tree we'd been sitting under. The man yelled and fell to the ground.

Talon turned to my guy, who had grabbed me again. He hurled his body into both of us, taking us to the ground. He grabbed the goon and started pounding his fists into his face.

The guy screamed and gurgled.

"Get off him."

Raj's voice. The big man approached us, holding his own attacker at gunpoint. He regarded the two unconscious, bloody men.

"Make sure they aren't armed, and then strip them. The two of you put those black clothes on over your own. This one will show us where we're going, or he'll get his fucking head blown off."

The man with Raj was also dressed all in black, including a black ski mask.

I grabbed Talon and pulled him into a stand, steadying him. His eyes still shone with a wildness, a primal fury.

"You okay?"

He nodded slightly but didn't say anything.

"Come on. Let's go with Raj."

"Not until we make sure they're not armed," Raj said.

I quickly frisked the two men, finding two pistols and three knives. I took one of the guns and gave the other to Talon, who still looked freaked.

"Take this, but be careful," I said.

He nodded slightly again. I'd need to keep my eye on him.

Then I stripped the clothes and masks off them. One was white and the other black. Without masks, they looked a lot less menacing. The masks were both tainted with blood, but Raj was right. We needed to put them on. I handed Talon the better mask of the two and took the gun from him for a minute.

"Come on," I said. "Put this shit on."

I pulled the shirt and pants on over my clothes. They were tight, but I was able to get into them. Then I put the mask over my head. It was made of a breathable cotton, thank God, but with the coppery smell of fresh blood...

I held back my puke.

Talon followed my lead. Once he put the mask on, I shuddered a bit. His eyes still looked wild, and with his face obscured...

I wouldn't want to run into him in a dark alley.

"Okay, mon," Raj said to his own attacker. "You take us in."

"The fuck I will."

"Let me make this easier. You take us in there, or your brains will be smeared all over your friends here."

"They'll kill me."

"Well, then, you'll have a few hours' reprieve while you take us there, then. A few hours is better than nothing, right, mon?"

Raj's attitude overwhelmed me. The man had nerves of steel. Quickly he pulled the mask off the man's face. He was white with darker hair. I couldn't discern his eye color yet, but the haze of dawn was just beginning to break. Had we really been up all night?

Raj stopped a moment and looked back at the two men. "You think they're out for a while?" he asked Talon and me.

"I'd say so," I said. "Talon went at them pretty good."

Raj regarded them for a few more seconds and then shook his head. "Can't take the chance." He produced some twine from his bag and bound their arms and legs. "I ought to put bullets through their brains."

I stopped myself from gasping and looked to Talon. He didn't seem fazed.

I quaffed down my astonishment—and a little bit of fear—and followed Raj.

The man led us to an SUV parked on a dirt road about

a half mile away. Raj pushed him into the driver's seat, still holding the gun to his head. "Get in," he said to Talon and me.

We got in the back seat, and I held my gun on the guy while Raj got in the passenger side of the front seat. He situated himself and then pointed the gun at the man's temple.

"What's your name, mon?"

"Fuck you," he spat.

Raj nudged the gun against his temple. "Your name, asshole."

The man winced. "Scotty."

"All right then, Scotty. Drive."

★ ★ ★

We arrived half an hour later at a large brick structure with lots of small windows. The area had been cleared of trees and brush. In fact, most greenery was gone. Strange.

"They won't let you in," Scotty said.

"Yes, they will. Take your fucking clothes off so I can put them on." He handed me his piece. "Hold it on him."

I forced my hand to remain steady as Raj changed in record time. Clearly he was used to changing clothes inside a car. Though I still didn't fully trust him, I was impressed so far.

He put Scotty's mask on and then said, "You'll take us in."

"They'll wonder where my mask is. Where my clothes are."

"Tell them you lost them. Make something up. I don't give a damn."

"Three of us left, and now four of us return?"

"Use your wits, if you have any. I'll have this pistol in your back the whole time. I'm betting it will spur your imagination."

He looked back at us. "You two ready?"

Ready? I had no idea what we were about to encounter, but I was armed with two guns. Talon still didn't look quite like himself, but we had no choice but to move now.

The time had come. Whatever was in that building was what we had come here for. I just wasn't sure I was prepared to see it.

"Ready," I said.

"Ready," Talon echoed.

CHAPTER EIGHTEEN

Ruby

I had only been to the main Steel house a few times. I'd spent most of my time on the ranch at Ryan's home, which was several hundred yards behind the main house, so I'd gotten some good views of the sprawling abode from the back. I was less familiar with the front, but from what I could remember...

I was looking at an exact replica of the main Steel ranch house. The house where Talon lived with Jade, Marjorie, and Brooke Bailey.

I blinked several times. The brick color was exactly the same—red with flecks of gold and yellow—the trim painted the same pale blue, like a robin's egg. I walked forward as if in a trance. I almost expected to see Talon's little mutt, Roger, appear in the window by the front door.

Then I stopped. Cold.

I turned around. I had completely forgotten about Juliet. She had emerged from the car.

I ran back to her. "I'm sorry. I didn't mean to leave you."

She stood on shaky legs. "Where are we?"

"I honestly don't know, but I recognize this house." I turned to Theo. "What's the meaning of this?"

"I promised you better accommodations. I trust this will suffice."

"I don't know. I haven't seen the inside yet." Visions of rooms filled with starving women and children chained up forced themselves into my mind.

"The inside is as pleasant as the outside. I assure you, no expense was spared. I should fucking know."

Resentment. Resentment in my father's voice. I didn't stop to try to figure out why. Right now, my main concern was Juliet. I felt a twinge of guilt that I couldn't focus more on Ryan, but at least I knew he could take care of himself.

"What's in there?" I demanded.

"Better accommodations, as I said. Follow me."

I took Juliet's arm and followed my father up the pathway to the front door. Oddly, my father rang the doorbell.

The door opened, and a woman in a maid's uniform stood there. "Mr. Theo. What can I do for you?"

"I've brought some guests for you, Marabel. These two ladies will need rooms and a shower, obviously."

"Who are they?"

"The dark-haired one is my daughter. The other is her... er...friend."

"We're happy to have your daughter here, of course. Please, do come in."

My father stood back and let Juliet and me in first. Gentlemanly of him, which surprised me. But I didn't doubt my father was a charmer if he had swept Brooke Bailey off her feet. Juliet was stone-faced and showed no reaction to the news that I was Theo's daughter. I turned to look at him.

He stared back at me with his natural brown eyes. When had he taken out the blue contacts? Sometime during the night, while I was asleep, I guessed. Funny I hadn't noticed until now.

"Come on, girls," Marabel said. "Don't just stand there.

You both look like you could use a good meal. I've got spaghetti sauce simmering on the stove for lunch. It's the lady's favorite. But it's a hearty breakfast for you first."

The lady? But I couldn't consider the implications of Marabel's statement at the moment. I walked in, guiding Juliet, and the spicy smell of tomatoes and basil drifted toward me. I inhaled.

A tear came to Juliet's eye. "Why are we here?" she asked.

"I honestly don't know," I said. "But let's make the most of it while it's happening."

"But the others..."

Her thought mirrored my own. I wouldn't rest until the others were safe as well, but for now, we could both use a good meal and a good bed. We'd be better able to help the others if we were well fed and rested.

Marabel led Juliet and me down the corridor to a door. "Here you go. One of you can take this one."

"You mean we're not staying together?" Juliet asked frantically.

I squeezed her hand. "Of course we can. We'll need just one room."

"All right." She led us farther down the hall. "Then take this one."

We walked into a room that had two queen beds. "You'll have to share the bathroom. There are robes and pajamas in the bureau. Leave your soiled clothing in the hamper, and I'll do your laundry for you later."

"You don't have—" I began.

"Don't be silly. I'm happy to do it. Now the two of you get cleaned up, and I'll get a hot breakfast ready for you."

"We will," I said. "And thank you." I looked at Juliet. I had no idea when she'd last had a proper shower. "Come on." I led her to the bathroom and turned on the shower. "You go first."

She looked at me timidly, biting her lip, her eyes darting back and forth.

"You'll be all right," I said. "I'll be right in the bedroom."

"Please. Don't leave me."

I smiled. "I can't shower with you, Juliet."

"No, of course not. Just stay in here while I shower. And then I'll stay in here while you do."

"All right. If it will make you feel better."

She pulled the dirty gray sweatshirt over her head.

I held back a gasp.

She looked nothing like the beautiful blond bombshell I'd met at the resort in Jamaica. Her curves were gone, and ribs showed through her skin that was red and dry in places. Her full breasts now hung limp. Though she was blond, her body hair was thick under her armpits and on her vulva. Her legs were unshaven. When she finished disrobing, I urged her toward the shower before she had a chance to look in the mirror. I needed to prepare her for that.

"I'm going to find you some moisturizer for your skin. Take it easy while you shower. Don't use a shower pouf. Just a soft cloth, okay?" I didn't mention a razor because her skin was in no condition to be shaved.

She nodded. Her hair was a raggedy mess, and I probably should have brushed it out for her before she washed it, but too late for that now. I'd help her with it when she was done.

She let out a wail when she stepped into the hot water.

"Is it too hot?" I asked.

"No. No. It's fine. It just feels...warm. It feels...good."

I smiled. When was the last time Juliet had felt good? Not

since that day on the beach. It had almost been worth it, to be drugged and hijacked by my father, just to hear Juliet say that the warm shower felt good.

Was my father still in this house? I wanted to explore, but I didn't dare leave the bathroom. Juliet would panic if she got out of the shower and found me gone. So I went through the medicine cabinet and other cupboards. I found some unscented moisturizer for Juliet's skin. Also some facial moisturizer. And a lavender toner. I also turned up three brushes and two combs—plenty for me to help Juliet work the tangles out of her wet hair.

She spent a long time under the pelting water, and I didn't blame her. I'd had a shower a lot more recently than she had, I'd bet, and I planned to take my time as well.

When she finally turned off the faucet and the water dripped to a stop, I grabbed a fuzzy bath towel and handed it to her when she stepped out. This time, I couldn't spare her the reflection in the mirror.

"Oh." She clamped her hand over her mouth.

"You're still beautiful," I said.

"How can you say that?"

"Because you're still you. We'll fatten you up. You'll see. And those red patches on your skin will heal. I found some moisturizer for you to use. Once your skin is back to normal, you can shave."

Without asking, I grabbed a comb and brush and began work on her hair.

"You don't have to do that," she said.

"I don't mind." And I didn't. It took about fifteen minutes, but I eventually worked all the snags out of her hair. I handed her a robe. "Put this on. I'm going to take my shower now."

"Can I stay in here with you?"

I wasn't one to undress in front of others, but she'd already seen me naked at the resort. Even if she hadn't, I had to give her what she needed now. I owed her that.

And again Melanie's voice entered my mind. You don't owe her anything. I ignored it.

The hot water was glorious on my tired and achy body, so I could only imagine how Juliet had felt. Once I was finished, we dressed in some of the pajamas we found in the dresser and left our dirty laundry for Marabel as she'd instructed.

Juliet eyed the bed. "I'm so tired. So damned tired."

"Lie down, then. Breakfast can wait."

"You won't leave me?"

"No, I won't leave you." Though I wanted some decent food, the bed looked pretty good to me as well.

She lay down and snuggled under the down comforter. In a few minutes, she had fallen asleep.

Though sleep beckoned me as well, I wasn't anxious for a repeat of the creepy dream I'd had about Ryan. Or rather, not about Ryan. I looked around the room a bit. I hadn't been in any of the bedrooms in the main Steel house, but I could only assume this one was identical to one of them. It was meticulously decorated with walnut furniture and hardwood floors. A beautiful ornate rug in reds and golds covered the floor, and my bare feet sank into it as I walked.

I jerked slightly when someone knocked. It was probably Marabel, but what if it was my father? I knew I'd have to deal with him soon, but I wanted a few more moments of peace for Juliet.

I opened the door.

A woman stood there—a beautiful woman with dark-brown hair and brown eyes, a long braid hanging over one shoulder. She was older, her skin lightly marred by age, but still she was stunning. She wore a lush robe, and in her arms she cradled a baby in a pink crocheted blanket.

CHAPTER NINETEEN

R y a n

Scotty led us to a door. He punched in a code, and the door opened. He walked in. We followed.

"That seemed to go all right," I whispered to Talon.

"Where to from here?" Raj asked.

"I have to sneak you in the back way," Scotty said. "I can't get you through the front way without IDs."

Raj fished in his pocket. "Seems I have your ID, mon."

I stuck my hand in the pocket of the pants I was wearing. Sure enough, I came out with what looked like the ID Raj was holding.

"Guess we don't need you at all, do we?" Raj smiled, his teeth nearly glowing.

"Uh...yeah. You need me. Like I said, there are four of us when only three left. And if you haven't noticed. I'm in a T-shirt and boxers here."

"That's not a reason to keep you around, dumbass," I said. "Seems like a reason to get rid of you." Not that I had any intention of pulling out my gun and doing the job.

Raj lifted his eyebrows and fingered his weapon, still smiling. Scotty went pale.

"We'll do it your way," Raj said. "But no funny business. We've all got guns on you, mon."

The man was visibly tense. He hadn't forgotten we were armed.

We walked down a dark hallway that appeared to be deserted, though we could hear muffled cries coming from... where? I wasn't sure.

My skin turned icy. Ruby was here. If any of those cries were coming from her... I was glad I was armed, because I'd kill any motherfucker who was making her wail like that.

We turned at the end of the hallway to another corridor. A group of women dressed in gray were sitting in the hallway, chained to each other.

I tried to breathe through my nausea, but I wasn't successful. These were the women they'd kidnapped, the women they were going to sell into slavery.

I ripped the mask off my head and heaved. Nothing came up.

Talon didn't seem as affected. After all, he'd been held in worse conditions than these. Though his stoicism was no doubt a cover.

I didn't realize I'd forgotten to put the mask back on my face until a soft voice invaded the quietness of the hallway.

"Ryan?"

I jerked and followed the voice. A pair of blank eyes met mine. The voice had come from a woman. A woman who had a familiar look about her.

"Ryan?" the woman said again.

A brick hit my gut.

"Oh my God. Anna."

Anna Shane. My ex-girlfriend, whose ranch had been acquired by the elusive Steel Family Trust. They'd sold the ranch and gone to Hawaii. I'd never heard from her again, even when I attempted to contact her through email and social media.

Now I knew why.

I knelt down next to her. "Anna, how did you get here?"

The scrawny woman next to her nudged her forearm. "Be quiet!" she whispered. "You know what happens when we disobey."

Raj doubled back to where I was kneeling. "Steel, come on, mon. We can't help them right now."

"Bullshit," I said. "Grab that bastard ahead of you and get his keys."

"Where would we take them? We don't know this place. We'll help them later, when we can."

"No way," I said. "I know this girl, and I'm getting her out of here."

Anna and I had been in a fairly serious relationship a couple years before. We'd ended it amiably—neither of us had heard bells—and decided to stay friends. I'd been surprised when she hadn't responded to my attempts to contact her. She'd probably never received any of my messages.

Talon knelt beside me. "Is it really you, Anna?"

The poor girl nodded.

"Ry," Talon said. "We'll get her out of here. We'll get them all out of here. But Raj is right. There's nothing we can do right now. They're all chained."

"Damn it, Tal. Your wife is safe at home. Safe. At. Home. My ex-girlfriend is here, being brutalized. I have no idea where the woman I love is. Please. I have to at least help Anna."

Understanding swept into Talon's eyes, and he nodded. "Raj, get his keys."

I took Anna's hand, her fingers thin and her nails cracked

and broken. "I'm so sorry you're here. What happened about Hawaii?"

"I never went to Hawaii. It's a long story. It's even hard to remember it all now."

"Jesus. How long have you been here?"

She shook her head. "I'm not sure. I went somewhere else for a while, where... I can't talk about it. But I know I never got to Hawaii."

My heart ached. "What about your parents?"

"I'm sure they think I'm dead by now."

Anguish consumed me. How had it all come to this? I hadn't been able to keep Anna safe, and I didn't even know it. I hadn't kept Ruby safe. I should never have let her go back to her apartment. Should never have let her out of my sight.

I almost smiled at that last thought. The idea that I had any control of what Ruby did was laughable. Maybe a little in the bedroom, which surprised the hell out of me, but I loved it. But in any other aspect of her life? She was in complete control, and she never failed to let me know it.

Raj tossed a set of keys to Talon. "Here you go, mon. I have no idea if any of them will help these girls." He kept his gun on Scotty, who seemed a lot less harmful in his underwear.

Talon started testing keys, first in the lock chaining Anna.

No dice. He tried the keys on a few of the other girls. Again, nothing.

My heart was breaking for these women, one of whom I'd cared for very deeply. None of them deserved this fate.

"I told you they wouldn't work," the boxer-clad smartass said. "This isn't my territory."

"We'll take them all, then." I looked around but then let out an anguished sigh. "They're chained to a bolt on the wall."

"We've got to move," Raj said.

"Listen," I said, still holding Anna's hand. "I'll come back for you. I swear it."

She nodded solemnly, but her eyes told a different story. She didn't believe me. She had given up hope.

Talon had talked about giving up hope. About how at first he'd thought about escaping but hadn't the strength. After that, he never tried again. He only got weaker the less they fed him and the more they brutalized him. That had been for a period of two months. Anna had been missing for nearly two years, as far as I could tell. God only knew what she'd gone through.

Then I looked into my brother's eyes, and I saw a glimpse of the tortured Talon. He knew. He was reliving it right at this moment.

"Hey." I squeezed her hand. "I'm so sorry the keys didn't work. I will be back for you."

"Yes," Talon said. "We will be back. Somehow, we'll shut this thing down."

Raj jiggled my shoulder. "We've got to go. It's still early, but people will be coming around anytime now. We've got to find a place to hide and figure out our next move."

I called upon every ounce of strength I possessed to let go of Anna's bony fingers. "I'll be back," I whispered, hoping I wasn't inadvertently lying to her.

I stood, along with Talon, and turned to Raj. "Now what?"

He poked his gun into the man's temple. "You tell us. Now what?"

"Now we—"

A blaring siren permeated the corridor.

CHAPTER TWENTY

Ruby

"Marabel said we had guests," the woman said. "I wanted to come welcome you."

"Thank you." I wasn't sure what else to say. "I'm Ruby. Thank you for letting Juliet and me stay here."

"You're most welcome. I love having visitors. Usually it's just me and Angela here alone all day. The boys are at camp."

I opened my mouth to reply, though I didn't know what I would say, but fortunately Marabel came walking briskly toward us from the direction of the kitchen.

"Goodness, ma'am, you shouldn't be out of your room. Where is Jocelyn?"

"She went to check on some formula for Angela." The woman turned to me. "I nursed my boys, but Angela would never take the breast."

Marabel took the woman by the shoulder. "Let's get you back. Angela needs her nap."

Angela was an extremely quiet baby. I hadn't heard so much as a gurgle out of her.

"I just wanted to welcome our guests, Marabel."

"Of course. I understand. But let's get you situated back in your room, okay? Come on, dear."

Was this the "lady"? I had no idea. Something in her eyes

seemed familiar to me, but I couldn't place it.

Marabel led her down the hallway, past the kitchen, and down another hallway, which I knew led to the master suite of the house where Talon and Jade lived in the original. Marabel led the woman into that very room.

An eerie feeling of unease swept over me. I turned toward a rustling. Juliet appeared to be fighting something in her sleep.

"No!" she shouted. "No! No! Don't take Lisa!"

I ran to her and nudged her gently. "Juliet, shh." I tried to make my voice as soothing as possible. "It's just a dream."

Her eyes shot open. "Where am I?"

"You're in the nice house, remember? It's me. Ruby."

She sat up, looking over one shoulder and then the other before clutching her chest. "My heart is beating so fast."

"It was just a bad dream. You're safe here. I'm not going to let anything happen to you."

She fell against me. "I can't believe I'm here. Out of there."

"You are. And we'll get the others out too." I rubbed soothing circles onto her back.

Then another knock at the door. I didn't want to let go of Juliet, so I said, "Come in."

Marabel entered. "I'm sorry about the lady. She's not quite right in the head. I can't believe her nurse left her alone."

"It's okay. If the baby needed formula—"

"The baby is fine," Marabel said. "If you and Miss Juliet are ready, I have breakfast for you. I can bring it in here if you'd like."

I nudged Juliet away from me. "Do you want to have breakfast in here?"

She nodded but then changed her mind and shook her head. "No. I want to get out of this room. I want to feel what it's like to be able to go into another room."

My heart broke for her all over again. I stood so she could get out of bed, and together we followed Marabel to the kitchen.

I'd been in this kitchen before. It was identical to Talon's, where I'd sat at the same kitchen table with the Steels and their spouses, discussing strategies for bringing my father down. Little did any of them know, my father appeared to be a regular visitor at an exact replica of their home.

Was I starring in a horror movie? Everything about this place brought out spooky feelings in me. The skin on the back of my neck prickled, and I expected the Psycho violin screech at any moment. But I had to allay my fears. They would rub off on Juliet, and she was already scared enough.

We each took a seat at the table. "Eat slowly," I told her. "You haven't had any decent food in a while, and your stomach might rebel."

She nodded and put a glass of orange juice to her lips. Then, "Ow!" She set the glass down harshly, spilling a bit.

"What's wrong, ma'am?" Marabel asked. "I squeezed that fresh just for you girls."

I touched Juliet's forearm. "What is it?"

"It hurts. Stings."

I sighed. "Open your mouth for me."

Several ulcers covered her tongue and gumline. Canker sores. Common enough among people with vitamin deficiencies and stress. Juliet no doubt had suffered both.

"Maybe some milk, Marabel," I said. "Does that sound good, Juliet?"

She nodded, and Marabel brought her a glass of milk a minute later. She took a long drink.

I took a sip of my juice, and it was delicious. But knowing Juliet couldn't drink it hampered my enjoyment of the citrusy beverage.

Marabel had fried some potatoes and peppers for us and had topped each mound with two eggs over easy. I was hungry—I'd lost most of the shitty food I'd eaten when I vomited on my father's desk—but I had a hard time eating. Ryan was somewhere close, and I was still worried about him.

Plus, this house... The woman and the baby... What the hell had Juliet and I walked into?

Juliet finished a little less than half of her breakfast and then stopped. "I can't eat any more."

"That's good for now," I said.

She nodded. I ate about half of mine as well, hoping we wouldn't be insulting Marabel by leaving food on our plates. She cleared our dishes without saying a word.

"Would the two of you like to go out on the deck for some fresh air?" she asked. "It's a beautiful morning."

What I really wanted was to get out of here and start my search for Ryan. At the very least, I wanted to find a cell phone or laptop so I could do some research. But fresh air would do Juliet's pale skin some good, and right now, she had to be my priority.

"That would be nice," I told Marabel.

I stood and strolled to the deck. Juliet followed me. Marabel opened the French doors for us. Again, an exact replica of Talon's deck, right down to the wrought iron and glass table and the Adirondack chairs and chaises longues.

In the distance, the guesthouse stood.

The guesthouse where Ryan lived in the original.

He was here somewhere. My father hadn't lied. I was

almost sure of it. He'd come for me, and I wished he hadn't. I had no idea what awaited him here—no idea what awaited me, for that matter.

Fear gnawed at my gut. Fear for Ryan. For Juliet. For all the other poor souls being held here.

Somehow I'd save them all. I had to.

"Oh!"

I turned at the sound of Juliet's voice. Three fluffy golden retriever puppies bounded up to us, and her eyes lit up with joy. For a moment, I saw the blond twenty-one-year-old I'd met at the Jamaican resort.

"Hello, babies!" she cooed.

I grabbed one ball of fur and picked him up. "Where did they come from?" I asked Marabel.

"They're Jewel's pups. Jewel is the lady's dog. She was a gift from the master."

Master? Strange. I couldn't help myself. I had to ask, given what else I'd seen on these islands so far. "Marabel, are you here willingly?"

"Of course! Why would you ask otherwise?"

"Just... Calling him the master."

"Out of respect. I'm not here against my will."

She seemed sincere. I couldn't think of any reason not to believe her. Except, of course, that I was near an island filled with evil—evil of my father's doing.

But I couldn't worry about that as I kissed the top of the pup's head. He wriggled in my arms and then licked my face. I laughed out loud.

Juliet was busy with the other two pups. She picked them both up and examined them. "So you're a boy," she said to one, "and you're a girl. Do they have names?"

"Not yet, miss," Marabel said.

I snuggled the pup to my cheek, thinking of Ryan's gorgeous golden retriever, Ricky. I missed him. So much.

"Then I'll name them," Juliet said. "You're Bo, and you're Beauty. Perfect."

I worried for a split second that Juliet was already getting too close to the dogs. But the happiness on her face made my concern short-lived. In fact, I kind of wanted to name the puppy I was holding. He was a boy. You're Ernie, I said to myself. A man named Ernie had lived above my mother and me in our small apartment when I was a kid. He was kind to me and gave me something to eat if I was hungry. Yes, this puppy would carry that name. Ernie. If I didn't say it out loud, maybe I wouldn't grow too attached to the little thing.

He squirmed out of my arms and raced to play with his brother and sister.

Juliet stood and followed the puppies out into the large yard. I thought about stopping her. She was still so weak. But I didn't want to take these few minutes of joy away from her.

I turned around and looked through the French doors into the kitchen. A man, his back to me, stood talking to Marabel. His hair was dark, and for a moment I assumed it was my father. He'd probably returned to take us back to the horror of the dorms, as Juliet had called it.

But no— This man was taller than my father, and he was wearing blue jeans and a black shirt. Not the black pants my father had been wearing.

He stood talking to Marabel for what seemed like forever. Turn around, I screamed inside my head.

When he didn't, I stood, my feet moving toward the door seemingly of their own volition.

I opened the door and walked in.
The man turned to face me.
And I gasped.

CHAPTER TWENTY-ONE

R y a n

I clapped my hands over my ears. The women in the hallway began wailing.

Raj was yelling at Scotty, but I couldn't hear what they were saying. The man started walking, Raj's gun never moving from his temple. I looked to Talon. As much as it pained me to leave Anna and the others, I followed.

The siren blared on and on for what seemed like hours. We followed Scotty down a flight of stairs and into a dark basement. The sound was muffled a little more here. I sniffed. No smoke, so it wasn't a fire alarm. We were safe for the moment.

"What was that?" Talon yelled to Raj.

"He said it's a signal of breach," Raj yelled back. "He doesn't think we've been seen. What most likely happened is that someone found the two guys we left behind. We should have killed them."

His use of the pronoun "we" disturbed me. As much as the jerks deserved death, I could never take a life. But I couldn't argue the point now.

"What's down here?" Raj yelled.

"You don't want to know," Scotty said.

As my eyes adjusted to the dark, I began to make out

images. A stockade. A— Fuck. Was it a guillotine? Christ. This must be where the goons doled out the severe punishment.

Raj was dragging Scotty along, clearly looking for something, though I didn't have the slightest idea what. Talon and I followed them as Raj pushed Scotty down onto a chair.

"It'd serve you right if I locked you in that stockade." Instead, Raj took a roll of what appeared to be duct tape out of his bag. The man definitely came prepared. He bound Scotty's hands and wrists together and then taped him to the chair. He held a piece of tape to his mouth. "Lucky for you I'm not a sadist. Any last words, mon?"

"Fuck you," Scotty spat again.

"Original." Raj taped his mouth shut. "But I respect the fact that you didn't beg." He turned to us. "He's taken care of for the moment. Since we're in our black outfits, we can fit in around here. Next step is going back up and seeing what this is about."

"No offense," I said. "But I'm sick and tired of smelling and tasting a guy's blood." I held my mask out to Raj. Since the masks were black, the blood didn't show. We could still smell the tang of it though. It was quickly making me gag.

"Me too," Talon agreed.

"Sorry. They're all we have. I can trade, but that'll only help one of you."

"You take it," I said to Talon.

He didn't try to argue. It was the least I could do. Talon had seen more blood in his lifetime than I had. He deserved the clean mask.

"Everyone armed?" Raj asked.

Talon and I both nodded and patted our weapons.

"All righty, then." Raj pulled Talon's bloodied mask over

his head, his brown eyes black in the dark cellar. "Let's go."

We walked slowly and quietly up the stairs. I still had Scotty's keys, though they hadn't helped me release Anna and the others.

"We need to find more keys," Raj said.

"Shouldn't we call the cops?" I asked.

"This is a private island. There aren't any cops here."

Of course. I should have known that. So we'd have no backup.

Shit.

Shit, shit, shit.

Ruby's beautiful face poked into my mind. How I missed her. If anyone had harmed her...

I couldn't go there. Not now. Right now, Talon and I had one mission. Find Theodore Mathias and take him down. In doing so, we'd probably find and rescue Ruby.

I hoped so. I prayed to a God I wasn't sure I believed in anymore to keep her safe. To keep the woman I loved—the woman I was going to marry—safe.

Raj opened the door slightly. The siren was still blaring. "Look," he yelled to us. "People in black are running around out here like a bunch of maniacs. No one will notice us. Follow me."

We exited the stairwell into the hall. He was right. Men in black were everywhere checking rooms. We blended right in. That siren had given us the perfect cover.

But where to now? I had no idea. We hadn't made any plans on the yacht because none of us had a clue what we'd find here. Talon and I had agreed to give Raj the lead, as he was the most experienced at investigating.

So far, he'd proven himself trustworthy, but I still wasn't

sure. Something niggled at the back of my neck. I thought again of Ruby, about how she'd said she'd learned not to ignore her intuition.

My intuition was telling me to tread carefully with Raj. He was hiding something. I was almost sure of it. As soon as I had the chance, I'd relay my concerns to Talon.

For now, we followed Raj, nodding to the other men in black who scurried down the corridors. Some wore masks and some did not. We didn't dare remove ours. They might not all know each other, but what if they did? What if they recognized that we didn't belong here? We couldn't take that chance.

We still had no idea what Scotty's keys opened.

Raj began stopping at doors. "Cover me," he yelled to Talon and me.

We stood in front of him while he tried all the keys. We did this at three doors before we hit pay dirt.

The door opened, and inside were two children. Boys. Both had blondish hair, could pass for brothers—maybe were brothers. They were dressed only in large T-shirts, and their wrists and ankles were bound with white rope. Both cowered in the corner when we entered the room.

Talon went rigid.

I could see it in his eyes. He was flashing back.

And that damned siren kept blaring!

"Hold it together, Tal," I yelled at him. "Please! We'll get them out of here!"

Then his eyes went feral. He ran to the two little boys and grabbed one of them.

"No!" The little boy yelled. "No! Please! No more!"

"We won't hurt you!" I yelled.

And the siren stopped blaring.

Thank God.

But the little boy was yelling, and the other was quietly weeping.

"Hey, hey," Talon said. "You need to be quiet if you don't want the bad people to come. We're not going to hurt you. I promise." He quickly unbound the little boy's hands and feet.

"Can he walk?" I asked.

"Of course he can't walk. Look at him. Look at both of them. They'll stumble. They're starved and malnourished. They'll need our help."

Talon knew. He knew just what these boys had been through. And it was eating him up inside. I could see it. See what it was doing to my hero.

This had to stop.

"Tal," I said. "Get a grip. We need them to be strong if we're going to help them. You walked out, remember?"

"I had help."

"You had Larry, who let you out, but you didn't have anyone to help you walk. They do. They have us. They'll be okay."

"Listen, mon," Raj interjected. "We can't take them right now. We don't know what we're walking into. The siren has stopped. Things will settle down and get back to normal. We need to find who's in charge here and get him taken care of. They'll slow us down."

"We are not leaving them here," Talon said through gritted teeth. "I'm paying your bills, goddamnit, and you're going to help me get these boys out of here."

My mind whirled. The fact that Scotty had a key to this room meant he'd probably had a hand in abusing these young kids. Abhorrence erupted in my throat. I hadn't been able to rescue Anna, but we could rescue these two little boys.

Not just for them, but for Talon. For the little boy my brother had been. For the little boy I had been, saved only because I had a different mother—an evil woman who had orchestrated all of this.

I so couldn't go there right now...

"Talon's right," I said to Raj. "We're not leaving them here."

The boy Talon held let out a scream.

I clamped my hand over his mouth. "Hey, I know you're scared. But we're going to help you. We need you to be quiet. If you scream, someone will find us and we won't be able to help you. Do you understand?"

The boy nodded shakily, but when I removed my hand, he let out another blood-curdling howl.

"He doesn't trust you, Ryan. He doesn't trust any of us. He can't. He's been through hell."

I hated what I was about to suggest, but we had no alternative. "Raj, you still have the tape?"

Talon turned on me. "We will not tape his mouth! Damn it, Ryan. We can't put them through more shit."

"Tal, I understand, but they have to be quiet."

"I'll get them to be quiet," Talon said. "I know what they need right now." He set the little boy down next to the other and then sat on the floor with them. He removed his mask.

The little boy let out a heart-wrenching shriek.

CHAPTER TWENTY-TWO

Ruby

He was tall. Tall and broad. In his hand, he held a black Stetson. His eyes were dark as strong coffee, and his hair was the same color, though silver streaked through it, especially at the temples.

In his sculpted jawline I saw Ryan. In his profile I saw Talon. And the rest was exactly what Jonah Steel would look like in twenty-plus years.

"Brad Steel," I said.

"Hello, Ruby."

"You know who I am?"

"You're Theo's daughter. My son's girlfriend. I helped bring you here."

I nearly lost my footing. I'd seen two blurry faces that day as I lost consciousness.

Two...

No. Ryan's father wouldn't participate in kidnapping me.

But I didn't know Ryan's father. After all, Ryan was nothing like his mother, thank God. His father could very well be just as monstrous.

"So Wendy was telling the truth. You are alive."

"I am. I'm sure you have a lot of questions."

Questions? They swirled through my mind at a hundred

miles an hour. What to ask first? But all that came out was, "How could you do this?"

"I need to tell my children the truth first."

I couldn't fault his logic, but damn, I was standing right here. "Please. Just tell me."

"I had reasons for everything I did. Reasons you—and my children—may not understand. But someone broke a promise to me, so all bets are now off. My children deserve to know the truth."

"They deserved that a long time ago," I said, seething.

"I was trying to protect them."

"By not letting them deal with anything? I'm sorry, but you were wrong. Talon is only now getting the help he needs."

"I know that. And I'm thankful."

"And Ryan..." I couldn't finish.

"Ryan was never supposed to know about his mother. His biological mother. Daphne was his real mother. She treated him as one of her own." He shook his head, his eyes heavy-lidded and sad. "He was never supposed to know."

"Well, he does now."

"I know, and I'm sorry. Daphne loved him as much as the others. She raised him as her own. She did that for me."

"But why—"

"That's all I can say for now. My children deserve to hear the truth before anyone else does."

"I understand." I did. Didn't make it any easier to have Brad Steel standing right in front of me and not get the answers I was yearning for. And then it dawned on me. "I do understand, really. But I'm Theodore Mathias's child, and I deserve some truth as well."

"I'm sorry to disappoint you, but I can't tell you anything

about Theo. He and I aren't friends."

"But you used to be. My uncle told me. Rodney Cates."

"That changed long ago."

"When he took your son."

"I can't talk about that yet."

"Or did your friendship end before that? When they went into this disgusting business they conduct on these godforsaken islands?"

He didn't answer.

"Why? Why did you build a replica of this house here? Who is the woman who lives here with you? Is that your baby?"

"Miss Ruby," Marabel said. "Please. The master is tired."

"It's only midmorning."

"The master gets up early to do his work."

"His work? What work? There's nothing here. Only this house. Outside these concrete walls, there are crimes being committed, Marabel. Vicious, heinous crimes!" I turned back to Brad. "What the hell do you do here all day? Whyever you did it, was it worth it to leave your family? Jonah is going to be a father soon, for God's sake. You're going to have a grandchild. So what did you do? Come here and start a new family with that woman and her baby?"

"Miss Ruby, please," Marabel said again.

"It's all right, Marabel," Brad said. "She is understandably upset."

Juliet's face flashed in my mind. She'd freak if she noticed I was no longer on the deck with her. I looked out the French doors. She was fine, still in the yard playing with Bo, Beauty, and Ernie.

I turned back to Marabel. "Do you have any idea what goes on here? On these islands? What these people are doing?"

"Enough!" Brad Steel's voice was loud without actually being a yell.

The fire in his eyes. I'd seen the same fire in Ryan's eyes. He meant to be obeyed.

I didn't care. I was in love with Ryan. I eagerly welcomed his commands.

I hated the man standing before me.

"Enough of what? You know what's true as well as I do. The least you can do is tell me the truth about you and my father. I deserve that much."

He sighed. "I can see why Ryan loves you. That fiery spirit. I couldn't resist it when I was younger either. It got me into a lot of trouble. A fiery woman was always my downfall."

Wendy. He was talking about Wendy. Maybe Daphne as well. I didn't know anything about her except that she'd been mentally unstable.

"I'll tell you what I can."

"Good. We'll need to go out on the deck. I can't leave Juliet alone. She's very fragile right now. Because of what my father and you have put her through."

"I'll sit with Juliet," Marabel said. "Why don't the two of you go into your study, Mr. Steel?"

"She needs me, Marabel."

"She'll be fine with me, Miss Ruby. Look at her. She's in love with those pups."

"Marabel will look after her. She's good with children. She's done this before."

I widened my eyes. Before? Did they rescue others and bring them here? Or was he talking about the boys the "lady" had mentioned?

"Follow me," he said.

I felt no fear of Brad Steel, though maybe I should have. Just because he resembled the man I loved and his wonderful brothers didn't mean he had the same ethics. I followed him into the corridor that housed the room Juliet and I were staying in. His office was on the other side of the hallway. Probably exactly the same room where Talon had his office at home.

He took a seat behind a large oak desk and nodded toward a few leather chairs on the other side of the desk.

I sat and looked down. I was wearing silk pajamas. I'd forgotten. Brad hadn't seemed surprised. Did they provide pajamas for a lot of women? I was about to find out.

He stared at me for a moment. "You don't look much like Theo. Just the hair color."

"Your sons and daughter all look exactly like you."

"They do. I must have dominant genes."

"Except Ryan has his mother's nose." I wasn't sure why I said that.

"He does." Brad sighed. "So you want to know about your father and me."

"Yes. The truth, please."

"What makes you think you don't already know the truth?"

"Were you there? Are you the one who drugged me with chloroform the night I was taken from my apartment?"

"Yes. And I'm sorry for my part in it, but I had no choice."

"There's always a choice."

"Not always. Not when the choice is to do something you find distasteful or see everything you hold dear destroyed."

"You're Brad Steel. Owner of Steel Acres. Billionaire. How exactly does anyone hold any power over you?"

"Your father has a little. But there's someone else who has

a lot. I won't discuss that. I will discuss your father."

"All right. I'm listening."

"We were friends once. We're not anymore."

"Then why did you go with him and drug me? Bring me here?"

"I had my reasons, and we'll get to that."

"Fine."

"Four of us—your father, Tom Simpson, Larry Wade, and myself—formed a club in high school." He sighed, threading his fingers through his thick salt-and-pepper hair. "God, how I've come to regret those innocent first days."

He pushed his chair back. "Tom and Larry were the actual future lawyers. Your father and I had no interest in the law. I knew I'd be running the ranch, and your father was bound and determined to become rich. He got Tom and Larry into that mindset, so we decided to start a business."

I knew where this was going. Wendy had told Ryan and me how it had started small. Just a reselling of products in demand at inflated prices. Innocent enough. Until they got into drugs...and people.

"I had money, so I offered to back the business for a quarter of the partnership. I'd be a silent partner. It started out innocently enough, and the four of us made some cash." He let out a heavy sigh. "Then we had two people approach us, asking to join the club. First was Rodney Cates. He'd been trying to date your aunt, your father's sister. He thought making friends with her brother would help his case. Turned out he had a mind for numbers."

"Numbers? He's a linguistics professor."

"I didn't say he was interested in numbers. But he was good at them. So we put him to work on the financials. Let him in for five percent."

"Okay."

"Things were going along pretty smoothly, until we had another person approach us for membership."

I sighed. "Wendy."

"Yes. Wendy Madigan. A junior varsity cheerleader. All-American girl. Sweet like the girl next door. Or so she seemed."

"She's crazy."

"She is. She's also got an IQ that's nearly off the charts, though we didn't know either of those things at the time."

"So I've heard."

"From whom?"

"My father. And Larry, before he died."

"Don't expect me to tear up on Larry Wade's behalf."

"Why would I expect that? I know what he and my father did to Talon. You don't owe any of them any sympathy. Frankly, I can't understand why you have anything to do with my father at all."

"We have a common enemy. A lethal enemy. And the enemy of my enemy is my friend. I don't have a choice. Larry and Tom are gone, and your uncle has enough to deal with, losing his daughter and his wife, for all intents and purposes. Your father and I are the only ones who can try to right all the wrongs now."

"My father's interested in righting wrongs? I witnessed him murder my boss less than a week ago, Mr. Steel. I don't think he's interested in righting any wrongs."

"He wasn't. Not until you got involved."

"Why would that matter? Maybe my father has neglected to tell you, but he tried to rape me when I was fifteen. I got away."

"No, he didn't tell me. But it doesn't surprise me in the least."

"I'm sure it doesn't. How could you let all of this happen? To your own son, for God's sake." I gripped the arms of the chair, my knuckles white.

"That is for Talon to know first, and I didn't let anything happen."

I rolled my eyes. "Fine. Just tell me about my father, then."

"He was greedy. He and the others didn't come from money like I did. When the money started coming in, they were astounded. They wanted more."

"I know all this. From Wendy."

"Wendy isn't the most reliable source of information," he said.

"Probably not, but what she told Ryan about your business makes perfect sense."

"Wendy tells the truth when she thinks it will benefit her. Unfortunately, this last bout she had with the truth broke a promise to me. I don't intend to let that lie."

CHAPTER TWENTY-THREE

Ryan

Raj covered his ears. "Damn it, mon! We've got to leave them."

I turned on him. "We are not leaving them." If we did, I didn't know what would happen to Talon...except that it wouldn't be good.

Talon held the boy to his chest. "Shh. You see? I took off the mask. I'm just a normal person, like you. Only the men who wear masks hurt you."

The boy still sobbed.

"You two," Talon said. "Take off your masks. Show him he doesn't need to be scared."

"Mon..."

"Do it!" I commanded Raj. "Just fucking do it!"

Raj sighed and pulled off his mask as I did the same.

"See?" Talon said. "We're not going to hurt you. I promise. As long as you're with us, you're safe."

The larger of the two boys still cowered in the corner.

"Ryan, get that one."

I walked forward, and the little boy cringed. My heart nearly broke in two. How could anyone hurt a child? "Please," I said. "It's okay. We're friends. I promise."

He choked back a sob but didn't recoil when I reached for him. I pulled him into my arms.

"We know you've been around some bad people who hurt you. We won't hurt you," Talon was saying. "I know how you're feeling right now. You're scared, and you're hurting, and you don't know who to trust. You're also a little embarrassed. You never imagined the things that have happened to you, that such horrible things could even exist. But there is good in the world still, and you'll be okay. You'll be okay again. I promise."

The good in the world... I wasn't seeing a whole lot of that at the moment, but Talon was finally, after twenty-five years, healing. Jade and Melanie had worked their miracles for him, but the true strength and wisdom came from Talon himself. He was trying to infuse his strength into these little boys. I hoped he'd be successful—at least enough to get us somewhere safe.

God, was there anyplace safe on this godforsaken island? This place was pure evil.

I half expected my mother to show up. Thankfully, she was safely locked up in the psych ward back home.

The smaller boy clung to Talon. Talon kissed the top of his head.

And for the first time, I saw my brother as a father. He and Jade would have children someday, and Talon would be an amazing and loving parent.

"I don't want to scare you guys," Talon said, "but we have to put the masks back on. We won't be able to get you out of here if we don't, because the bad men will recognize us and know we're not supposed to be here. Will you be okay if we put the masks back on?"

The little boy in Talon's arms choked out, "Yes," but the older one simply nodded against my neck.

"All right," Talon said in a soothing voice I didn't know he possessed. "I'm going to put the mask on now. And the others will too. Then we'll go."

We put our masks on.

"Are you both ready?" Talon asked.

Again, the boy I held only nodded, but Talon's said softly, "Uh-huh."

"I still think you're crazy," Raj said, donning his mask.

I glared at him. Talon would break if he said much more. Right now, the most important thing in my brother's world was saving these two kids. They represented the innocent little boy he'd been, and damn it, I was going to help him.

There were other keys, other rooms. What if Talon insisted on looking in all of them? Rescuing every child and woman here?

We were only three people.

I didn't voice this concern. Right now, Talon was immersed in saving these two little boys.

We left the room stealthily. Now that the siren had stopped blaring, the hallways were, thankfully, mostly vacant.

"Be quiet," I said to the boy in my arms. "If you see another masked person, just be quiet. Act scared."

The boy wouldn't have to act. They were both still frightened out of their skin. But we hadn't hurt them, and that would eventually dawn on them.

For a moment, my mind wandered back to Anna, chained up in the hallway with several others. I hadn't been able to help, but somehow, I'd get back to her.

And then there was Ruby. Somewhere on this island. Possibly being held against her will.

I couldn't let my mind go there. Couldn't...

But it went there anyway. Images emerged of her being bound, raped, sodomized...

"No!"

Talon turned around. "What is it, Ry?"

I hadn't realized I'd spoken out loud. "Nothing. I'm fine."

But I wasn't fine. I might never be fine again if I didn't find Ruby alive and in one piece.

I love you, Ruby, I called out to her in my mind. Whatever happens, we will get through it. I'll do whatever I need to do. I'll put you back together piece by piece if I have to. I promise.

"This is ridiculous," Raj said. "We don't even know where we're going."

"We'll take them back to the yacht. One of us will have to stay with them," Talon said.

"Then it'll be one of you," Raj said. "I'm not paid to babysit."

"You're paid—and very well—to do what we say, damn it."

"Tal," I said. "We can't get them back to the yacht. They're in no condition to swim, if they even know how." My brother wasn't thinking clearly. All he could focus on was getting these boys out of here. Not that I could blame him for that.

"All right. All right. We'll find somewhere safe to hide them." Talon moved forward. "But damn it, we're getting them out of here."

We moved toward the back where we had entered the building. When we went outside, the little boys both wailed when the sun hit their eyes.

"Shh," Talon said. "You have to be quiet so the bad men don't hear you."

They got silent quickly. We began walking through a wooded area, avoiding the road that had brought us here. But soon it was impossible to navigate, so we made our way back to the road.

We'd been walking for an hour, and my arms were growing tired of carrying the bigger of the two boys, when a black SUV pulled up beside us.

"Get in," a masked man said.

"Hell, no," Talon said, reaching for his gun.

"Get in, or you're dead out here. I can take you someplace safe."

"Who the fuck are you?" I asked.

"I'll take you to Ruby," the man said.

My heart lurched.

"He's lying to you," Talon said.

"You're a fool if you get in that car," Raj agreed.

"Look, I'm not asking you for your gun. You can shoot me in the head if you want. But if you want to save those two boys you're carrying, I'm your only shot."

I made a spontaneous decision. "I'm going. I'm armed. If you two don't want to go, don't." I handed the boy to Raj.

Talon and Raj looked at each other.

They got in the SUV.

CHAPTER TWENTY-FOUR

Ruby

"Wendy is locked up in psych back in Grand Junction," I said. "She can't get out."

"You're underestimating her."

"Look. You're not going to tell me about some things, but can't you at least tell me about Wendy? Why the hell you slept with her in the first place? She's crazy and evil."

"Again, this is something I should tell my children first."

This was a man who still was trying to hold on to some semblance of honor. After all, he'd waited until all his children had reached adulthood before disappearing into thin air. He cared about his children.

Well, I cared about his children too.

"They won't forgive you," I said. "Ryan and the others. They won't forgive you for leaving them."

"After they hear the whole story, they might."

"What if they don't?"

He sighed. "Then I'll have to live with that. Everything I ever did was with their best interests in mind."

"Even Talon?"

"Yes, even Talon. What happened to him was a travesty. There's not a day that goes by that I don't hate myself for it. Wendy is a vengeful woman. An evil woman."

The ring. The quote.

"Who designed the future lawmakers ring?" I asked.

"She did."

"Did she ever tell you what the symbol on the ring meant?"

"Not in so many words. But we figured it out."

"So did your sons. We've all figured it out. Wendy was the mastermind behind all of this."

"Yes, she was."

"I hope you know that doesn't absolve you or my father or any of the others of any of the guilt."

He sighed again. "How well I do know that."

"Talon was taken because your wife got pregnant with Marjorie. What do you think that is going to do to Marj when she finds out? And she will find out. We can't keep that from her."

His eyes pleaded with me. "Please. She can't know that. I wasn't able to shield the boys, but Marjorie... My baby girl..."

"More secrets? No." I shook my head vehemently. "This all ends now."

Before Brad could respond, someone knocked on the door.

"Yes?" Brad said.

Marabel entered and brought Juliet inside. "Miss Juliet is tired from roughhousing with the pups. I'm going to take her to lie down."

"I need to go with her," I said. "I don't want her to be alone."

Juliet looked visibly relieved.

I turned to Brad. "This isn't over."

★ ★ ★

When I opened my eyes, darkness had fallen. I had no idea how long I had slept, but I must have been exhausted. Nothing else would have let me fall asleep in this strange place. I'd been fighting it, frightened I'd have another freaky dream. Juliet was still snoring softly in the other bed.

I rose, went to the bathroom, and then I tiptoed out of the room, sliding against the wall. The door to Brad Steel's office was ajar, and voices spoke within.

"She's not ready." Brad Steel's voice.

"They're on their way. She'll need to get ready quick." Shit! My father's voice.

"She can't yet. She'll go off the deep end."

"She's already off the deep end."

"Damn it!" A fist hit a hard surface, probably the mahogany desk. "You're still a sick man, Theo. The fact that we're working together now doesn't change that."

"I won't try to atone for my crimes. It's impossible. But I'm willing to do what I need to do, for my daughter's sake as well as my own, though I don't expect you to believe that. I want out. But I need what you owe me."

A ringing commenced in my ears. Had I heard him correctly? He was actually thinking of me? He wanted out for my sake? I must have misheard. Mere days ago he'd been trying to get me to call off the Steel brothers.

"Why now? After...everything?" Brad asked.

"I've tried to get your kids to stop this manhunt, but they're determined. I'm too old and tired to run anymore. And you may not believe this, but there are times I regret...everything."

"Even torturing my son?"

My father sighed. "Especially that. All of it. I mean all of it."

"It seemed easy enough for you at the time."

"It gets easier after a while. After you've..." Silence for a few seconds. Then, "You don't know what she's capable of."

"I don't know what she's capable of? You're forgetting who you're talking to. She turned my life upside down. And not just mine. My wife's. My children's."

It didn't take a genius to figure out they were talking about Wendy Madigan.

Silence for a moment. A muffled buzzing sound. Then, Brad's voice. "They're here."

I tiptoed silently back to my room and closed the door.

Who was here? My father had said Ryan had arrived on the other island. Was he here? My heart jumped in anticipation. But if it was Ryan and his brothers, who was the "she" they'd been referring to? The "she" who wasn't ready for "them" to be here?

Three choices.

The woman with the baby.

Juliet.

And me.

They could have been talking about any of us, depending on who was here. It couldn't be the Steels. I certainly was ready for them to be here, and they wouldn't harm Juliet. And the woman with the baby should have no problem with them either.

Juliet was still sleeping soundly.

I quietly stole out of the room again. The office was now empty. I traipsed down the corridor, shielding myself as best I could against the wall.

Marabel was nowhere to be found, nor were my father or Brad. Perhaps they had gone out the front door. I sneaked down the other hallway to the master suite. The door was ajar, and I opened it slightly and peeked inside. The woman in the robe was sitting in a rocking chair, looking lovingly into a bassinet. The baby must be inside.

A slight whoosh. Maybe the front door opening? We were far from the foyer, but the noise had been muffled.

The woman got up swiftly. I flattened myself against the wall. She didn't appear to notice me. I breathed a sigh of relief.

Once she had left, I walked into the room.

I peeked into the bassinet. Angela slept soundly.

I touched her baby soft cheek...

"Oh!" I gasped.

The skin beneath my fingers was soft but not warm. Not... human. Not at all. It looked human, yes, but it wasn't.

The child didn't move, didn't react at all to my touch.

No wonder Angela never made a sound. She was a doll. A very lifelike doll—the size of a real baby, but a doll nonetheless.

If I hadn't thought I was visiting crazy town before, I knew I'd arrived now. I stood, motionless, but then jerked as I heard bustling. I sneaked back down the hallway.

Then, a feminine voice—the lady.

"You've brought the boys home, finally! Jonah, Talon, Mama has missed you so much!"

CHAPTER TWENTY-FIVE

R y a n

We had driven up to and walked into a replica of our ranch house at home. Neither Talon nor I had reacted, other than a confused glance at each other. We couldn't upset the boys. But inside, my nerves were a jumble, frantically crawling underneath my skin. Was I in a science fiction novel? Had we walked into a parallel universe?

When I heard the woman's voice, I nearly dropped the child I was holding.

My heart pounded against my sternum.

In front of me stood two phantoms. My father, who we expected. He thanked the driver and handed him an envelope.

But the other one...

My mother. The one who'd committed suicide over two decades ago.

Daphne Steel.

I couldn't breathe. Couldn't...

The woman took the trembling child from my arms. "My sweet Joe," she cooed. "Mama has missed you so." She turned to Talon, eyeing the child he was holding. "And Talon. You look so tired. Do you need a nap, sweetie?"

The man with my father's face said, "Darling, what are you doing out here? Where's Angela?"

"She's asleep. You know I couldn't miss my boys' homecoming. It seems like they've been away at camp for years."

The older boy struggled in her arms. "Help! Help me!"

"She won't hurt you," I said, hoping I was right.

"Of course," she soothed. "Mama would never hurt her babies."

Talon had gone nearly catatonic beside me. The woman had called the boy he was holding by his name. These boys were blond and looked nothing like Joe and Talon had as kids.

And then it hit me like a boulder dropping onto my skull.

She hadn't called out for me. She'd called for Joe and Talon, welcoming them home.

Not for me.

I was not her son.

A long-forgotten memory tugged at the corner of my brain.

★ ★ ★

"Get that woman out of my house!"

I covered my ears. I missed Talon. He was my big brother. My hero. But now that he was back, he wanted his own room.

Maybe soon he'd move back in with me.

Maybe not.

He had changed since he'd come back. He didn't play with me much anymore. He was quieter now. More like Joe.

Mom and Dad were fighting again. They did that a lot these days.

My baby sister wailed from the nursery.

"Damn it, Daphne. You woke the baby!"

"I'll take care of her. At least she's my child."

"We've been through this. You made a promise years ago."

"A promise I regret."

"You love him. You've always treated him like your own."

"But he's not mine. He'll never be mine. She's always around to remind me. So I'm done with this charade."

My mother's footsteps echoed down the hallway until I heard her open and shut the door to the nursery where my baby sister slept.

I tried closing my eyes again.

They fought a lot now. More than they ever had before.

Now that Talon was home.

I didn't understand what they were talking about. I just wanted the fighting to stop.

It made my stomach hurt.

★ ★ ★

I'd been too young to realize it—only nine when she died—but she had treated me differently after Talon returned. Only slightly, but now, as an adult, it was clear as a sunny day. After Talon came home, my mother became peculiar. She didn't hug me as much, didn't read to me anymore. I'd always chalked it up to Talon's ordeal, but it was more. Much more.

I inhaled, willing my mind to calm. Now wasn't the time to lose it.

But then all became right with this fucked-up world again.

I saw her face.

The face of the woman I loved.

Ruby peeked around from the hallway leading to the master suite. Thank goodness the child had been taken from my arms, or I might have dropped him.

I ran to Ruby and grabbed her, inhaling her vanilla scent, pressing my lips to her neck.

"My God. Ruby. My baby. Thank God you're here and you're okay."

She pulled away, cupping my cheeks. "Are you okay? Where have you been? What did they do to you?"

She was wearing silk pajamas, very un-Ruby like. Her hair was fresh and hung below her shoulders in a dark-brown waterfall. Her cheeks were a bit ruddy, but her lips were red, plump, and perfect. She looked like an angel from heaven. I bent toward her and kissed her.

She opened for me instantly, and we kissed madly for only a few seconds before she pulled away.

"What?"

"They're all watching."

I didn't much care. "Are you all right?"

She nodded. "Are you?"

"Yeah. We're okay."

"Ryan, I found Juliet. She's here with me. But the others..." She choked and then cleared her throat, her eyes glistening. "We have to help them."

"We will."

She looked toward Talon. "Where's Joe?"

"Still at home. It's a long story. I'll tell you everything as soon as I figure out what the hell is going on here."

"I understand." She lowered her voice. "That woman is crazy. She keeps a doll in a bassinet that she swears is a baby. I don't know who she is."

"Ruby," I said. "She's my mother. My other mother. She's Daphne Steel."

★ ★ ★

The housekeeper, a Jamaican woman named Marabel, took the two boys to get cleaned up and fed. Daphne saw to their needs herself, convinced they were young Joe and Talon, with a woman who appeared to be her nurse supervising. She clearly wasn't distraught over a missing young Ryan.

The thought left a lump in my throat.

Now, Talon and I sat in the office—Talon's office at home—to hear our father's side of this twisted tale.

"First, your mother," he said to us.

"Uh...which one?" I hadn't meant to sound sardonic, but my words came out with an edge to them.

"I'm sorry. Daphne. If I'd had it my way, Ryan, you would never have known Daphne wasn't your mother."

"Would that have been fair?" Talon asked.

"Wendy broke a promise to me by telling you," he said to me. "When I found out, I got your number and tried to call you to explain, but you didn't say anything."

"I was speeding across Colorado at about one-sixty when I got your call. A call from my dead father. Then my Porsche went over a cliff. Sorry I couldn't get back to you. And by 'sorry,' I mean fuck you."

He ignored me and turned to Talon. "None of this is fair."

"And whose fault is that?" I wasn't in the mood for niceties. Not only had my father come back from the dead, he'd brought Daphne with him.

"Mine," he admitted.

"We knew you as a man of honor," I said. "A man who instilled in us a work ethic like no other, the value of a job well done, the importance of being a good man with integrity.

You're none of that."

He said nothing.

"You let my mother hurt my brother," I continued. "How can I ever forgive you for that?"

"I'll explain everything as well as I can, but I don't expect your forgiveness. I never did, though I hope you might grant it. I never meant for you to find out I was still alive. But then things went terribly wrong."

"Then they went terribly wrong?" I clenched my hands together. "Things have been terribly wrong for a while. You've had Daphne here since Marj was two. You deprived our little sister of a mother. The rest of us too, for that matter."

"Daphne was no longer fit to be your mother. As you can easily see, she lives in her own delusional world now. She keeps a doll that she believes is Marjorie, though she uses her original given name, Angela."

I well remembered the first piece of evidence we'd uncovered in this whole mess—Marj's original birth certificate that listed her name as Angela Marjorie Steel. Marjorie had never known her real name because her certificate in the database had been altered to read Marjorie Steel, with no middle name.

"Wendy"—I refused to say "my mother"—"told Jade that Daphne named our sister Angela because when she was born prematurely, she knew she'd be an angel soon. Then, when Marj lived, she decided not to call her Angela after all because it would be a bad omen."

"Your mother—"

"She's not my mother!"

"I was speaking of Wendy, who is your mother."

"If it's okay with you, I'd rather not lay claim to any of my so-called parents, including you." I gripped the wooden arms of the chair I sat in.

"Ryan," Talon began.

"Tal, don't try to stop me from having my say here. My life has been shattered into a million pieces and—" I sighed, feeling like complete crap. "I'm sorry. You've had to deal with way worse shit than I ever have. I'm being selfish."

"That's big of you, Ryan," my father said.

"I said it out of respect for Talon, not for you." I gripped the arms of the chair again, my ire rising. "I lost all respect for you when I found out about my true parentage."

My father sighed, his eyes glassy. "I'm not sure I can do this now. Let's all sleep on this."

"Are you serious?" Talon this time. "I just find out that both my parents, who I thought were dead, are instead alive and well, and you want us to sleep on this?"

"Your mother is far from well. That should be patently obvious." Bradford Steel rubbed at his forehead. "I swear to both of you that I'll tell you everything, but not until your brother and sister are with you. I can't go through this twice."

"They're not coming here," I said. "This place isn't safe for Marjorie, and Joe's wife is pregnant. His place is home with her. So get it off your chest now, Dad, or goddamnit, I swear I'll beat you into tomorrow."

"Ry..." Talon rubbed his palms on the black pants he still wore.

"What? You think just because I'm the most jovial Steel brother I can't have a fucking temper? I may not be as dark as you and Joe, but Jesus Christ, Tal, this motherfucker owes us an explanation."

"Yes," Talon said. "He does."

Our father cleared his throat. "And you'll get it. Back home. If Marj and Joe can't come here, we will go home to them."

"We're not going anywhere until you release every woman and child who is being held against their will in that place," Talon said, his dark eyes glaring. "I can't believe you ever had a hand in this."

"I would release them all in a minute," he said. "But it's not that simple."

"Make it simple, then," I said. "Make it simple and get it done. Or I will kill you where you sit."

He didn't bat an eye at my words. "You have every right to. Believe me, I'm working on it."

"Start talking, Dad," Talon said.

"In the morning. I'll tell you what I can. The rest when we're all together. That's the best I can do."

I stood, advancing toward my father behind the desk. I wasn't the biggest or the strongest of the Steels, but right now I was the maddest. I pulled my father up by his shirt collar. "You'd better thank God Joe didn't come with us. Talon will keep me in line. But no one keeps Joe in line." I threw him back in his chair, walked to the door, and left, rage consuming me.

What I needed at the moment was not in that office.

It was somewhere in this house, though, and I was going after it.

CHAPTER TWENTY-SIX

Ruby

I was back on the deck with Juliet and Marabel when Ryan stalked outside.

His eyes were feral, primal.

The way he looked at me...

Juliet cowered against Marabel.

"It's okay," I said to her. "He's here for me."

I knew what he wanted, what we both wanted and needed. I expected him to yank me out of my chair, but he pulled me up gently.

"Come with me."

I looked toward Juliet. I didn't want to leave her, but my physical needs were bearing down on me. I needed to be with the man I loved, and the look in his eyes told me he needed the same. She was cuddling Beauty, and Marabel gave me a slight nod. I took that as my okay.

The guesthouse sat in the distance—the guesthouse that was Ryan's home, or at least looked just like it. Would it be furnished the same way? Would it be furnished at all?

As we walked toward it together, I knew I'd soon find out.

"I want to scoop you up in my arms and run to that house," Ryan said quietly. "But I don't want to upset Juliet."

"I appreciate that." Though part of me longed for the

same. I'd felt so helpless since I'd been brought here, so unable to have any control. And now, with Ryan, that's what I longed for. To submit to his control.

What the hell was wrong with me?

Nothing. I heard Melanie's soft voice in my mind.

But I couldn't help but think she was wrong. Here Ryan and I both were, stuck on this island in the Caribbean where so many suffered. And right now, all I could think about was getting to that guesthouse faster and having Ryan fuck me into oblivion.

Oblivion sounded like heaven.

When the door to the house was within a hundred feet, I ran, pulling Ryan along with me.

I turned the knob, but it was locked. "Damn!"

We tried all the doors. All locked.

"This is fucked up," he said. Then, "Fuck it. I don't care." He put his fist right through the front window.

I gasped, worried. "Are you hurt?"

"Don't care," he said again, reaching his long arm through and undoing the window lock. Then he opened the window and crawled through. "Wait here."

A few seconds later, he'd unlocked the door. "Hurry," he said.

I entered and gasped again. The place was decorated nothing like Ryan's at home but was certainly decorated. Probably by a woman, I'd guess, though none of it was to my taste. The living room was done in pure white, including a white lacquer baby grand piano. It was a muted white rather than stark, but still, I almost had to squint to look at it.

Then I remembered Ryan's hand. "Let me see."

"Just a few scratches. Forget it. Let's find a bedroom." He

raked his fingers through his hair, looking around. "Screw it. We're doing it here."

"On this white stuff? You'll get blood on it."

"Do I look like I care?" He grabbed me and crushed his lips to mine.

I opened to him, exploring his soft mouth. I'd missed him so much, but I hadn't let myself think much about him, at least so far as I could control myself. Thinking about Ryan too much would have overridden any logical part of my brain, and I'd had to concentrate on Juliet and the others. I hadn't been able to control my dreams, though.

But now...

I finally gave myself the freedom to melt into the man I loved.

He cupped my cheeks with his warm hands, thumbing my skin softly. Then he brushed his hands over my shoulders and around to my breasts. He began unbuttoning the silk pajama top, but then ripped it open down the middle, baring me. The fabric landed in a heap at my feet.

He roughly shoved the silk pants over my hips, and within seconds I was naked, my nipples so hard I swore they could have cut through glass. I inhaled. Already I could smell the musk of my arousal.

He thrust his fingers between my legs. "God. Fuck. Ruby. Ruby." Single words came out as groans.

"Please, Ryan. Please. Now," I moaned in whispers.

He set me upon the keyboard of the piano—discordant notes rang out, oddly unsettling yet perfect for the moment—and then pushed the black pants he wore over his hips and thrust into me.

Steadying myself, I hit the keys with my left hand, and

more disharmonic chords swirled around us. I let out a long moan, letting him seat himself to the hilt inside me. We hadn't been separated long, yet this felt like a homecoming. Like a deliverance from evil—which, in some ways, it was.

With my other hand, I touched Ryan's rough cheek and stared into his dark and fire-filled eyes.

We didn't speak, but our gazes spoke volumes. He thrust into me again and again, each thrust evoking more obscure notes from the piano.

The position was different somehow, and each thrust rubbed at my clit until soon I was ready to explode into orgasm.

"Yeah," Ryan grunted. "God, yeah."

I screamed as the convulsions started deep within me, traveling through my core to my limbs, and then returning at light speed to my pussy, exploding like fireworks.

Ryan thrust into me one last time, groaning, as he emptied inside me.

When he came down, he kissed my forehead gently, sighing.

My hand fell from his cheek to the piano keys, eliciting higher notes this time.

"Baby," Ryan said. "Let's find a bedroom. I'm going to lick every drop of my cum out of you, and then I'm going to fuck you again and again."

CHAPTER TWENTY-SEVEN

Ryan

We found a bed in the master suite. Again, all in fucking white. I didn't give a rat's ass if we soiled every inch of this house. I wasn't stopping until I'd had my fill of Ruby...and that wouldn't be for a while.

I undressed so we were both naked, and I pulled her against me. God, her skin, so soft and supple against my own. How had I never stopped to just feel her? Enjoy the sensation of our skin touching? I hardened again, my cock pushing into her soft belly. Her effect on me hadn't lessened at all. I closed my eyes and inhaled. The sweetly pungent smell of sex coiled around us. I touched her between her legs. My semen had dripped out of her, wetting the inside of her thighs.

I hardened even further. I pushed her down upon the bed and spread her legs. Licking my lips, I dived in.

Sweet heaven. She tasted of a mixture of us, of our lust. Of our love. I pulled at her clit. She grabbed two fistfuls of the white duvet, moaning my name.

Her moans fueled my desire, and I tugged at her labia, swirled my tongue around her wet lips and then thrust it inside her hot channel. She arched her back, her hips rising, as she ground against my face.

God, she was so hot, and she knew just how to turn me on.

I flipped her over onto her stomach and pushed her thighs forward so her beautiful ass was mounted for my view. Her pale skin shone against the stark white of the comforter. I leaped back into her wet heat, sliding my tongue from her clit all the way up to her pink and puckered asshole. She shuddered beneath me, grasping the covers once more, her hips undulating as she pushed her ass back into my face. I wanted to lick every inch of her, drown in her sweetness.

My cock throbbed, but I hadn't had enough of tasting her yet. I lay down next to her, positioning my head at the edge of the bed, and then pulled her onto me. "Sit on my face, baby." Her cream coated my cheeks and chin, and I reveled in it.

And then... Oh God... Her tongue was slithering over my cockhead, invading my tiny slit, and then her mouth was upon me until I nudged the back of her throat.

Good God! That was the farthest she'd ever taken me, and I concentrated all my willpower on not unloading again right there.

I couldn't hold out much longer, so as much as it pained me, I pushed her off my face. "Take my cock, Ruby. Ride me."

She turned to face me, her cheeks rosy, her blue eyes afire, and grasped my cock with her fist. Slowly she nudged it against her swollen pussy and sank down on me inch by excruciating inch.

She gloved me like no other ever had. So tight, so perfect around me, hugging me, clasping me with her ridged walls. I reached up to her breasts, which I hadn't paid any attention to yet. How could I have neglected such perfection? I smoothed my hands over her silky skin, but I couldn't keep my hands off her nipples for long. I thumbed them, loving how they hardened further at my touch. I tugged at them, and she moaned.

"Ryan, God. That feels so good!"

I twisted them harder, and she began riding me faster. I jerked my own hips up and down with her rhythm, and when my balls tightened against my perineum and the tiny convulsions began, I yelled at the top of my lungs.

"Ruby. God, Ruby! I love you!"

I erupted into her, pulsating wildly, exploding into her willing body. When she followed me into ecstasy, clamping around me, I pulled her down to me and took her lips with mine, kissing her deeply.

I couldn't kiss her hard enough, fast enough, and through our orgasms we remained kissing, our mouths fused together as were our bodies.

Finally, I broke the kiss and inhaled harshly. She collapsed on top of me, and rather than roll her over to her side, I welcomed her weight, her body against mine. Our skin stuck together with perspiration. After a few moments, she slid off me and sighed.

"Wow," she said.

"Wow times a hundred," I replied.

She sniffled against my arm.

I pulled her close. "Anything wrong?"

"Are you kidding? Everything is wrong. Everything except the two of us. Here. Together."

I knew what she meant. "We'll fix this, baby. I promise. Somehow."

"What did your father say?"

I rolled my eyes. "He refused to tell us much until the morning. Even then, he said we have to wait until Joe and Marj are with us. He can't tell us until we're all together."

"I suppose I can see his point."

I stiffened. "I can't."

"I know. I haven't gotten much information out of my own father either. Only that he wants out. That he has regrets. Too little too late as far as I'm concerned."

"Me too. I'll never forgive him for what he did to Talon. I'll never forgive any of them, my mother especially."

"What did he say about..." She hedged. "Daphne being alive?"

"Not much, except that she became unfit to be our mother. Why she's here, and why she carries a doll around thinking it's Marj—"

Ruby sat up. "She thinks the doll is Marj? She calls it Angela."

"I know. Remember when we told you about the birth certificate we found?" I quickly told her the story of Marjorie's original name.

"Oh. Wow." She shook her head. "I feel incredibly stupid. It never even dawned on me that she could be Daphne."

"There's no reason why it should have."

"Of course there is. I'm a detective. I—" She looked down at my hand. "We need to get you cleaned up. You're pretty scratched up." She moved toward the edge of the bed.

"It can wait." I pulled her back and kissed her.

She responded, but after a few beautiful minutes, she pulled away again. "I'm taking care of you. I hope this house has first aid supplies." She stood and held up her torn pajama top. "What am I going to wear out of here?"

I smiled. "Don't care."

She shook her head. "You're incorrigible. I guess I'll go walking around this strange place naked, then."

"You won't get any complaints from me."

A few minutes later, Ruby returned with some washcloths, antibacterial ointment, and Band-Aids.

"Ow!"

She rubbed at my scratches with the warm cloth. "Sorry. But some of these gashes are pretty deep. You're a good clotter, though."

"You sweet talker, you."

She laughed. "Hey. Go with it. You're lucky they're clotting up. Still, they need antibacterial ointment and bandages." She looked at the bed. "You bled all over the white comforter."

"Again. Don't care."

"Truthfully, neither do I." She applied some ointment to the largest of the wounds and added a bandage. "The rest of these aren't too bad. What were you thinking? Breaking a window with your fist and then sticking your whole arm in?"

"I was thinking if I didn't get you inside this house and me inside of you I was going to fucking explode."

She nodded. "I felt the same way. I felt really guilty about it too. We're surrounded by people being held against their will and being abused in the most horrible ways. Plus, Juliet is fucked up and needs me. But all I wanted was you."

"Don't feel guilty. Juliet seems like she's doing okay, and there's nothing else we can do without backup right now. Not until our fathers decide to be truthful with us."

What I didn't say was that I was feeling guilty too. I'd left Talon alone with my father in that damned office. He was the one who'd suffered the most because of our father's little business venture, and he didn't have his woman here to comfort him as I did.

Guilt.

All three of us had harbored a ton of it over the years,

probably Joe most of all. Part of me wished with all my heart that he was here with us, but part of me knew it was better that he wasn't. Joe would have done what I hadn't. He would have taken a fist to our father...and then another. Brad Steel would have fought back, but Joe would have won. He was younger, bigger, and stronger. Not that the asshole didn't deserve it, but if we were going to figure this out, we needed him in one piece.

"Who do you think decorated this place?" Ruby asked. "When I was looking around for first aid supplies, I wandered into the kitchen and family room. They're all white too. It's freaky."

"Hell if I know." And I didn't care.

"Just seems strange. All the white." She sighed. "There. You're all set. I'm no nurse, but I think I did a pretty good job."

"Baby, you're the only nurse I'll ever need. You can be my naughty nurse." I pulled her down to me and kissed her.

And I hardened once more.

CHAPTER TWENTY-EIGHT

Ruby

His lips were so soft, so gentle with me now. We'd both gotten the urgency out of our systems, and now our lovemaking was tender and slow. He laid me back down on the bed and kissed my cheeks, my ears, my neck, sending shivers coursing through me. He swirled his tongue inside my ear, and goose bumps erupted on my skin. I tingled all over, and my core began to flutter.

How could I want him again? So soon? But wanting had never been an issue since I'd met Ryan Steel. I'd been in heat since I first laid eyes on him when I was an inexperienced virgin.

I had a lot of experience now, but there were still more things to share with this amazing man. I couldn't get enough of his lips and tongue on my skin. He seemed determined to cover every inch, and I had no plans to stop him.

He did stop, though, for a moment, and he gazed into my eyes, his own burning. "You're so beautiful, Ruby. Your dark hair is fanned out on that white pillow like a soft curtain. Your eyes are sparkling. You look so gorgeous, so thoroughly used." He smiled.

Then he went back to work.

Lips on my shoulders, my chest, the globes of my breasts.

Tongue on my abdomen, in my navel, in the crease between my thigh and groin.

Then fingers...squeezing my nipples, twisting them. I gasped, squirming, my pussy wanting attention. But as he moved his lips downward, kissing my inner thighs and then my knees, his fingers left my nipples and trailed over my abdomen, and then he entwined them in the short hair of my bush.

My clit was throbbing, crying out for attention. Our combined musk wafted in the air, and I inhaled, letting it infuse my body.

Ryan traveled down my calves to my feet, kissing my toes, sucking them, tickling my instep with his tongue.

"Turn over, love," he said.

I obeyed, and he began his way back up my body, his lips journeying over my heels, my calves, tickling the inside of my knees. Then up my thighs and between the cheeks of my ass.

I shuddered when he licked me there. So wrong yet so right.

"Spread your legs, Ruby," he commanded.

I hadn't disobeyed him yet, and I had no desire to begin now. I complied, and he spread the globes of my ass.

"So beautiful," he said. "I'll have you here one day. When you're ready." Then he gave one cheek a light slap.

I shivered. The dream... He'd slapped me in that creepy dream, and I'd liked it. Loved it...but then the dream had gone down a different path.

I erased the fractured images from my mind and tried to concentrate on how I was feeling now. I'd longed to be reunited with Ryan, and no way was some stupid dream going to spoil it.

He'd slapped me there once before, and my reaction had been ambivalent. It was now as well, but I couldn't escape the fact that beneath my contradictory feelings was a heat from his hand that traveled to my clit.

He tongued my asshole, gently at first and then more forcibly, seeking entrance. "Relax," he whispered.

I tried. I'd enjoyed this before, but this time he was jabbing harder.

"Better. Yeah, that's better, baby. Let me in. Mmm." The point of his tongue breached my rim. "So sweet."

I buried my face in the white pillow and let him do what he was determined to do.

And God...it felt so fucking good.

I closed my eyes, drowning in the pleasure as he pushed in and out and then soothed me with long licks all the way down to my clit. Then he moved upward, kissing my back, trailing his lips along my spine until I quivered. Then up my neck to my head, where he kissed my hair and inhaled.

And then he slid his cock into me gently.

I let out a soft moan.

I was sore from all the frantic fucking we'd done, and his entrance this time was oddly soothing, as though I was meant for this. We, together, were meant for it.

He made love to me slowly, sweetly, my walls hugging his cock every time he entered me. I felt so full, so complete. That emptiness I'd felt since I'd woken up in that room with Juliet was gone now.

Gone for good.

"So nice, baby," he whispered against my neck, kissing it. "So perfect."

He continued to pump in and out of me, and soon the familiar tingles in my clit emerged and I soared into climax. Every time was different yet the same. The feeling of two souls meeting and becoming one.

"That's it, love. Come. Come for me. For us." He thrust forcefully into me, his own orgasm erupting.

When his cock stopped pulsing, he withdrew and lay on his back. I turned to face him. His face and body were gleaming, his hair sticking to his neck. He'd never looked more magnificent.

"Three times in a little over an hour," I said. "That's got to be some kind of record."

He chuckled. "I wanted you. Needed you. When I saw you... I was just so relieved that you were safe, and after talking to my father..." He sighed. "It's all just too much to handle. Both he and Daphne have been alive all this time."

"I know it's a lot to digest. But you'll get through it. You and your siblings are some of the strongest people I've ever met. Your sisters-in-law too. You're all amazing."

He opened his eyes and rolled onto his side so our gazes met. "And so is my wife-to-be."

My skin prickled. He'd proposed in the heat of passion a few days ago, and I hadn't answered. I wasn't about to hold him to anything he shouted out during climax.

"You're not saying anything," he said.

Warmth crept up my neck and into my cheeks. "I'm not sure what to say."

"'Yes' would be a good start."

I smiled. "I want to say yes. But we haven't known each other that long and—"

He covered my mouth with his fingers. "I was with Anna— Oh, God...Anna!" He sat up, pushing his damp hair off his forehead.

"What is it?"

"Anna. She's here. They took her. She never went to Hawaii. I think the reason my father bought her ranch was... Oh my God."

"Ryan. It's okay. None of this is your fault."

"If it hadn't been for me... Shit, if it hadn't been for me, Anna would still live on the little ranch next to ours. My mother wanted her away from me. That woman is pure evil!" He stood and paced around the bedroom, his feet imprinting the plush white carpeting.

I went to him, wanting to offer comfort but not knowing how. Anna was here? "You saw her?"

"Yeah. She was chained up with some other girls in the hallway of this place. A big building with rooms."

"The dorms."

"Yeah, like dorms. Wait...what?"

"They put me there my first night."

He turned to me and gripped my shoulders. "What? Did they hurt you? Chain you?"

"No, no. I swear. Just put me in a room with a concrete floor to sleep off the drugs they gave me. Juliet was there." Images flooded back to me, and tears welled in my eyes. "Two masked goons came in and raped her right in front of me."

Ryan embraced me. Hard. "My God, I'm so sorry. But they didn't touch you, did they? Swear to me that they didn't." His muscles were tense and rigid, as if they'd hardened into rock.

"No. They didn't." And the guilt I still felt from that was overwhelming.

"Ruby...don't lie to me."

"I'm not. I swear!"

"If you're thinking you have to keep me out of trouble by lying—"

This time I placed my fingers over his mouth. "I'm not. It was terrible. I couldn't help her. All I could do was watch. She didn't even react."

"I'm so sorry. We have to put a stop to this. We have to get Anna and Juliet and everyone else out of here."

"Juliet is safe for now."

"So are those two boys Talon insisted we rescue."

"I can understand. I'm sure he saw himself in them."

His features twisted into anguish. "But I couldn't help Anna. She was locked up. I couldn't get her away."

"We're going to get them all out. As soon as your father tells us what we're dealing with. I swear it." I touched his cheek.

He placed his warm hand over mine and lowered his head—

A cell phone rang.

He dropped his hand. "That's me. Sorry."

"Get it. It's probably important."

Ryan dug through the pockets of the black pants he'd been wearing and put the phone to his ear. "Tal, what's going on?"

CHAPTER TWENTY-NINE

R y a n

"I talked to Joe," Talon said over the phone. "He's fit to be tied, but the good news is the Grand Junction PD has dropped their investigation of him for accessory to the murder of Larry Wade."

"That's good." A load should have lifted off my shoulders, but so much weighed me down, I didn't feel any lighter.

"So Dad chartered a plane. Joe and Marjorie arrive late tomorrow morning."

Ire prickled my spine. "Marjorie is coming here? That's insane."

"That's what I said, but Dad says he won't talk unless we're all here. He has assured us of her safety."

"And you believe him?"

"No. I don't believe a word that comes out of the bastard's mouth. But we can't keep this from our sister forever, and with the three of us here, no one will get near her."

"Bringing her here is nuts."

"Well...I think we can safely say Dad is nuts. As are both your mother and mine."

"At least yours isn't a psycho." I sighed and closed my eyes. "I'm sorry, Tal. You've been through so much more than—"

"For fuck's sake, Ryan, this doesn't always have to be about me! I'm so sick of you tiptoeing around me. You're entitled to your own pain. Own it, for God's sake."

"I just meant—"

"You just meant that anything that has happened to you can't possibly be as bad as what happened to me. Maybe it isn't. Maybe it is. But what happened happened. I've had to own it. It's time for you to own your own pain. Finding out you have a different mother than the rest of us couldn't have been easy. None of us think it was. So stop feeling guilty for wanting to own your pain. It doesn't lessen mine for you to keep belittling yours. I'm your brother, for God's sake. I feel it with you."

I had no words. Talon was so wise. He always had been, despite trying to push everyone away for so long. Joe was strength and Talon was wisdom. Where did that leave me? For now, I'd give my brother what he seemed to need and want. "All right, Tal. I get it."

"Good. Because I have more news, and it's not good."

Chills raked over me as I prepared for the worst. "What is it?"

"Raj is missing."

★ ★ ★

"Hey, he came highly recommended." I gripped the edge of the table where I sat with my father and my brother over breakfast. Ruby was having breakfast with Juliet and the boys on the deck. Talon and I were eating with our father in the formal dining room, where no one on the deck could see us or hear us.

My father shook his head.

"I hear what you're not saying," I said. "You think we made

a mistake hiring him. Well, you weren't around to advise us, Dad. You were supposedly ashes in the earth."

"I'm not in any position to give either of you advice."

"You can say that again," I said.

Talon was eerily quiet.

"What is it?" I asked him.

"Something was never right about him," Talon said. "Someone on that yacht tampered with my oxygen tank or regulator."

"We don't know that for sure. It could have been a malfunction." Though I couldn't fault my brother's observation. I addressed my father. "What were we supposed to do? Leave him when we got to this place? He was all we had."

"No one's criticizing," Talon said.

"Bullshit." I pointed to our father. "He is."

"I'm not."

"Tell me why you took Anna. I saw her there. Did you know that? She was chained up in a hallway like a prisoner, and I couldn't help her. How do you think that makes me feel?"

"I know how it makes you feel. You watch something horrible happening, and you're powerless to stop it. I've felt it every single day since high school."

"How could you have funded these people?" Talon asked.

What was more important was what Talon hadn't asked yet. The question we both wanted the answer to. Why had he allowed Wendy to have Talon abducted? Surely he could have stopped it.

"I made some mistakes," he said. "Some grave mistakes."

"Sell it somewhere else," I replied. "I, for one, am not buying it."

"Look," he said, "I'm not flying your brother and sister

186

here so you can believe me, much less forgive me. But I'm going to tell you the truth. You all deserve that much. Besides, there's something else you need to know."

"What's that?"

He cleared his throat. "I'm dying."

CHAPTER THIRTY

Ruby

Juliet and I sat on the deck with Marabel and the two little boys Talon and Ryan had rescued. They had showered and were dressed in T-shirts and sweatpants that were a little too big on their skinny frames. Marabel had fed them a light meal. Too much too soon, and they'd get sick. They hadn't told us their names yet, but the puppies were bringing out a few smiles in them. They were handsome boys, both blond with green eyes. Probably brothers. The younger boy spoke a little. I hadn't heard the older one utter a sound yet.

I tried not to worry, even though Ryan had told me that the private detective they had arrived with had disappeared. I wasn't sure how anyone could disappear from this strange Steel compound. We were fenced in by twenty-foot concrete walls. He'd be found soon.

Juliet was improving. In twenty-four hours, she had regained some color to her cheeks and was shivering a little less. Her appetite had improved as well. She'd eaten two whole eggs this morning, though she still skipped the orange juice.

We expected Joe and Marj anytime now. They were coming straight here, so Marjorie wouldn't be subjected to the dorms or any other heinous things.

The older boy was petting the puppy Juliet had named

Bo. He was a little less rambunctious than Ernie and Beauty, and he allowed the boy to hold him and stroke him without wriggling away.

I'd heard of pet therapy, and now I was a true believer. Bo was helping this boy. I walked over to where he sat on the deck with the puppy.

"He's cute, isn't he?"

The boy didn't answer.

"Can you tell me your name?"

Nothing.

"My name's Ruby, and that puppy's name is Bo."

Still no answer. If only Melanie were here. She'd know how to talk to these kids.

"If you can tell me your name, we can call your parents. I'm sure they'll want to know where you are."

Again, nothing.

So I sat with him, just let him feel my presence. Sometimes that was all I could do. Made me feel pretty useless.

A few minutes later, Ryan came to the door. "Joe and Marj have arrived. They'll be here in about fifteen minutes."

I stood. "I'll be back as soon as I can," I told the boy. "Stay here with Marabel and the others, okay?"

He didn't respond, but he did give me a slight nod of his head. I smiled at him and secretly jumped up and down in my mind. I'd gotten through to him. This was the first time he'd responded in any way to any of us.

I walked into the kitchen with Ryan. "Do you want me to come with you?"

"Yeah. This concerns you as much as any of us."

"I'm not sure it does. This is family stuff, Ryan. I'm not family."

"You will be."

I hadn't yet given him an answer to his proposal. We'd been interrupted.

"I don't think it's appropriate for me to be there if Jade and Melanie aren't. This is between you, your siblings, and your father."

"I want you there, Ruby. I need you there."

"I want to be there," I said. "But it's not fair to the others."

He sighed. "All right." He pressed a kiss to my lips. "We'll be in my dad's office. It's not going to be pretty. I hope Tal and I can handle Joe. He hasn't even come into the house yet, and already I can feel his anger permeating these walls."

"You're imagining things."

"I hope so." He kissed me again and walked out of the kitchen.

I would join the others back on the deck, but first I was going to change clothes. I had worn another pair of silk pajamas to bed, but Marabel had ordered clothes for Juliet, the boys, and me, so I wanted to put on something other than nightclothes.

I walked toward my room, when voices—one that was very familiar—came from Brad Steel's office again.

"This is my business too," my father said.

"I'm not denying that, but you can't be here right now. Leave. Use the garage entrance. Make sure no one sees you."

"You owe me."

"I owe you nothing. So I welshed on a bequest. So what? You didn't need it. You, Wade, and Simpson were pulling in millions at the time of my supposed death."

"Well, Wade and Simpson are dead now, and I'm rapidly going broke."

"Not my problem. Now leave."

"It is partially your problem, Brad. Do I need to remind you?"

Silence for a few seconds. Then, "All bets were off when you brutalized my son. I could've had you arrested, tried, and convicted, and you'd be living out your days as a prison bitch. Or maybe you'd enjoy that?"

"You wouldn't have found me. Not even my daughter could find me, and she's a first-rate cop."

"She didn't have my resources. Most importantly, one resource that could have done you in with a phone call. Just leave now. Let me deal with my children. I'll take care of you later."

Footsteps advanced toward the door, and I scurried into the bedroom I shared with Juliet.

CHAPTER THIRTY-ONE

R y a n

Talon and I met Jonah and Marj at the front door. They had arrived in a black SUV—was that the only car on this island?—and their driver pulled away as I watched.

I looked at my brother.

Joe was angry. A vein pulsed in his neck. They'd been flying all night, so he was also no doubt sleep-deprived. An invisible shield surrounded him. Talon and I knew better than to mess with it.

Marjorie, though, fell into my arms and held on for dear life. A few seconds later, though, she pulled away and punched my arm. "How could you not tell me any of this? What kind of brothers are you?"

"The kind who put your safety before everything else," I said.

"That's no excuse." She punched me again and then headed to Talon. She fell into his arms as well and then repeated the punches.

"I'm so angry with both of you, but so happy—" Her eyes turned into circles, and she ripped herself away from Talon. "Daddy!"

I turned. Our father had indeed entered the foyer. He hadn't elaborated earlier on his statement that he was dying, as we'd gotten word right then that Joe and Marj were arriving soon. Talon and I hadn't pushed. He looked the same as he always had, and I couldn't help wondering if the statement had been some kind of ploy to gain our sympathy.

Marjorie launched herself onto him, hugging him hard.

"Hey, there, baby girl," he said softly. He kissed the top of Marj's head. "I've missed you."

I expected her to pull back and punch him as she had Talon and me, but she didn't. Instead, she burst into tears and cried into his chest. He rubbed her back and let her sob, saying nothing.

Finally, when she pulled away and sniffled, I saw the pain in my baby sister's eyes.

"I want to see my mother."

The truth of that statement struck me. Marjorie had only been two when Daphne had presumably died. She had no memories. She would truly be seeing her mother for the first time.

"Later," our father said. "She's not...well."

"Talon explained everything. I understand. But damn it, I want to see my mother!"

"Not now," he said.

I walked toward him and stood in his face. "You take our sister to see her mother right now. She's never laid eyes on her, at least not that she can remember, and she wants to see her."

"It's not the right—"

In a flash, Joe was on our father and had him in a headlock. "I'd like to see her as well. She's my mother too. Take us to her. Now, you bastard."

So much for Talon and me being able to keep Joe in line. But his demand was not unreasonable. After a pained look from Marj, Joe released him.

Our father rubbed at his neck. "She won't know you. She thinks you and Talon are still little boys." He turned to Marj. "And she thinks you're a baby. She carries a doll around, believing it's you."

A knife hit my heart. Again, no mention of me.

Because I was not hers.

I attempted to swallow the lump in my throat that formed whenever I thought about Daphne Steel.

"Don't care. You've kept her from us for twenty-three years, and we will see her now." Joe hardened his lips into a thin line.

"All right," my father relented. "I'll take you to her."

Joe gripped his shoulder. "I'll hold myself in check for now. I want to see my mother, and I don't want to upset her. But after that, you will answer to us."

Brad Steel nodded with resignation. "Follow me."

I nudged Talon. "You should go with them."

"I've already seen her. Besides, she doesn't know who I am."

"Still, you should share this moment with them. With your brother and sister."

"Thanks," he said, "but I'll stay here. With my brother."

My eyes moistened, but I held myself together. No time to get weepy over Talon's and my brotherhood. How had I ever thought for a second that my having a different mother would matter? It did matter, but it had not affected my relationship with my siblings. I was especially glad that Talon still felt bound to me by blood. He was still my hero, even though he most likely wasn't the reason I'd escaped his horrible fate. My biological mother was.

Ruby walked out from the hallway, clad in a pair of gray yoga pants and a tank top. Even with everything else going on, the sight of her still made my groin tighten.

"Hey. I just wanted to change my clothes. I'm going back out." She turned to Talon. "The older boy gave me a little nod when I talked to him outside. It's not much, but it's more than he's responded to anyone since he got here. Slowly, they're coming around."

Talon smiled. "Good. I hate what they've been through. I hate it. I want to kill the people responsible, even though two of them are my father and yours."

"I feel you," she said. "Believe me."

"How's Juliet?" I asked.

"She's better. As with the boys, it's slow, but it's steady. She's eating more now, and those pups are like magic to her and the boys."

"You know," I said to Talon. "This place is huge. I bet we could bring all the women and kids here and get them healthy while we search for their parents."

"I'll mention it to Dad," Talon said.

"Dad? Are you kidding? Dad's been here this whole time. No, we're going to take care of this ourselves. You'll help, won't you, babe?"

"Of course. But Ryan, this isn't our house. It may look just like your house, but it isn't. We can't control what goes on here."

"The hell we can't."

"She's right, Ry," Talon said.

I balled my hands into fists. "I have to get Anna out of there!"

"We will," Ruby said. "Somehow. Believe me. I'm just

as determined as you are." She sighed, her eyes misting. "We won't be able to save them all. My father told me that my cousin Gina had been sold. Sold like a fucking animal!"

I went to her and embraced her. "We'll find her. We won't stop until we do."

She sniffled into my shoulder for a few seconds and then pulled away. "I can't lose it. Too many people need me right now."

"I know. I feel the same way. We'll do everything we can, baby. I promise."

She nodded, wiping at her eyes. "This isn't like me. I'm not a crybaby."

"Ruby, you're about as far from a crybaby as anyone I know," I said. "But this is getting to all of us. Why do you think Tal insisted we bring those two boys with us? They slowed us down, but he would not be deterred, and he was right to bring them. I wish I could have released Anna and the others. I wish..." Now I was choking up. We all needed to get hold of ourselves.

Footsteps alerted us to Joe and Marj's return. Marj's eyes were red and swollen. Joe's face looked like it had been carved in white granite. Neither were good signs.

"Ruby, I'm glad you're here and that you're all right." Marj gave her a quick hug.

"We're all hanging in there," Ruby said. "How are you?"

"Seeing my mother was a shock, but I'll be okay. At least Talon prepared us when he called. We came for the truth, and you've promised to give it to us, right, Daddy?"

My father nodded, clearing his throat. "Let's go to my office."

I kissed Ruby quickly. "I love you."

"I love you too. I'll be on the deck with the others if you need me."

I needed her. But this had to be done with my siblings alone.

I followed behind them to the office.

CHAPTER THIRTY-TWO

Ruby

"Miss Ruby!" Marabel greeted me. "I have wonderful news. The little boy finally revealed his name. It's Donny, and his brother's name is Dale."

The older boy sat where I had left him, still playing with Bo. I walked toward him and sat down. His too-long sandy-blond hair blew into his eyes with the subtle breeze, and gray circles marred his sad emerald-green eyes. Bruises and scratches soiled his arms, making anger boil within me. But even so, he was an extraordinarily beautiful child. His beauty—and his brother's—was probably what had made him a target. "Dale. That's a nice name. Can you tell me how old you are?"

"He's ten," Donny said. "And I'm seven."

The same ages as Talon and Ryan were when Talon was taken. Coincidence, obviously, but I was understanding more and more why Talon had refused to leave without them. Dale clearly wasn't ready to talk yet, and while I knew I could pump Donny for information, I felt strongly that my place for now was next to Dale.

We didn't talk. He just stroked Bo.

Juliet walked over to join us. She had also changed clothes and wore a black T-shirt and gray yoga pants. "I know they hurt you, Dale. They hurt me too. But we're going to be okay now. It will just take time."

Dale nodded slightly, just as he had for me before. Juliet was reaching him. I smiled. This would be good therapy for both of them and would give me a chance to speak with Donny.

"Would you stay with him for a little while?" I asked.

She nodded, stroking Bo's soft head. "We should take the puppy down into the yard so he can play. Would you like that?"

No slight nod this time, but Dale stood, releasing the pup. He followed Juliet out onto the green grass.

Now was my chance to talk to Donny.

He sat next to Marabel. The other two puppies squirmed away from him and joined their brother and the others on the grass.

"Are you hungry, Donny?" I asked.

"Yeah. A little."

"Do you think we could give him something to eat?" I asked Marabel.

"Just a little. I'll get him something." She walked into the house.

"Do you remember your last name?" I asked him. "Or your mommy's or daddy's names?"

"We don't have a daddy. Just Mommy. Our daddy died when I was a baby."

"I grew up without a daddy too." Until I was fourteen, anyway. "Do you remember your mommy's name?"

"Her name is Cheri. She has blond hair too. Our last name is Robertson. We live in Colorado."

"Really? That's where I live too."

"I like the mountains. We could see them outside our back window. They look purple."

Far enough away to look purple most likely meant Denver

or Colorado Springs. Now we were getting somewhere. I could ask him how long he'd been held captive, but he probably wouldn't be able to answer me. Days had no doubt blended together.

Then he squirmed in his chair. "My bum hurts."

A spear entered my heart. God only knew how this sweet young boy had been used. I took only a smidgen of solace that my father hadn't inflicted it the way he had on Talon. And that was only if he'd been telling me the truth.

"I know you took a shower, but have you had a bath? That might help a little."

"No, not yet. The bad men did things to us."

"I know. But you're safe now. And you will heal. I promise." I could easily make the promise that his body would heal. His mind? He could heal, but he would need help. A lot of help. Help Talon hadn't been given until much later in his life. Help that Gina had been getting, but they'd taken her anyway.

"Dale protected me a lot. They hurt him worse. He stopped crying after a while."

My heart splintered in two. "He's a good big brother, isn't he?"

"He's the best. He's my hero."

★ ★ ★

After Donny had eaten the snack of apple slices and peanut butter that Marabel brought him, I took him inside to my bathroom and ran a warm bath. I found some lavender bubble bath in the cabinet.

"Mommy used to give me bubble baths," he said.

"Your mommy is going to be so happy to know you're

okay. You and Dale both." I turned off the bath water. "You're a big boy. You probably don't need my help to take a bath."

"Right. I can do it myself."

"I'll just stay in here, in case you need me."

"No. You don't have to."

"Donny, have you ever taken a bath by yourself before?"

"Yeah. Dale doesn't get in with me anymore. He says he's too old for that. So I have to do it alone."

"You mean your mommy doesn't stay in the bathroom with you?"

"Sometimes. But sometimes not. I'm getting too big for that too. I mean, I'm a boy and all."

"You sure you'll be okay?"

"Yup. I'll be fine."

Still, something poked at me. "I'm not leaving you."

"Please," he said, his voice taking on a whine. "I'm... embarrassed."

"You don't have to be embarrassed. I'm a police officer, and I'd never hurt you. I just want to make sure you're okay."

"But...they did things... Please."

I shuddered. I knew exactly what had happened to this sweet boy. He wanted some privacy, which made complete sense. Maybe I could give him a minute or two.

"Okay. Just sit in the water for a while. It will help. There's a washcloth and towel on the rack. Some shampoo on the shelf if you want to wash your hair. I'll be right in the next room. Just holler if you need anything."

"Okay."

I closed the door behind me, leaving it cracked so he'd know I was here...and also so I could keep watching him without him knowing. The water sloshed as he got into the tub and sat down. I quietly moved a chair so I could sit and still see Donny in the tub. Across the hall, the Steels were having their conference. I could sneak out and probably hear what they were saying, like I'd heard Brad with my father before. But I couldn't. First, I couldn't leave Donny alone, and of course, it was none of my business. This was between Brad and his children—four children who were mad as hell.

I didn't envy Brad Steel his task, but he deserved it nonetheless.

Donny wasn't using the washcloth. He was just sitting there, silent. Poor ba—

Crash!

And then a high-pitched scream.

I jerked toward the bedroom door. The sound had come from the office. Ryan had warned me that Joe might get physical. Marjorie had probably been responsible for the scream.

I walked to the door but then hurried back.

I couldn't leave Donny.

I peered back through the cracked door. He was no longer in the tub. He must be drying off behind the door. "Donny? Do you need help?"

No answer. I jerked the door open. No Donny.

I ran toward the tub.

His little body was floating. Facedown.

CHAPTER THIRTY-THREE

Ryan

Joe took charge, as the rest of us knew he would.

"Talon has filled us in on the bullshit you've spewed so far," he said to our father, "so start with something new. Like why the fuck you faked your own death. I can't believe I let that lunatic Wendy Madigan—" He looked to me. "Shit. I'm sorry, Ry."

"She is a lunatic. I can't help that I'm her progeny. No need to tiptoe around it. I'm not the idiot who slept with her." I couldn't resist the dig at our father. It was a hell of a lot less than he deserved.

He remained silent, his lips pursed.

Joe cleared his throat. "As I was saying, I can't believe I let that lunatic Wendy Madigan identify your body. It was my job as the oldest."

I saw where this was going. Joe was a master at harboring guilt. "Don't do that to yourself," I said. "We were all adults. It was all our responsibility."

"Still, I should have—"

Marjorie stood. "Stop it! Stop this right now. We all should have looked at the body. We all should have stopped this long ago."

"Marj," Talon said. "You didn't even know anything about

it until the guys and I told you."

"Well, stop protecting me. I'm not some fragile glass ornament that needs to be wrapped in bubble wrap. I'm as strong as the rest of you."

Our father smiled from across his desk. "Yes, baby girl. You are."

Marj's eyes began to soften. When he'd tried to keep her away from ranch work, she'd had none of it. She learned to run the ranch right alongside the rest of us, all the while remaining Daddy's girl.

She was our father's Achilles' heel. Maybe that could come in handy. Though Marj was nobody's fool. She wouldn't appreciate being used. Plus...she'd held on to him for dear life when she saw him. She wouldn't harden easily.

"Start talking, Dad," Joe said icily. "And don't leave out one single solitary detail."

Brad Steel coughed into his fist. "What you all need to understand is that everything I've done was for your protection."

"What about the future lawmakers?" Joe demanded. "Why did you fund them? How couldn't you tell they were bad people? You can't say you did that for our protection. We weren't born yet."

"I've made many mistakes, and I have many regrets."

Joe scoffed. "Sell it to someone who gives a damn."

"I did the best I could by you."

"By keeping our mother from us? By keeping us from our father as well?" Joe stood, grabbed an empty chair, and hurled it at the wall. It crashed against a framed photograph of Aspen trees, and the wooden legs splintered from the seat.

Marjorie screamed. Talon sat, rigid, while my body went

tight, as if I were a balloon and the air was being squeezed out of me.

Our father had no reaction to Joe's outburst except for a slightly raised brow. "You will understand after you know everything."

Joe snarled like an animal. "Don't bet on—"

"Help!"

Fuck! That was Ruby's voice. Coming from her room. I stood and bolted.

Ruby was administering CPR to one of the little boys, who lay, naked and wet, on the floor of her bedroom. She pumped at his heart ferociously. "Come on, damn it. Breathe, Donny, breathe!"

Then she tilted his head, pinched his nose, opened his mouth, clamped her lips over it, and delivered two rescue breaths.

After she lifted her head, she began chest compressions again. "Call 9-1-1, damn it!"

I pulled out my cell phone and dialed, and then it occurred to me that there probably wasn't any 9-1-1. My father and siblings had congregated in the room. I grabbed my father's shirt collar. "Who do we call in an emergency? Damn it, who?"

"I'll take care of it," he said and returned to his office.

Talon knelt down beside Ruby, his hands shaking. "What the hell happened?"

"Come on, damn it!" Ruby punched on his chest again.

And the little boy coughed and sputtered up water.

Ruby sat back, weeping. I went to her and held her. "It's okay, baby. He's okay. He's breathing."

Talon touched the little boy's forehead. "Can you sit up?"

Donny, still coughing, choked out, "No. I was supposed to

die!"

"You're alive," Talon said. "And we're all glad you're alive. Your brother will be glad."

He coughed again. "No, he won't. We made a pact. If either of us had the chance to end our own life, we'd do it."

Talon shook his head. "Why?"

"So the bad men wouldn't hurt us anymore."

Talon held the boy to his chest. "The bad men won't hurt you anymore. I promise. They won't. You're going to have a long life. I promise that too." His eyes glossed over.

Talon seemed to have the boy under control, so I tended to Ruby as she sobbed against my shoulder. "Shh, baby. It's okay."

She rubbed her nose on my shirt and sniffed, facing me. "It's my fault."

"How is this your fault? Ruby, you saved him. He's alive because of you."

"No." She shook her head, sobbing. "I put him in the tub. He said"—she glanced at Talon—"he said his bum hurt. I thought sitting in a tub would help. He said he could do it himself. But I kept watch. The door was cracked. It was only a few inches of water. I didn't leave him!"

"Of course you didn't. You didn't do anything wrong."

"But then I heard something from the office."

Joe's tantrum. Damn it. "I'm so sorry. That was—"

"It doesn't matter what it was. I shouldn't have stopped watching for a second."

"He's old enough to take a bath by himself."

"He's only seven. What was I thinking?"

"Ruby, how old were you when you started taking a bath by yourself?"

"I don't know. Five, I think."

"So was I. You didn't do anything wrong."

"He was doing so well. He was talking. He was eating. Playing with the puppies." She pressed her head back to my shoulder. "I never imagined..."

"You couldn't have known what he'd try. Please. You didn't do anything wrong, baby."

Talon was rocking Donny in his arms. "You're safe now. There's no need for your pact anymore."

"But Dale said—"

"Shh. When was the last time you talked about the pact?"

"In the room. Before you came."

"Well, things are different now, aren't they? You're here, and no one here will hurt you."

"But Dale won't talk. Not even to me."

"Dale is just..." Talon paused. Then, "Dale's going through some stuff. But it's over now. He'll come around. I'll make sure he's okay."

Donny nodded and sank his head against Talon's chest. My brother would make a good father when the time came. A damned good one. Ruby still sobbed softly against my shoulder.

Suddenly the door slammed open, and Dale ran in, Marabel at his heels.

"Donny!" he yelled. "Are you all right?"

Donny lifted his head from Talon's chest. "I'm sorry, Dale. I tried."

"No!" He grabbed his little brother into a bear hug. "No, God. I'm so sorry. I never meant... I'm so glad you're okay. That you're alive."

"But we made a pact."

"It was a stupid pact. We were starving and hurting. But

now we're not. I want to live, Donny, and I want you to live too."

It was a stupid pact, but to a seven-year-old little boy, it was a blood promise between brothers. Little boys couldn't see past tomorrow, and I knew exactly why Donny had tried to drown himself. Because his brother had told him to. I would have done anything Talon told me to do when I was seven. I would have fought with him and gone to the bad place. But he'd told me to run.

And I had.

Donny was me. Only he hadn't gotten away.

I looked into Ruby's eyes, and she curved her lips upward ever so slightly. For a moment, I thought she had read my mind, but then I noticed her gaze wander to Dale. He was talking.

"Hey," I said to her. "Tal has this under control, and my father is calling...well, whoever they call around here for an emergency so we can make sure Donny is truly all right. Let me take care of you."

I stood, bringing her with me. She needed some TLC. I knew just how to take care of her and just where to do it.

★ ★ ★

Back in the guesthouse decorated all in white, I searched the kitchen for something to help Ruby relax. All I could find was some regular black tea bags. It was better than nothing. I quickly put some water to boil on the stove.

She sat at the table, her head in her hands. When I brought her a cup of tea, I kissed the top of her head. "He's fine. And we'll keep extra eyes on both of them now."

"His bum hurts. That's what he told me. And we all know why it hurts. This is all so horrid!" She rubbed at her temples.

"He's seven, Ryan, and his brother is ten. The same ages you and Talon were when..."

My heart jolted and broke at the same time. Her thought was something that had already occurred to me. This little brother hadn't gotten away.

I sat down in the chair next to Ruby. No words came to me. All I could think about was little Donny's fate—a fate I'd been spared.

Then Ruby looked at me with fire in her blue eyes.

"Take me to bed, Ryan. Now. Please."

As much as I always wanted her, I wasn't sure sex was what she needed. "Ruby—"

"Don't argue with me. Just fuck me. Fuck me until I can't stand. Show me that something wonderful still exists in this horrible place."

She stood and pulled me out of my chair. She quickly undid my belt and zipper and tugged my jeans and boxers over my hips.

I couldn't help myself. In spite of the horror we'd both just witnessed, my cock sprang out, ready, as always, for her sweet lips, her sweet cunt. I expected her to kneel down and take me into her hot mouth, but instead she shed her slippers and yoga pants and sat down on the kitchen table, legs spread.

"Please, Ryan. I need you. Now."

I pushed into her wet heat.

She was ready, her vanilla musk wafting to my nose. I inhaled. Sweet magic. She was right. This was what was wonderful in this horrible place.

I pumped in and out of her. When she lowered her hand to her vulva and began fingering her clit, I nearly lost it.

But she had wanted a fuck, a fuck until she couldn't stand.

So I held myself in check and kept thrusting until her breath quickened and she moaned, soaring into climax. Once she slowed, I pulled out, turned her around, and pushed into her from behind.

"Is this what you wanted, baby?" I whispered against her neck. "Is this the fuck you wanted?"

"God, yes," she gasped, her hips meeting me at every thrust.

I cupped one of her butt cheeks and squeezed it hard, still pummeling into her. "Come again for me, baby. You're so beautiful when you come. You make such beautiful sounds."

As if on cue, she shattered around me once more, and though I wanted to continue to give her the fuck she needed, I found release within her tight walls.

"God, Ruby. Please. You have to marry me."

CHAPTER THIRTY-FOUR

R u b y

I collapsed on the table, my legs barely holding me up. Well, I'd told him to fuck me until I couldn't stand. My pussy was still contracting lightly from my second orgasm, and my breaths came in rapid puffs.

His words echoed around me, as if being carried on sound waves through the house.

You have to marry me.

He didn't repeat them. Instead, he rubbed my still-clothed back, my shoulders, my neck.

"Relax, baby. Everything's okay."

But everything wasn't okay. Nothing in this godforsaken place was okay. He knew it as well as I did.

When I had the strength to stand, I turned and gazed at Ryan. He'd pulled up his pants but hadn't zipped or buckled them. They hung loose around his muscular hips.

"Thank you," I said.

"For what?"

And I realized how stupid "thank you" had sounded. "I don't mean thanks for the sex. I mean thank you for taking me away, if only for a few precious moments."

"Baby, I needed that as much as you did."

I pulled at my hair, which was now in disarray. My cheeks

were hot with sweat. "I'm such a mess."

"A beautiful mess."

I gave a slight smile. "Ryan, I—"

"You saved him. Believe that. This wasn't your fault."

I nodded. "And Dale is talking."

"Yes. Dale is talking. Donny's action snapped him out of his stupor. So they're going to be okay." Then he let out a sarcastic laugh. "Well, at least they're not in any imminent danger. It'll be a long time before they're really okay. But they have each other, and when we find their mother, they'll have her too."

I went into his arms for a hug.

We held each other for a long, long time.

★ ★ ★

We took a shower before heading back to the main house. Ryan walked straight to the office while I checked on the boys. They had both been exhausted and had gone down for a nap, with Marabel holding vigil over them.

For a moment, I panicked. I'd forgotten about Juliet! But I found her on the deck, sipping water and eating a plate of fruit while the pups and their mother, Jewel, frolicked around her. She was doing better. I smiled.

A doctor—I assumed he was a doctor—arrived a few minutes later to examine the boys. When he returned in half an hour and pronounced that Donny was fine, I was relieved, but I knew it would be a while before Donny was truly fine. I asked him to examine Juliet out on the deck. I went along and was relieved again to hear him say she should make a full recovery. He hadn't, at my request, done a pelvic exam. I wasn't sure she was ready for that. I could only hope that she hadn't been damaged and could still bear children if she wanted to in the future.

Daphne Steel was nowhere to be found. Since she thought of those little boys as her sons, she would no doubt be distraught if she knew what had happened. Likely, Brad had kept her safe in her suite with her nurse to avoid any disruption to her routine.

If Melanie were here, she could examine and diagnose Daphne and tell us what was going on. But she couldn't be here. She was pregnant, and she needed to stay safe. So far, her pregnancy was progressing well with no complications. She'd confided in me that her age worried her. Melanie was forty, but she had the best care available. I had no doubt that she would carry a healthy baby to term.

I jerked backward when lips caressed my neck.

Ryan had come up behind me as I gazed out the window at Juliet and the dogs.

I turned toward him. "I thought you were in the office getting the scoop from your father."

"That was the plan, but Daphne needed him for something. My guess is she's wondering where the boys are."

"I was just thinking about that," I said. "Has there been any luck in locating their mother?"

"Not yet. Now that we know their last name, my father has been looking, but it could take a while."

"Where is everyone else?"

"Talon went to check in with the boys and Marabel, and Joe and Marj are in the office. Marj is having a hard time with all of this. Wait until she finds out Talon was taken for revenge on our father for getting our mother pregnant with her." He shook his head, sighing. "I didn't want her involved in this. None of us did."

"You can't keep the truth from her, Ryan, no matter how much you want to protect her."

"I know. It's been doubly hard on Joe. He feels like he has to protect all of us, and this is killing him. I'm glad Marj is with him. If she weren't, he'd no doubt go ballistic and do some serious damage to our father."

"Maybe that's what your father needs." I regretted the words as soon as I said them. "I'm sorry. My father deserves way more damage than yours."

"I'll agree that he deserves a lot of shit, but at this point, my father deserves just as much. Part of me wants to see my big brother pummel him. He's quick to act without thinking, and his temper gets the best of him sometimes."

"He won't, though. He has a pregnant wife at home who needs him."

"True," Ryan said. "She's the best thing that's ever happened to him. She's really grounded him."

"I'm happy for him. And for her. She's an amazing person. She's helped me a lot."

"I'm glad for that." He pressed his lips to mine in a soft kiss.

His phone buzzed against my side. He pulled it out of his pocket.

"Time to congregate in Dad's office again." He sighed. "Maybe I'll get some real information now."

I squeezed his hand as he turned to leave.

CHAPTER THIRTY-FIVE

Ryan

Joe and Marj were already sitting in the office, as I'd known they would be. Marj's eyes were still red-rimmed and puffy.

"I'm all right," she said before I asked. "I had pulled myself together, but then the little boy..." She shook her head. "I can't say it. I'll start up again."

"You cry as much as you need to, baby sister," Joe said. "This has all been a big shock to you."

"I can't tell you how it felt to look at my mother for the first time. She's beautiful, but she's a shell of a woman. What happened to make her like that?"

"He'll explain it all," Joe said. "He'd better, if he knows what's good for him. Where the hell is Talon?"

I strode to the bar on the side wall of the office and helped myself to a bourbon. Yeah, a bourbon. Wine wasn't going to cut it. "He's probably with the boys. He feels responsible for them. They're the same age Talon and I were when..."

"Wow," Joe said.

"I know." I rubbed my temples, trying to alleviate a tension headache that was springing up. That was what the bourbon was for. "You two want anything?"

They both shook their heads.

Our father walked in then. "You sure you want to be

drinking?"

I took a long sip of the hard stuff. It burned my throat with spicy warmth. "Hell, yeah. How's Daphne?"

"She's all right. Well, all right for her. I had to calm her down and assure her that the boys were fine. She still insists that they're Talon and Jonah."

"But not me," I said, acid in my voice. "She doesn't think I've come back from camp."

My father walked behind his desk and sat down. "No. In the world she's living in, she only has three children—the three that came from her body. I'm sorry. I hope you believe me, Ryan, that I never meant for you to find out about your maternity. Everything was going well until..."

"Until Talon was taken," Joe said.

I clenched my fists. Was Joe about to spill the beans as to why Talon was taken? Marj was not ready for that.

"Yes. Your mother never recovered from that."

"You let us think she was dead," Joe said, his voice dark and deep.

"I did what I had to do to protect you kids and her. I'm hoping I can make you understand all of that." He turned to me, regarding me with what at first glance seemed like paternal pride and love.

But I had to be mistaken. My father couldn't possibly feel those things for any of us, or he wouldn't have left us.

"Ryan, Daphne loved you like one of her own."

"Doesn't seem that way now." I swirled the amber liquid in my glass.

"She did at first. She agreed to raising you at Steel Acres. Her name is on your birth certificate. In the eyes of the law, you're her child. She forgave me, and she didn't hold you responsible for my mistakes."

"How did you manage it? Joe says he remembers her being pregnant."

"We used a graduated prosthetic. When you were born to Wendy, we invented a story about a home birth and had a doctor and nurse attend to you and your mother."

I took another drink. "Are you saying I was born at home?"

He nodded. "The doctor and nurse were well paid to keep quiet. As was your mother. She broke a vow to me when she told you the truth."

"Christ!" Joe stood, pacing. "How could you put our mother through this? How could you fuck that crazy woman?" He turned to me. "No offense, Ry."

"None taken." After all, I wasn't the only one who had a crazy woman for a mother. At least Daphne Steel wasn't evil, though.

"It's a long story, and Talon isn't here yet."

Silence. What the hell could any of us say to that, anyway?

"You might as well know. I'm likely to be imprisoned when this all comes out. Ruby's father will be too. You may want to warn her," he said to me.

"Are you kidding? She's been trying to get him behind bars since she became a cop. She'll be thrilled."

"He's slippery," my father said. "He's eluded arrest all these years. He's a master of disguise and aliases. So good that he got complacent. That's how you boys were able to track him down through his tattoo. But there's another reason he got lazy as well."

"Why is that?" I asked.

"He wants out now."

"Out of what? This crazy trafficking ring? It's not

possible."

"I can understand why you'd think it isn't possible. But he wants it bad enough that he has switched alliances. He's working with me now."

Joe's eyes went feral. "What?"

"Before you ask, no, I don't trust him. He probably doesn't trust me either, but we're all each other has. You kids were never supposed to know that your mother and I were alive or that Ryan is your half brother. Wendy is going to pay for all of this."

"I don't get it, Daddy. You had Mother, the most beautiful woman in the world. Why would you stray? You said she was devoted to us, even to Ryan, who she didn't give birth to. I don't understand." Marj wrung her hands together.

"Sweet baby girl," he said, gazing downward. "Your mother will always have my heart, but my soul? Without meaning to, I sold my soul long before I met her." He paused, exhaling and looking back up. "I sold it to the devil herself."

Three pairs of eyes settled on me.

My cell phone vibrated in my pocket. I picked it up, trying to ignore the heat of my family's gazes. From Ruby.

I just got a text from my father. Something big is going down.

CHAPTER THIRTY-SIX

Ruby

This is your father. Take cover.

That's all the text said. I didn't know my father's cell number, and it was untraceable. It could be a hoax, but I doubted it. Oddly, he seemed to be on my side now, and previously he hadn't usually bothered telling me who he was when he texted. At least that was what my intuition said.

I quickly texted Ryan.

I just got a text from my father. Something big is going down.

Seconds later, he found me in the kitchen. "What's going on?"

"I don't know yet. He told me to 'take cover.'"

"Take cover? What the—"

Brad Steel's footsteps thumped loudly down the corridor, followed by Joe and Marj. "I just got word. The FBI has raided the compound. I need to get your mother out of here."

"And go where?" Ryan said.

"What the hell is the FBI doing on foreign soil?" Joe said. "If you're lying, I'll fucking kill you with my bare hands."

"Why would I lie?"

"I don't know," Ryan said with sarcasm. "You've been so honest with us for the past thirty years."

"If it's truly the FBI, we're not going anywhere," Joe said. "The only guilty person here is you. The rest of us are innocent."

"And if the FBI is here," Ryan said, "they're rescuing Anna and the others from that horrible place. So yeah, I'm with Joe. We're going to let them do their job."

"I have contacts at the FBI," I said. "Let me see what I can find out." I left the kitchen and made a quick phone call to my confidante at the FBI. Armed with new information, I walked toward the kitchen, listening.

"This isn't going to end well," Brad Steel said.

"For you, maybe," Ryan said.

He didn't deny it.

Marjorie went into his arms. "I forgive you, Daddy. I don't want you to go to prison."

"Nothing can stop that now, baby girl."

"Christ, Marj," Joe said. "What is this about? He kept you from knowing our mother. He kept her from all of us."

"That doesn't mean he should go to prison."

Joe rolled his eyes. "Maybe not, but the shit going on here does."

Brad nodded. "Your brother is right. I had nothing to do with any of it, but I did know about it. That makes me an accessory."

"How could you know about this and not do anything about it?" Marjorie asked.

"For you," he said. "For all of you. Everything I did was to protect my children. My legacy."

That was as good a time as any to interrupt with my

information.

"It is the FBI. My sources confirmed it. And your PI, Raj? He's an FBI attaché in Jamaica. He's actually an American citizen, a captain in the Marine Corps who masquerades as a private investigator. He didn't disappear. He rendezvoused with the other agents when they arrived."

"How did your father know there was going to be an FBI raid?" Ryan asked.

"I'm not sure. We'll probably find out when he contacts me again in the same enigmatic way he always does. Unless they already have him in custody, and I hope they do."

"Theo will get away," my father said. "He always has before."

"Seems the two of you have that in common," Ryan said.

"No, it's over for me," he said. "I'll die in prison. But at least Daphne will be taken care of."

Talon finally arrived. "Hey, what's going on? I looked for you in the office."

"The FBI has raided the compound." Joe quickly filled him in. "It won't be long before they come here."

Talon eyed Brad. "I see."

"So we'd better get to the whole truth before they get here," Joe said. "Back to the office."

I squeezed Ryan's hand. "Go ahead."

"No, this time you're coming with us," he said.

"I don't think that's approp—"

"Ryan's right," Joe said. "You're as involved in this as any of us. Come to the office. You deserve the truth as well."

Brad had taken a phone call and appeared to be listening intently. I looked to Ryan for guidance, and he nodded.

We all followed Brad back to the office.

CHAPTER THIRTY-SEVEN

R y a n

I walked numbly, Ruby's hand in mine, to the elaborately decorated office across from the bedroom Juliet and Ruby were using.

Would we finally get the answers we sought? Or would the FBI interrupt us? Only time would tell.

Joe took the lead. "Start from the beginning. The future lawmakers. We know you funded their business. We know you once considered them friends. Ruby's uncle even said you were the one person Theodore Mathias trusted. So how the fuck did a club based on brotherhood—Mathias's words, according to Ruby—turn into a million-dollar human-trafficking business? And we already know you got greedy."

"I'm going to be getting another call. I don't have much time."

"Talk fast, then," Joe said through gritted teeth.

Our father sighed. "They got greedy. I had money."

"Whatever. You funded them, so you're just as much a part of this," Joe said. "Explain how Wendy was in control. She was a sophomore JV cheerleader, for God's sake."

"Shit," he said. "Where to start?"

"The beginning, Daddy," Marjorie said. "Jade says Wendy told her you and she were soul mates and always wanted to be together."

"Yeah," Joe said, "but that didn't add up because you didn't get together with her after Mom died. Of course, now we know that Mom was never dead."

"Wendy does indeed own my soul, but not in a good way."

"So you've said."

"We did date and become"—his face reddened—"intimate during high school. She joined the future lawmakers, and it turned out she had an amazing head for business. She was creative as well. She liked to paint, and she also dabbled in metalsmithing."

My hand drifted absently to my pocket. My father's ring. I'd been carrying it with me all this time. Why? I had no idea.

"She made this." I held it up to my father.

"She did. I see you found it. I left it on the cushion of the couch at Ruby's apartment."

"You fucking drugged my girlfriend!" I stood, clenching my palm around the ring.

"I did." He looked to Ruby. "And I'm sorry. You were never in any real danger. In his own warped way, your father loves you."

She didn't respond. Hell, what could she say?

"It was between the cushions. I only saw it when I sat down."

"It must have rolled a bit. But you found it, and it brought you here." He cleared his throat. "The rings. Wendy designed them and made one for each of us."

"And who paid for them?" Joe asked.

"Who do you think? She designed the symbol and engraved my name on the inside of mine."

"And the GPS coordinates?" Talon asked.

"I had those added recently. So you could find me."

"Hold on," Joe said. "We're digressing. This is all important, but we need to keep it chronological. Back to Wendy and the club, please."

I couldn't believe he had said please. The tone of his voice and expression on his face didn't seem pleased at all.

"Wendy moved away after her sophomore year, and I thought it was over. She had other ideas though. She kept in contact with me and the other guys in the club, specifically Larry, Tom, and Theo. She watched us grow our business, watched them get greedy, and when the time was right, she swooped in. She's very intelligent and shrewd and cunning. She put ideas into their heads without them even knowing it. As for me? I funded them and continued to do so before I realized they were getting into illegal stuff. They started with marijuana, which was of course illegal in Colorado back then. But face it, pot is pretty harmless. I didn't see any real reason to get out at that point."

"You said yourself that it was illegal," Joe said. "That wasn't reason enough for you?"

"Yeah, but I was seventeen and rich. I figured I was untouchable." He closed his eyes. "Remember those days? When you're young and carefree, and you don't think anything can harm you?"

"No, we don't remember those days," I said. "We were busy dealing with fallout from Talon's abduction the best we could, since you wouldn't allow us to get the help we needed."

Ruby touched my forearm. She was trying to soothe me. Too bad it wasn't working.

"This is all shit you taught us not to do," Joe said. "Didn't your father teach you the same thing?"

Brad Steel opened his eyes and coughed. "As a matter of fact, no, he didn't. The Steel fortune has some precarious history. Your ancestors left their scruples at the door sometimes to build their fortune."

"You're saying our fortune is dirty money?" Joe said.

"No. I'm saying they didn't practice the best ethics. Our money is clean."

"Why were you so adamant that we be so ethical, then?" Joe asked.

"Why do you think? Because of what I had gone through— was going through—with the future lawmakers. I'd thrown caution to the wind when I was too young to know any better, and it cost me dearly. It still is."

"You've been dealing with these people since then? Our whole lives?" Talon rubbed his forehead. "The people who tortured me?"

He nodded. "I promised you the truth. I never promised it would be pretty."

"Christ." Joe stood. "We knew it wouldn't be pretty. Frankly, it's pretty unbelievable."

"I never wanted you kids to get involved in anything like that. I was determined that you would be protected at all costs."

"Get back to Wendy," I said. "How did a fifteen-year-old girl have any hold on you at all?"

"She blackmailed me."

"How? She couldn't have had any power over you."

"She became pregnant after she moved away. We hadn't been together in a couple months, but she claimed it was mine and that she'd just found out. Remember, there was no DNA testing back then. The best we could do was a blood test that might or might not have indicated paternity. My father would have disinherited me if he knew I got Wendy pregnant."

Joe sat down, fingering his hair. "Always about the money, huh?"

"I was seventeen, Joe, and afraid of my father's wrath."

"What happened to thinking no one could touch you?" Joe rolled his eyes.

"Please, let him talk, Joe," Marj said.

"Anyway, I begged her to get an abortion and not tell anyone. I offered her money, but all she wanted was me."

Joe harrumphed. "You're not going to try to get us to believe that all of this happened because of an unwanted teenage pregnancy."

"Partially. I know it sounds crazy, but remember that Wendy is psychotic. More than that, she's exceedingly good at hiding it. Anyway, she ended up having a tubal pregnancy that went undiagnosed until about ten weeks, and then her tube ruptured. She had vast internal bleeding and nearly died."

"So I would have had a true sibling," I said, astonished.

"Maybe," my father said. "If Wendy was telling the truth. We'll never know. Anyway, after nearly losing her life, Wendy changed. She became even more obsessed with me and the future lawmakers club. To her, the loss of her pregnancy was a message somehow. A message that she needed to make others pay for the loss. To make me pay."

"So she spoon-fed Tom, Theo, and—to a lesser extent— Larry all the information they needed and exploited their greed. She figured because I was the financier, I'd always be involved, so she could punish me through the evil deeds of the others. She counseled them to form a corporation."

My mind whirled. "The Fleming Corporation."

"How did you know about that?" he asked.

"It was easy enough to find. It's the corporation that owns the house where Talon was held captive," Joe said. "It also owns another house, where my wife was left to die. I tried getting information out of the registered agent, but he wouldn't budge. My threats had no effect on him."

"He's well paid to stay silent, and your threats are nothing compared to the threats from others."

"What others? From Wendy? She's locked up in psych. Simpson and Wade are dead. That leaves only Mathias."

"As dangerous as Wendy and Theo are, they're nothing compared to the elusive ring they work for. That's who controls them and the Fleming Corporation."

"What ring?" Talon said.

My father shook his head. "I don't even know that. Wendy wouldn't tell me. She said it was for my own protection. In her own twisted way, she cares for me."

"My father must know," Ruby said.

"He doesn't. Only Wendy knows. And she's not talking."

My mother was truly evil. Evil, psychotic, and a creative genius.

"Again, goddamnit, you're digressing," Joe said.

"By the time we'd all graduated and Larry and Tom had finished law school, they'd gotten into the business of...slavery." He gulped audibly. "Even now, I find it difficult to say."

"Of course it's difficult to say. It's the abusing and selling of human beings. Christ," Joe said.

"Wendy set them up with a bigger trafficking operation. Tom, Larry, and Theo became suppliers. They were responsible for finding and training the slaves and then transporting them to the pickup location, which was usually on foreign soil somewhere, but sometimes in the US."

Ruby sat beside me, her face pale. I squeezed her hand. "You okay?"

She didn't answer me. Instead, she addressed my father. "How did they"—she swallowed—"learn how to train these people?"

"Baby..."

"No, Ryan. I need to know."

"Are you sure?" my father asked.

"For God's sake, tell us the fucking truth!" Joe yelled.

He looked to Ruby, his black eyes sunken. "They went through the same training themselves."

CHAPTER THIRTY-EIGHT

Ruby

My mouth tasted like battery acid. I clamped my hand over my lips.

"Baby?" Ryan said.

I shook my head. I'd get through this. So my father had endured things I hadn't. So what? He'd wanted to inflict those same things on me. I'd just been able to escape before he could.

I could not—would not—feel sorry for the man, even if I owed my existence to him.

"You mean..." Talon began.

"Yes," Brad Steel said. "Everything those monsters did to you had once been done to them."

Marjorie gasped and clasped her hand over her mouth. Joe put his arm around her and whispered something that I couldn't hear.

"At least they weren't ten years old," Ryan said. "I don't feel the least bit sorry for them. But I don't know why anyone would voluntarily put himself through that."

"Easy," I said, my voice cracking. "They were paid well, weren't they?"

"Two million dollars each," my father said. "Their drug business was going well, but this was more money than they'd ever seen."

"Two million dollars for their humanity." Talon shook his head. "Not fucking worth it."

"They didn't have a choice at that time. They'd entered into an agreement. It was fulfill it or be killed."

"I think I'd have chosen death," Ryan said.

Talon shook his head vehemently. "You wouldn't have. You wouldn't believe the survival instinct when you're in such an insurmountable situation. It kicks in whether you want it to or not."

"It didn't kick in for little Donny."

"No. Because he was doing something he thought he was supposed to do, something that someone he trusted told him to do. But when you're in command of yourself and think you want to die? Unless you're truly suicidal, you'll do anything you can to survive. You submit to things you never thought you'd submit to, say things that make you gag to get the words out, just for the promise of one more minute in your hellish existence." He looked up at the ceiling. "You just don't know."

"Easy, Tal," Ryan said. "I'm sorry."

"It's okay," he said. "I'm all right."

"He's right, Ry," Joe said. "Melanie told me the same thing when she was left in that garage to die. She was willing to do anything to get out alive."

"I'm so sorry about what happened to you, Talon," Brad Steel said.

"You let it happen," he said, his words caustic.

Marjorie still didn't know why Talon had been taken. I hoped Ryan would stop this. It wasn't my place. I squeezed his hand, hoping I was conveying my concern.

"I did," Brad admitted. "But it was never my intention."

"Let's get back to the discussion," Ryan said.

I breathed a sigh of relief.

Steel cleared his throat. "After they were trained and had regained their strength, they were required to participate in the training of others. Once they were deemed ready, they were let go and then required to train and supply a steady source of people. They were paid very well for this, and they were soon all worth over a hundred million dollars."

"So they no longer needed your money," Joe said. "Why the hell are you still involved, then?"

"They didn't need my money. Even Wendy didn't need my money, because she got a cut of everything they got. But Wendy wanted one thing money couldn't buy."

"You," Talon said.

"Right." He sighed. "I had married your mother by this time, and Joe and Talon, you had already been born. God"—he sank his head into his hands—"I'm not sure I can do this."

"Do it," Joe said through clenched teeth. "The truth, or I'll beat it out of you."

Ryan's knuckles whitened, his hand still clasping mine. Neither he nor his siblings said a word.

"Wendy came to our home one night. Your mother was tired from dealing with a toddler and an infant and had already gone to bed. I found Wendy in your nursery, Talon, holding a knife to your throat."

Marjorie gasped.

"I knew she was crazy," Steel continued, "but would she harm a child?"

"I think we all know the answer to that question," Talon said quietly.

"Yes, now. But then, I wasn't sure. She'd been broken up over her ectopic pregnancy. And she'd never married. Still, I wasn't going to take a chance with your life, Talon. I asked her what she wanted. Of course, she said she wanted me. I told her I had a family now. I needed to be there for them. She said she could take care of that, and she pressed the knife against your flesh. I lunged for her and took her down to the floor. Thankfully you slept through the whole thing."

Silence. I looked at Ryan. His skin had gone pale.

Steel cleared his throat and continued, "I decided to cut a deal with her. For the first time in my life, I was truly afraid. Afraid for my family. I had to protect you boys and your mother, no matter what. She wanted two things, she said. First, my will had to include a bequest to the Fleming Corporation for a hundred million dollars."

"It was only fifty," Joe said.

"Right. I changed it later. But she demanded a hundred million dollars. She also demanded my child."

"She wanted me?" Talon asked, incredulous.

Ryan stiffened beside me. "No, Tal," he said. "She wanted me."

CHAPTER THIRTY-NINE

Ryan

"Yes," my father said solemnly. "She wanted a child by me. Of course I told her 'hell, no.' But remember, she was a gifted journalist. She produced a trail of documents linking me to the Fleming Corporation and threatened to leak them if I didn't comply with her demands. I would have been imprisoned. I couldn't leave a wife and two children who I loved more than my own life. So I gave in to her demands. I promised to have sex with her one time, thinking I could keep from impregnating her. She only had one fallopian tube, and if I didn't ejaculate, I figured there wasn't a chance."

"How could you?" Joe said. "How could you do that to our mother?"

I stiffened. This was all about me. They were wishing I hadn't been born. Maybe not consciously, but that was what it amounted to.

"I didn't think I had a choice. She said she'd accept the chance of not getting pregnant just to be with me again. I had no idea, but she'd been keeping track of her cycles and was at her most fertile time."

"What? So this wasn't an accident?" Joe shook his head.

I wasn't sure whether I should feel better or worse. So I hadn't been an accident due to my father's infidelity. He'd allowed my birth to happen.

"Being unfaithful to your mother was the hardest thing I've ever done."

"Yeah, fucking a beautiful woman is a difficult thing," Joe said sardonically.

Our father seemed to ignore him. "So I had sex with her in this office. Well, the office that looks just like this one back at home. Your mother was asleep, and I hoped like hell she wouldn't wake up. I figured I could control the situation. I tried not to ejaculate, but unfortunately I wasn't successful. I did pull out as soon as I could."

"But one of your little buggers got in anyway," Joe said. "This is farfetched."

"It is," my father agreed. "But that's how it happened. She did become pregnant, and the timing worked out."

"Didn't you think it might not be yours?"

"Of course I did. But I had slept with her, and I knew that it could be mine. No way was I letting her raise any child of mine, so I began manipulating her into giving the baby up."

"She let you manipulate her?" Joe said.

I piped in. "Yes. I can see that. I've been able to manipulate her. She has very strong feelings for both of us. That's her Achilles' heel."

"Exactly," my father said. "Of course, giving up a child required a lot of manipulation, and I knew I couldn't get her to do it without payment of some sort. I paid for all her medical bills, of course, and arranged for her to have the baby at the ranch house. I also gave her a lump-sum seven-figure payment."

"How the hell did you talk our mother into this?" Joe was riled. "Did you manipulate her too?"

"Sadly, yes, I did. I asked her forgiveness for my infidelity and begged her to raise the child as her own. I promised I'd never stray from her again, and I never did. We had some knock-down, drag-outs about it, but finally she forgave me."

"Was that it? All it took for Wendy to get rid of me was money?"

"Don't think of it that way, Ryan. She wanted you. She wanted you desperately. But I worked her and worked her and convinced her you would have a better life on the ranch with two parents and two big brothers to protect you."

I looked to my sister. Our father hadn't mentioned the other thing he'd promised Wendy to get her to give me up. I sincerely hoped he wouldn't, but I knew it was coming. If he didn't say it, Joe might beat it out of him without thinking of how it would affect our baby sister.

True to form, Joe said, "What else did you promise her? Say it, Dad."

He raked his fingers through his salt-and-pepper hair. "I promised to be celibate from that time on."

"What?" Marjorie clamped her hand to her mouth and shook her head. "But then who's my father?" A pause. Then, "You are. We had the DNA test done on all of us."

"Yes, baby girl. You're my biological daughter."

"Then was I..."

"An accident? No." He smiled. "More like a surprise. Of course I had no intention of keeping that promise to Wendy. Your mother and I loved each other, and I intended to continue sleeping with her. I figured our family was complete with three boys, and your mother had been on the pill since she stopped nursing Talon."

"But birth-control methods fail..." Joe exhaled. "That's

how Melanie got pregnant."

"Yes, they do. Your mother had bouts of mild depression sometimes, and sometimes forgot to take her pill. I didn't know about that until she admitted it to me when she became pregnant with you, baby girl.

"But back to Ryan's birth. When you were delivered, Ryan, and I held you, I knew without a doubt that you were mine. You looked exactly like your brothers as newborns, and you grasped my thumb almost immediately." Tears misted his eyes. "You were mine, and when I looked into your eyes—you were very alert for a newborn—I knew I hadn't made a mistake by sleeping with Wendy that one time. I'd made you."

My eyes welled. Ruby put her other hand over our clasped ones, offering her support. Invisible ropes pulled me in myriad different directions. My father. My mother. Without them, I wouldn't be here. I wouldn't have my life. I wouldn't have the beautiful woman beside me whom I loved more than anything.

But how I'd gotten here... What a fucking mess.

"I loved you, just as I loved my other two sons. And I vowed from that day forward to protect all of you with my life if I had to."

"That didn't work out so well for Talon," Joe said.

"No, it didn't."

Here it comes. I braced myself for the pain my sister was about to endure.

But my father's cell phone rang. He checked it and then said quietly, "I have to take this." He put the phone to his ear but said nothing. After several seconds, he took it from his ear but kept it in his hand.

"I'm afraid we need to table this discussion." He stood and walked out from behind his desk, tapping something into the phone.

Marabel appeared at the door almost instantly, opening it without knocking. "Code five?"

"Yes. In ten minutes."

"Jocelyn and I will have her ready." Marabel hurried away.

"What the hell is going on here?" Joe asked. "There are still a ton of unanswered questions. What happened to Mom? Why did you build this place? Why did you fake your death?"

"Another time, Joe."

"Fuck that. I told you I'd beat the truth out of you, and I aim to." Joe lunged toward our father, who was still standing in the doorway.

"You will not!"

And I hurtled back in time to when I was a kid. Our father's voice. No one argued with that tone.

"If you love your mother and want her protected, you'll leave this for now."

"You're taking Mother?" Marj asked. "What's going on?"

"There's a helipad on the top of the house. It's well-hidden, so you probably didn't notice it when you came in. The FBI are on their way here. I need to get your mother out of here and to someplace safe."

"But you—" I started.

"I will surrender myself to the authorities when the time is right," he said. "Right now, your mother is my priority. I must take care of her and get her to a safe place. If the FBI swarms in here..." He shook his head and left quickly.

I stood and ran out the door, my siblings and Ruby behind me. Soon, the whirring helicopter propellers buzzed above us. We all covered our ears.

Minutes later, Marabel hurried down the hall, our

mother in tow. Our father took her in his arms and shouted something inaudible to Marabel. Then he raced toward the garage entrance.

"What do we do?" Marj screamed.

"We haven't done anything wrong," Joe yelled. "We'll stay here and answer their questions the best we can. Then we'll go home."

CHAPTER FORTY

Ruby

Three days later, we arrived back in Colorado. Ryan and I said nothing during the drive to the ranch. I had no job to go to, so I was going home with him. After everything we'd been through, I didn't want to be alone. The silence was soothing. So much had gone on during the last seventy-two hours, and we'd hardly slept.

The FBI had swarmed in and questioned all of us. They'd taken the names of the two little boys and Juliet and arranged to get them home. As far as I knew, they still hadn't found the boys' mother, but they had found a great-aunt who was willing to take them until their mother turned up.

To Juliet's and my delight, Lisa had been found. She hadn't been killed, as Juliet had thought. Anna Shane had also been rescued. In all, twenty-nine women and seventeen children were recovered from the compound. One child wasn't so lucky. A little girl was found dead in one of the dorm rooms.

Of the total of forty-six, forty were American.

There had been no sign or documentation of Gina Cates, my cousin. That saddened me, but I tried not to dwell on it. The FBI was on it now, along with Interpol. They were determined to take this investigation all the way to the top and take this trafficking ring down.

One fact, though, I couldn't help but dwell on.

My father had not been taken into custody. He had disappeared.

Again.

Ernie sat on my lap in a small kennel. Juliet had taken Bo, Beauty, and their mother, Jewel, home with her, with a promise to send the two puppies to Dale and Donny once they were situated.

When we walked into the house, Ricky ran to us, tail wagging. I let Ernie out of his kennel to meet his new big brother.

"Hey, boy," Ryan said to his dog. "Have the hands been taking good care of you?"

Ricky stopped only for a few seconds to let Ryan pet him, and then he was preoccupied with the little ball of fur scampering around.

"You two better go outside." I walked to the kitchen and opened the French doors.

Ernie was a little inhibited but eventually followed Ricky outside.

Ryan had wandered into his family room and plopped on the plush leather couch. I went to join him.

"Before I sit down, do you want anything?" I said. "Because once I sit down, I don't think I'm getting back up for at least a day."

Ryan smiled. "Does that mean I have to carry you to my bedroom to have my way with you?"

"Yup, that's exactly what it means." I plunked down beside him.

"I can't believe this is really over," he said, taking my hand and pressing his lips to my palm.

I shivered just from the innocent contact...and because of something else. "It's not quite over."

He nodded. "Your father. We'll find him. And if we can't, surely the FBI or Interpol can."

"He has all those aliases, and he probably has documentation for each one. He could be across the globe by now."

"He could be. But I have a feeling he's not going to stray too far. You are all he has left, Ruby."

I doubted Ryan's words. My father hardly thought of me as family, but he did have a sister. "Maybe. He could be hiding out with my aunt and uncle."

"The Cateses? Yeah, maybe. But would they take him in after what he did to their daughter?"

Gina. I had no idea if she was alive or dead. My father had claimed she was alive, but he could have been lying. If she was dead, at least she wasn't in any more pain.

"I don't know. I've given up trying to understand my relatives," I said. "They're all nuts."

"Tell me about it," Ryan said, squeezing my hand.

"Where do you think your father went?"

"I have no idea. But he's a planner. He probably had something set up for every contingency. And I do believe he will take care of Daphne."

The reality was still so jarring. Not only Brad Steel but also Daphne Steel was alive. We still didn't know the story behind that, and who knew when Brad Steel would surface again to tell us.

Talon and Jonah were no doubt filling their wives in on everything right now.

I closed my eyes and sighed.

Ryan leaned over and kissed my cheek. "Want to go to bed?"

I laughed. "Sure."

He stood and then swooped me into his arms.

"Hey!" I said.

"You said you weren't moving until tomorrow, so I figured I had to carry you." He smiled down at me and walked up the short staircase, through the kitchen, and down the corridor to his master suite. He nudged the door open, walked in, and laid me gently on the bed.

He positioned himself beside me, and I snuggled into his shoulder, closing my eyes.

★ ★ ★

I awoke in the middle of the night, still dressed. Ryan was snoozing soundly next to me, also still dressed.

I was parched from the travel, so I rose, walked to the kitchen, got a long drink of water, and let the dogs back in. Little Ernie needed to be fed, so I gave him some of Ricky's kibble. I'd have to get puppy food in the morning.

Soft padded steps came up behind me, and then Ryan's firm lips grazed my neck.

"Hey," he said.

"Hey yourself. I'm just feeding the puppy and getting some water. I'm so dehydrated."

"Yeah, me too." He went to the sink, got himself a glass, and drained it in one gulp. In seconds, he was back behind me. "I'm sorry I fell asleep."

"Last time I checked, so did I."

"You want to take a dip in the hot tub? I know it's the

middle of the night, but it would feel great."

Sounded like sheer bliss to me. Plus, the dogs could go back outside and do their business.

"Mmm, perfect. I'll need to borrow one of your robes."

"There's no one here, Ruby. We can just use towels." He padded back to his room and returned a few minutes later with two king-sized bath towels.

We undressed in the kitchen and wrapped the towels around us. I couldn't help lasciviously appraising Ryan's masculine beauty. I'd never grow tired of looking at him. I untangled my hair from its band and piled it in a messy bun on the top of my head.

"Ready," I said.

"You look good enough to eat."

"Nothing stopping you that I can see."

Without ceremony, he lifted me onto the kitchen table, the towel around me sparing my behind from the cold surface.

I squeezed my eyes closed against the harsh fluorescent lighting.

The first time Ryan had set me on this table, I'd freaked, resulting in a nightmare after which I ended up in the shower trying desperately to wash the filth of my father from my body. It was the harsh lighting that had taken me back to the time my father attacked me. He'd started in the kitchen.

But this was Ryan Steel. A man who loved me, who wanted to marry me. This was his kitchen, not my father's. And I was here willingly. Oh, so willingly.

"You okay, baby?" Ryan whispered against the flesh of my neck.

I nodded. I'd be okay. I had to be. No more would Theodore Mathias rule my life.

"Good. Because I can smell you already. I need to taste you." He sat down in a chair and positioned himself between my legs. "Mmm, so wet. I love how wet you get for me." He slid his tongue over my clit.

I gripped the edges of the table. So good. His tongue swirled around every part of my vulva, and then he lapped at my clit before forcing his tongue inside my wetness. He groaned as he ate me, and I closed my eyes, tilting my head back, letting only good thoughts in.

Only good thoughts...

"Baby, you taste so good," he said against my pussy. "Come for me." He inserted two fingers, hitting that place that made me go instantly crazy. My skin tingled, and every cell in my body tensed and then released, pure pleasure flowing through every part of me and grounding itself in my pussy. I throbbed and throbbed, and he sucked on my clit, bringing me to new heights each time he twisted his fingers inside me.

After my fourth consecutive climax—how was that even possible?—I grasped his damp hair in my fists and pushed him away from my pussy. "Enough. I can't take any more."

He rose and kissed me, giving me a taste of my own tangy musk. "Oh, you can," he said. "And you will." He tucked my towel back around me and then led me outside to the hot tub, the dogs cavorting at our heels.

CHAPTER FORTY-ONE

Ryan

Had to have her. Had to get inside that tight little pussy. We hadn't been together in three days, with all the goings-on. Someone from the FBI was always in the identical house wanting to talk to one of us, and we'd had no chance for any alone time.

I needed her. Needed to claim what was mine.

I ripped the towel from her body and regarded her in the moonlight. A goddess, even with her hair piled in a mess on top of her head. Her skin was opulent, her breasts perfect round globes. Her red nipples were puckered and hard. I reached forward and gave each of them a pinch.

She gasped, closing her eyes.

A waft of her vanilla scent drifted toward me, and I inhaled deeply. No sweeter perfume. I took her hand and led her into the steamy water.

I sat down and pulled her onto my lap facing me. The steam floated around us, a mesmerizing cloud.

She inched down on me slowly, and with every millimeter of her pussy surrounding me, I was convinced I'd entered heaven itself. She sat on me, my cock totally embedded in her body, for what seemed like forever.

I wanted to lift her off, to thrust in and out of her, yet I also wanted to stay like this. Joined to the woman I loved, for a lifetime.

Within a few minutes, though, she rose, moving her hips in a tantalizing figure eight, and began fucking me slowly.

Oh. My. God.

This woman, who'd had no experience whatsoever when we met, had turned into a sexy seductress, a tempestuous siren who knew how to drive a man into madness.

Her breasts jiggled as she fucked me, her nipples bobbing like tiny berries on the surface of the water, begging me to catch them. I caught one between my teeth and tugged, eliciting a soft moan from her sweet red lips.

"Touch yourself, baby," I commanded. "I want you to come."

She reached down and began playing with that beautiful pussy, and that's all it took to catapult me over the edge. I thrust upward, giving her all of me, ramming against the entrance to her womb as I spilled everything I had inside her.

"Ruby. God, Ruby. I love you so much!"

She burst into climax at my admission, clenching around my convulsing cock like a perfect vise.

And we soared together.

★ ★ ★

The next morning, I awoke to the smell of bacon frying. I inhaled, went to the bathroom quickly, and then pulled on a pair of boxers and walked to the kitchen. Ruby stood at the stove wearing nothing but one of my T-shirts. It covered her cute little ass as a miniskirt would. I walked up behind her and cupped one of those luscious butt cheeks.

She swatted me away. "You're going to get splattered with grease."

"I'll splatter you with grease," I said, laughing.

"Ha ha." She turned off the burner and placed the fried slices of bacon on a waiting paper towel. "Sit down. I'll bring you some breakfast and a cup of coffee."

She moved about my kitchen as if she already lived here. I liked what I saw. I liked the idea of her here always. I'd tried to get her to move in with me a few weeks ago when I feared for her safety. I still wanted her here forever.

Damn it, she was going to have to marry me.

We hadn't had a chance to talk about my proposal—I'd asked twice now—in a while, due to all the other shit going on.

I smiled. "I never imagined Detective Ruby Lee would be making breakfast and serving me."

"Hey, don't get used to it. I just got up first. I had to tend to the puppy, and we were both hungry," she teased.

"Sorry, babe." I pulled her into my lap after she'd set my plate and coffee on the table. "I'm already used to it." I gave her a long, deep kiss.

She broke away, laughing. "You know? I kind of like getting up and making you breakfast. I'm just not sure I can do it at five in the morning, when you usually get up. Plus, I have to get another job at some point."

"Why?"

"It's kind of how I make a living."

"Baby, I have enough money to support you for ten lifetimes. You don't need to work anymore."

She punched my arm. "I want to work, you idiot. I'm a good detective."

"Yes, you are."

"So maybe I'll start my own private investigating service or something."

"Or maybe you could move in an entirely different direction," I suggested.

"Meaning...?"

"Meaning...you told me you wanted to learn more about wine. I just happen to know a winemaker who needs some help."

"You do?"

"I do. Jade was helping me before she landed her job as city attorney, and I haven't had the time to hire anyone new."

She lifted her brow. "I don't hate the idea."

I laughed. "I guess that's good."

"But being a cop is all I know."

"Silly, I'd teach you about wine. You are capable of learning new things."

I started to kiss her again, but the sound of my ringtone interrupted me.

"You need to get that?" She moved off my lap.

"Yeah, I should. It could be Joe or Talon." I stood and walked to my bedroom. I didn't make it in time, but the phone showed Joe's number. I quickly called him back.

"Hey, Ry," he said.

"Sorry. The phone was in another room. What's up?"

"You need to get over to Tal's place. Dad's here."

★ ★ ★

Ruby had stayed at my place to take care of the dogs and go into town for puppy food. I'd tossed her the keys to one of my extra cars and then walked over to the main house.

Jade let me in. "Hey, Ryan. They're all in the office."

"You and Melanie aren't joining us?"

She shook her head. "It's too much. This is really between all of you. We'll know everything soon enough. Besides, my mom is still here, and it's the nurse's day off. Someone has to deal with her."

"Okay." I walked down the east hallway to Talon's office.

My father sat behind the desk, which unnerved me a bit. This was Talon's office, no longer his.

Before I could say anything, Talon said, "Hey, Ry. It was my idea for him to sit there. That way he's talking to all of us, not just one of us."

Joe and Marjorie were sitting in the office, Marjorie's eyes already red-rimmed and swollen. I hated what all of this was doing to her.

"Are you okay, kiddo?" I asked, rubbing her shoulder.

"Dad just told her why Tal was taken," Joe said. "But she's doing okay."

"Hey," I said to my little sister. "None of this is your fault. Talon doesn't blame you, and neither do the rest of us."

She nodded and sniffled, but said nothing. It would take some time. I knew only too well. It had taken me some time to realize that my brothers and sister didn't think of me as any less of a brother to them even though we didn't share a mother.

I looked at my father icily. "I hope you're happy. Look at your daughter."

"None of this makes me happy, Ryan."

"Where's Daphne?" I asked.

"She's safe at a top-quality mental hospital in California. I admitted her under an alias."

"She should be here at home," Talon said. "We're her

children. We should be taking care of her."

"She requires round-the-clock care, Talon," our father said. "You're newly married, and so is your brother. And baby girl, you don't want that for your life."

He hadn't acknowledged me in that comment. She wasn't actually my mother. Still, it stung.

"She's my mother!" Marjorie cried. "The only one I've got. I want to get to know her."

"You can travel to visit her as often as you like, but she can't live here. Neither you nor Talon can handle it."

"I can handle anything you throw at me," Marj said adamantly. "I've proven that."

"Doing men's work on a ranch and caring for a mentally ill parent are two different things."

"You did it," she countered.

"I did. Because what befell your mother ultimately rested on my shoulders. But you kids are faultless. Let the professionals care for her. She doesn't even know who any of you are."

"What if she gets better?" Talon asked. "What then?"

"Talon, she has been this way for twenty-three years. She's not going to get any better. Now my decision on your mother is final. She is my responsibility. Not yours."

Joe said nothing, which surprised me. His demeanor was noticeably less combative than it had been on the island. Now he was home, back with his pregnant wife. He'd no doubt been reminded of what was truly important.

Though it was none of my business, I decided to speak. "Why can't she be someplace closer, where her children can visit her once a week at least?"

"The place in California is the best."

"So?" I said. "Create a place in Grand Junction for her. We have the money. Hire the best. That way Tal, Joe, and Marj can visit her whenever they want."

"Ryan's right," Joe said. "She needs to be closer to us."

"I did a lot of research finding her the right place—"

"Bullshit," Joe interjected. "You kept her on that island for God knows how long. You had a doctor and nurse for her there. Bring them here. You owe us that much."

"You owe us a hell of a lot more than that," I said. "For God's sake, let my siblings have a relationship with their mother."

"She's not capable of—"

I stood. "You're not listening! They know that. They don't care. She's their mother. They want to be there for her."

"No." He shook his head. "She can't be in Colorado. I can't run the risk of Wendy finding her." He looked me straight in the eye. "What about your mother? Do you want a relationship with her?"

CHAPTER FORTY-TWO

R u b y

After picking up puppy food and some other necessities, I headed to my car when my phone buzzed. It was a text.

You and I aren't through yet.

Of course I didn't recognize the number, but I didn't have to guess who it was. My father. I knew he'd turn up. I didn't bother texting or calling back. He was playing his usual head games, and I wasn't interested.

I stashed the groceries in the car, and my phone buzzed again. This time it was a call, another number I didn't recognize.

I shook my head, deciding to ignore my father, but then changed my mind. Maybe he was ready to turn himself in.

Probably not, but I had to find out.

"Yes, what the hell do you want?" I nearly yelled into the phone.

"Uh...hi. Ruby?"

Shit. A female voice. One I recognized from the phone calls I'd received after our first return from Jamaica.

"Shayna! Is that you?"

"Yes. It's me."

"I'm so sorry. I thought you were someone else. Are you okay?"

"I'm...fine. Now. I just heard from Juliet. She's home, Ruby, and she said it's because of you. Thank you so much."

"I didn't do anything, really."

"That's not what she says. She says you were captured and you told her you'd get her out of there. To trust you. And you did. You got her out of there. Her and Lisa both."

"Lisa's in bad shape, Shayna. But she's going to be okay."

"That's what Juliet says. She says I can't see Lisa yet. She's severely malnourished and is in the hospital in LA. She had to have IV fluids before the flight home. But she's stable, and she's alive, Ruby. She's alive."

Relief swept through me. I hadn't realized how much I'd been worried about Lisa making it home in her condition. "They both have a long road ahead."

"Of medical and psychological treatment. I know."

"They'll need you, Shayna. They'll both need a friend."

"I'm here for them. I swear it."

I smiled into the phone. "I know you are. This whole thing is a miracle. Many women and children were rescued."

"I can't even begin to imagine what they've been through."

"You don't want to. It wasn't pretty."

"I won't press them for details."

"That's good. Let them come to you. They'll both have therapists they can talk to. Just be there for them."

"I will be, Ruby. Thank you for everything."

I was smiling when the call ended. Though the FBI had done much more than I had, at least I had fulfilled my promise to Juliet. I had gotten her out of the dorms and into the nice Steel replica.

Damn. The Steel replica. Ryan was hearing the story of how and why that house had been built at this very moment.

I couldn't imagine the stories he'd have to tell me when I saw him this evening.

I got into the car and readied for the drive home, when my cell buzzed yet once more.

Sheesh! Again, a call from a number I didn't recognize. It could possibly be Juliet, and I didn't want to ignore a call from her.

"Hello, Detec— Er...Ruby Lee," I said into the phone.

"We need to talk," my father said.

Something surged within me at his voice—an emotion I didn't quite recognize. "I don't know what about. You should have surrendered yourself to the authorities, but as usual, you did your disappearing act."

"How much did Steel tell you?" he asked.

Despite the fact that I'd learned my father had been to hell and back learning to train potential human slaves, I had no sympathy for him. He'd been well paid, and he'd gone into the whole thing with his eyes open. The same thing couldn't be said for the poor innocent souls he ripped from their lives without their consent. Especially the children.

My heart squeezed in my chest.

As far as I knew, the mother of Dale and Donny Robertson still hadn't been found. At least they were out of the hellhole they'd lived in for several months. Poor babies.

"Enough to make me question why you wanted to lure his children there. Why, Theo?"

"Because I knew it would draw someone else out, and I wanted to be done with this, once and for all."

"You're talking about Wendy," I said. "She's locked up. And you'll still be put away for what you've done."

"I told you I'd never see the inside of a prison cell, Ruby," he said. "And I meant it."

"Brad Steel told us you wanted out. You told me you wanted out."

"I do. I will get out one way or the other."

"Why now?"

"I'm old and tired," he said, "but there's something I have to do first. And I need your help."

CHAPTER FORTY-THREE

R y a n

"Why in hell are you even asking me that? She's a lunatic. You know that as well as I do."

"She's still your mother."

"Do you want a relationship with her?"

"What I want has never mattered to her. Until she leaves this earth—or I do—our lives are intertwined. She's seen to that."

"She won't entangle me in her web," I said. "You can count on that."

"Let's get back to the subject at hand," Joe said. "Like how the fuck you ended up on some rock in the Caribbean in a replica of this damned house."

"You know that your mother got pregnant with Marjorie, and of course Wendy found out. She knew I valued my children more than anything, so the best way for her to get to me was to hurt one of them."

"Larry always said that Talon wasn't meant to be taken."

"He wasn't. Not permanently, anyway. They knew friends and family members were hands off."

I wondered for a moment about Ruby and her cousin Gina, but didn't want to sidetrack the discussion. That had happened much later, anyway.

"Wendy came to me and confronted me about your mother's pregnancy. Then she demanded another payment for me breaking my vow. Five million dollars."

"That's the withdrawal that Jade found," Joe said. "Wendy told us it was a payment for giving up her son. Though that didn't make sense, since Ryan was already seven at the time."

"No. I'd already paid her handsomely to give Ryan up. This was another payment, and again she threatened to take the documents linking me to the trafficking ring public. I felt I had no choice. Then she did the most heinous of things."

"Really? Something more heinous than having a young boy tortured?" I said.

"Not more heinous than that, but she made it very clear to me that she paid Mathias and Simpson off with that five million. She paid them with my own money to take my son!" He clenched his hands into fists. "Wendy would have been satisfied to hurt either one of you, but Talon was younger and easier prey. She paid Mathias and Simpson to take him and... Well, you all know what happened. I don't want to repeat it."

"No." This time, Talon stood. "I'll say it for you. Don't think you shouldn't have to hear what those bastards did to me. They starved me, beat me, raped me, inflicted such pain on me that I couldn't have ever imagined. They told me I was worthless. An animal. They made me beg for food, for a blanket. They taunted me with ice water when I was so thirsty I couldn't even make tears. They made me say that I liked being raped...that I liked their big cocks up my ass."

Our father closed his eyes, cringing.

"A ten-year-old boy! Your son! I cried out for you that first time. I cried out for Mother. No one listened. No one came. My twisted half uncle finally let me go. He did more for me than you did."

My father's head sank into his hands.

"Easy, Tal," I said.

"Oh, hell, no," Joe said. "Our father needs to hear this."

I looked to Marjorie, who was about to burst into tears. "I don't disagree. But she doesn't."

Marjorie choked back sobs. "It's okay. I'm okay."

Joe and Talon both shifted their gazes to our little sister.

"God. You're right. I'm sorry, Marj," Joe said.

"Yeah, me too." Talon sat back down.

She nodded. "I know. I'm okay."

"And I know I was spared because I was Wendy's son." Acid burned my tongue. "Let's get on with it."

Our father lifted his head and nodded. "Daphne was pregnant, and due to the added stress of Talon's kidnapping, she went into premature labor. You all know that Marjorie wasn't expected to live. But our baby girl did."

"And I came home to a new sister," Talon said. This time he had a soft smile on his face. "A beautiful baby doll. The only thing that convinced me there was some good left in the world."

Marj smiled through her tears.

"But Daphne was never the same after that. She did her best, but dealing with a newborn out of the NICU and then with a child who'd been through hell... She loved you both very much, but it was too much for her. She began to fade away, until the mother you knew and loved was no longer there. She couldn't touch any of you anymore."

"Why didn't you get her help?" Talon asked.

"I did, of course. But then someone else got involved."

"Let me guess," I said sardonically. "My mother." This had Wendy Madigan written all over it.

My father nodded. "She began to threaten your mother, and in her already precarious mental state, I couldn't have that. After what had happened to Talon, I knew Wendy was capable of anything. The best way to deal with it was to fake your mother's suicide. Even Wendy never knew."

I couldn't find fault with my father's words. If Wendy had known Daphne was alive, she would have told me. No one knew. Not until we found her on the island.

"All this time, you were the only one who knew she was alive?" I said.

"Yes. Until now."

"Do you think Mother is safe where she is?" Marj asked.

"As long as Wendy's locked up in psych, yes."

"You stayed with us then," Marj said. "Why did you eventually leave us?"

"I stayed until you were of age, baby girl. That was the promise I made to you the day you were born, and I fulfilled it. After that, I knew your brothers would take care of you, and I needed to go to your mother."

"Does she know you?"

"On her good days, she does. I visited her often before I left here. She was in a private compound in Florida."

"How did she end up in a replica of our house on that godforsaken island?" Talon asked.

"Another long story." He sighed. "By the time you all were adults, your mother had made a bit of progress—she remembered the three of you that she had borne, though she was convinced you were still young—and she kept asking to 'go home.' I couldn't actually bring her here, because everyone thought she was dead. Plus, I couldn't risk Wendy finding her. Wendy had uncovered almost everything about me, so I had to use kid gloves where your mother was concerned. So I did the next best thing. When I 'died,' I knew I couldn't move assets around because you kids would go looking. So instead, I took the money earmarked for my bequest to the Fleming Corporation and used it to construct the replica. It calmed your mother to be 'home,' but sometimes she still needed an escape from the sensory disruption. So I built the guesthouse."

"The muted white," I said, more to myself than to my father.

"Yes. Sometimes your mo— Daphne needs to be free from all stimulation, so I'd take her there."

"Why that island?" I asked. "Adjacent to that awful place."

He cleared his throat. "Because I own it."

CHAPTER FORTY-FOUR

Ruby

"If you think I'm helping you do anything, think again."

"You'll help me with this," he said, his tone low, and...was that a touch of remorse?

I must have been imagining it.

"What makes you think I will?"

"Because I'm going to find Gina."

Franticness clawed at my gut. "Gina? After what you did to her?"

"I don't expect you to understand."

"Good thing."

"I can say only this. I was desperate."

"Desperate enough to rape your niece for years?"

"Yes. I know this doesn't make sense to you."

"This wouldn't make sense to anyone, Theo."

"I wasn't in my right mind. I'm still not, but I'm not where I was. Things were...done to me. Things you wouldn't understand."

He had no idea that Brad Steel had told us about the training the three of them had endured. Still, I didn't buy this remorseful act. I knew better than to believe his bullshit. But he knew how to get to me. No way would I say no to finding Gina.

"How could you let them have your own niece?"

"We were short. We had a contract to fulfill."

"God. Do you even listen to yourself?"

"Ruby..."

"Really, Theo. You didn't have to 'groom' her by raping her for eight years. You could have just taken her when you needed her."

"It's not that simple."

"You got that right. None of this is simple. It's sick and twisted."

"I was messed up."

I scoffed. "You think?"

"There are things you don't know, that you wouldn't understand."

"I know the whole story, Theo. You were tortured and raped for money, to learn how to do it to others. One thing was different. You consented to that vileness."

"Actually...I didn't. None of us did."

A brick dropped into my stomach. I said nothing.

"Wendy blackmailed us. All three of us."

I stayed silent a few more seconds until I snapped myself out of my stupor. "What the hell could she have had on you? You hadn't even gotten into anything that bad yet."

"Wendy always had the upper hand. I tried to figure her out over the years. I never could. She was always one step ahead of us."

"What was her failsafe?" I asked, not sure that I actually wanted to know.

"Documents, mostly. They linked us to some bad shit. More than just narcotics dealing."

"Were they forged?"

"Most likely some of them were." He paused for a minute. Then, "She dropped bits of information into the laps of her fellow journalists. They'd come after us, and then they'd hit a dead end. Sometimes they got pretty close, and we had to sweat it out. It was enough that she could keep us doing what we were doing."

"She had that kind of power?" I said the words, but I knew the fallacy within them. She did have that kind of power. I'd seen it.

"Finally, she found out about you, Ruby."

"So what?"

"She threatened you. That was enough to keep me in line."

"Please spare me your father's pride," I said, trying to keep from gagging.

But he didn't elaborate. "Ruby, listen to me. If you help me find Gina, I'll make it worth your while."

I would already do anything to help Gina. He didn't have to bribe me. But what he didn't know wouldn't hurt him. "You don't have anything I want."

"You're wrong about that. I can take you to your mother."

★ ★ ★

I sat immobile for what seemed like hours after the call from my father. I hadn't looked for my mother. Never. I'd been told she was dead when the authorities took me and made me a ward of the state. Then, when they found my father, I'd gone to him. That had lasted about six months before he tried to rape me and I escaped at age fifteen.

He'd told me recently that my mother had voluntarily given me up because she couldn't take care of me. I'd thought he was lying.

He still might be.

But if there was a chance...

If my mother was alive, I had to find her.

My phone buzzed. My contact at the FBI.

"Hey, Finley," I said. "What's the good news?"

"Hey, Lee. Mostly good," he said. "We've found the parents of all the missing children except for young Dale and Don Robertson."

My heart sank. "Oh?"

"I guess I should rephrase that. We did find their mother. We found the remains of a woman near Estes Park. Gunshot wound to the head. No weapon found. She's been identified as Cheri Robertson, the boys' mother."

As a cop, I was used to getting bad news. But those poor little boys... Tears welled in my eyes, but I choked them back. I needed to find out more. "So what now?"

"The local police are treating it as a homicide for now, but it looks more to me like a suicide. Just a hunch, though, because no weapon has been found yet."

Finley had been in the business a long time. His hunches were usually correct.

"The boys are staying with their great-aunt, but she's elderly and can't take them permanently. We'll begin looking for alternate arrangements."

Alternate arrangements...

Two boys with mental health issues, ages seven and ten... The outcome wouldn't be good. Alternate arrangements would be a group home. Adoption was almost unheard of for children past toddler age. And children who would need years of therapy to deal with the trauma they'd experienced? Not likely. Even if one found a home, it was unlikely the brothers could stay together. And they needed each other.

I bit on my lip. "I don't know what to say."

"I wish I had better news, Lee. I do. I know how much you care for the two boys."

"Yeah." I sniffed. "Thanks for the update, Fin."

"You got it. I'll be in touch."

I was supposed to meet my father the next morning. Right now, I had to drive over to Talon's and tell the Steels the news about Dale and Donny. They would want to know. Maybe they could pull some strings somewhere, or at least throw some money at a home to make it a better place for them. I didn't relish telling them this.

Those poor boys had lost their mother after everything else they'd been through.

Swallowing back the sobs that threatened to overtake me, I began driving.

CHAPTER FORTY-FIVE

Ryan

"Say what?" I said incredulously.

"I own the island."

"The one where all that horror took place?" I shook my head.

My brothers said nothing, but their faces said it all. They were numb with shock.

"No. That one is owned by the Fleming Corporation. I own its sister island."

"How in the hell did that ever happen?" I asked.

"Your grandfather bought the two islands from a private landowner before I was born. It was cheap land back then, and your grandfather believed real estate was the safest and best investment. After all, it was limited. He had an idea to build a lavish Caribbean resort someday, but that day never came. The ranch took all of his time, and between production here and other more lucrative investments, he was close to becoming a billionaire, so the islands fell onto the back burner. After his death, I decided to get rid of them."

"So you sold one to the Fleming Corporation?"

"I did. That was before I knew the extent of what they were doing. I didn't see the value your grandfather had seen in real property. I saw only a big expense. Do you know the kind of money it would take to build a resort of that magnitude?"

"Probably around the same amount it took to build a replica of this house behind concrete walls," Joe said, rolling his eyes.

My father ignored the sarcasm. "Much more, actually."

"So Wade, Mathias, and Simpson owned the island."

"They did. Until they sold it to the company they worked for. And even I don't know who owns it now. But I kept the other one. When it came time for me to 'die' and move your mother 'home,' I used the other island to accomplish that goal."

Joe shook his head. "Crazy. You can't make this shit up."

"Why don't those islands appear on our list of assets, then?" Talon asked. Finally, the voice of reason.

"They're owned by a special trust, for which I am the beneficiary. I set it up after your mother's 'death' to make sure she was taken care of. Of course I couldn't let anyone know it existed."

"The Steel Family Trust," I said. "We found it. You bought the Shane ranch and transferred it to the Steel Family Trust. You have loyal attorneys. They wouldn't budge an inch."

"They're well paid," my father said.

"How did you keep all of this from Wendy?" I asked.

"After so many years of dealing with her, I learned how to stay one step ahead of her. She can be manipulated. As you said, Ryan, you and I are her Achilles' heels."

"She told you to keep Anna away from me. I found the note in with your papers."

"That shouldn't have been in there."

"Well, it was."

"I'm sorry."

"They took Anna. Did you have anything to do with that?"

"Of course not! I bought their farm and later set them up to relocate to Hawaii."

"Somehow they got hold of Anna."

"That must have been your mother's doing. If she wanted Anna away from you, that would have been one way of getting rid of her."

My throat burned. So much evil, and a big part of it was sitting across from me behind that fucking desk, looking so high and mighty. The great Bradford Steel.

"You never stopped dealing with Wendy, though," Joe said through clenched teeth. "She's the one who identified your body when you 'died.'"

"Yes. I needed her help with that."

"Why?"

"Why do you think? I couldn't have one of you identify me, because I wasn't dead. I couldn't pay off a doctor or nurse at the hospital and risk a paper trail. She was my only option."

"Maybe you needed a better option," Marjorie said, choking back tears. "Like staying with your children."

"I'm sorry. Your mother needed me. You were all good, strong adults. I knew you'd be okay."

"Okay?" Talon stood. "I was so far from okay. You never let me, or any of us, deal with what happened to me. You swept it under the rug. I needed help, damn it. So did Joe and Ryan. They suffered every bit as much as I did."

"Tal," I began. "You can't equate—"

"It's not a matter of equating anything. Joe suffered with all the guilt of not protecting me. You with the guilt of getting away. It's apples and oranges, but we all suffered, including our mother and sister."

"I did what I thought was best at the time. Your mother

was unwell. Your sister was a premature newborn. Plus, I knew Wendy would interfere if any of it was made public. I couldn't risk any of your lives. I wish I could make you understand."

"How could we understand any of this?" Joe demanded. "Logic flies out the window. You put your allegiance to some stupid high school club above your own family."

"I did not," my father said calmly. "I've explained all this to you."

"But it all comes back to that stupid club," I said. "The money you gave them. The money you promised them and then reneged on. Your association with Wendy. That's what this all boils down to. That fucking club at that fucking prep school. You even lied about that. You told us you had gone to Snow Creek High School. That's why you wanted us to go there, you said. If it was good enough for you, it was good enough for us. We didn't need any expensive private school, right, Dad?"

"You didn't," he said solemnly. "You see what my expensive education cost me."

"You could have left the club."

"I could have. You have no idea how much I wish I had."

"Why didn't you?"

"I was young. I had money. They needed money. They were my friends at one time. I was in love with one of them."

"You did love my mother?" I asked.

"I was seventeen, Ryan. No one understands love at seventeen. She was beautiful and brilliant. She had that fiery spirit that you love so much about Ruby."

"Don't ever say that again," I said, seething. "Ruby is nothing like my mother."

"Your mother does—or did, at one time—have some good qualities." He sighed. "And yes, at that time, I thought I loved her."

I supposed that should have made me feel better about the whole thing.

It didn't.

"I kept in touch with your mother, Ryan, after my supposed death. I had to. But she never knew where I was. I told her not to ask, and she didn't. She will submit to me when pressured."

"How did you get her to agree to that?" I asked.

"How do you think?" He shook his head. "I told her your safety depended on no one, not even her, knowing where I was."

Yes, her other Achilles' heel.

Silence for a few seconds.

Then, "There's something else you all need to know." He looked down at his hands.

"What's that?" Joe asked.

"I'm dying."

He'd said that before but hadn't elaborated. Talon and I hadn't told Joe and Marj. We'd been so angry, I'd nearly forgotten.

"What's wrong?" Marj asked, chewing on her lip.

"Cancer. Pancreatic. I've chosen to forego treatment. I have no more than about six months. That's why your mother needs to stay where she is. She'll be safe, and the Steel Family Trust will take care of her for the rest of her life."

"Is there treatment available?" Marj asked.

"There is, but the odds aren't good. I'm going to prison, treatment or not."

"No." Marj sniffled.

"It's all right, baby girl."

I hated to see my little sister cry—and over our father? My brothers and I weren't buying it. He'd done enough damage to all of us for several lifetimes.

"Marjorie," Joe said, his voice serious. "Our father is an accessory to human trafficking."

"He's right," I said. "You didn't see the people in that dormitory, but Talon and I did. Women were chained up. Little boys were locked in rooms and starved, beaten, and worse. You know as well as we all do what went on there."

Marj wiped a tear from her cheek. "I get it. I do. But I just got my parents back. My mother is off in some place in California."

"We'll bring her here," Joe said softly.

Our father shook his head. "You can't. She needs to be kept hidden."

"Why?"

"Why do you think? If Wendy finds out she's alive..."

Of course it all came back to my evil mother.

"I'll talk to my mother," I said as calmly as I could. "I won't allow her to hurt Daphne."

"No, Ryan," my father said. "She might actually listen to you even more than me, but where Daphne is concerned, there are no guarantees. The jealousy is too much for Wendy. In her mind, Daphne stole what Wendy considered hers. Me. Our life. And then you. Do you think I would have taken your mother away from all of you if I'd had another choice?"

"Honestly, Dad," Joe said, "I'm not sure any of us even know you anymore."

"For God's sake!" Marjorie cried. "Our father is ill. He's going to die. In prison!"

As much as we three brothers adored our little sister,

not one of us reacted to her outburst—a fact that didn't go unnoticed by our father.

"I deserve your resentment. Even your hate," he said with resignation. "And I deserve to spend my last days in prison."

My siblings and I said nothing. Even Marj, Daddy's girl, couldn't deny the truth of his words.

Silence, until—

Someone rapped at the door.

"Come in," our father and Talon said in unison.

This was still Talon's office, after all.

Jade entered. "I'm sorry to interrupt, but Ruby is here. She says she needs to talk to all of us."

CHAPTER FORTY-SIX

Ruby

Telling the Steels about Dale and Donny had taken its toll on everyone involved. I couldn't help shedding some more tears, and even Jonah misted up a bit.

Telling Ryan that I was going to go with my father to find Gina, and that he'd promised to take me to my mother...

That had gone even worse.

I'd gotten him alone after I told the others about Dale and Donny, and then he'd dragged me out by my arm to the deck and picked me up and carried me as if I were a small child all the way to his guesthouse in the back.

He hadn't said a word.

Now, as we entered, he still didn't speak. He let Ricky and Ernie out back, and then he turned to me.

"Undress."

"We're in the ki—"

"Undress," he said through clenched teeth.

"Ryan, I—"

"Haven't I made myself clear? I said undress."

What if I didn't? I'd always obeyed him before. And even now, my muscles were itching to do as he'd commanded. I had to force my fingers away from the buttons on my blouse, my feet from kicking off my shoes.

Melanie's words rang in my mind. You might finally be finding yourself.

Why did I have this urge to obey Ryan Steel? I'd never obeyed anyone in my life. I questioned everything, even my superiors at work if I disagreed with their handling of a case.

Why not Ryan Steel?

His cognac eyes blazed into me, burning into my own. He wasn't joking around.

He meant to be obeyed.

I fingered the collar of my blouse, slowly. The cotton was textured beneath my fingertips. Slowly I trailed down to a button and played with the smooth plastic.

But I did not unbutton it.

"My patience is wearing thin, Ruby," Ryan said.

Still, though my fingers itched to rip my shirt open and let the buttons fly across the tile floor, I stood my ground.

What would he do?

My curiosity was eating me alive.

I knew this man. He was not violent, nor was he evil. He was a good man. An honorable man.

If I was going to consider his marriage proposal—and I'd already pretty much decided—I had to know how he would react to my defiance.

He could not keep me from my cousin or my mother, even if it meant forming an alliance with my father. Surely he would understand that.

He advanced toward me, his gaze never leaving mine. His eyes were hard and determined, and when he lifted his hand to me, I fought back a flinch.

With a touch more gentle than I expected, he reached behind me and tugged on the band that was holding my hair in a long ponytail. My hair fell down my back and around my shoulders.

"You should wear your hair down more often."

"It's not practical." True. But even as I said the words, I knew I'd wear my hair down more often from then on.

"Why aren't you doing as I ask?" he said.

"I'm afraid."

"Of me?"

"No. Not of you. Of me."

He stalked out of the kitchen. A few minutes went by, and then he returned. I didn't ask why he'd left because I already knew. He'd left to get a grip on his temper.

He reached for my hair, and I expected him to yank on it. Instead, he sifted my long tresses through his fingers. "You're so beautiful. What are you afraid of, baby?"

"Of losing myself."

"Losing yourself? With me?"

"Yes. I haven't had a lot of time to think about it with all that's been going on, but every part of me screams at me to obey you. To bend to your will."

"All the time?"

"Well...no. Just in the bedroom." I looked around. "Or the kitchen, apparently. Or anytime you make one of your demands that will lead to sex."

"And that's a bad thing?"

"Yes. I mean, no." I shook my head. "I don't know. It's not...me."

"Maybe it is."

Melanie had intimated the same thing. I opened my mouth to speak, but nothing came out.

"I want you to undress. I like watching you undress. And

right now, I'm hard as a fucking rock for you. I won't deny that I'm angry—no, more frightened, actually—of you going off with your father. And when I get that way..." He laughed softly. "You scare the hell out of me, Ruby. I don't want you going off with your father on some wild-goose chase after your cousin. It's not safe. If you want to look for Gina, I'll help you. My brothers will help you. We have unlimited resources."

I dropped my mouth open.

He pushed my chin upward. "You need to cut ties with your father, baby. For good. It's not safe for you to be around him."

"But Gina—"

"If Gina is anywhere to be found, we will find her." His face became hard. "Now. Undress."

My hands shook as I fingered the same button, working it through the hole.

"Faster."

Why was I quivering so? I wanted to please him. And he was right about me going off with my father. It wasn't safe. I honestly didn't think Theo would hurt me, but he might not protect me either.

Ryan would protect me. And I'd protect him.

We were equals in life. Damn it, just because I wanted to submit to him during sex didn't make me any less his equal.

I smiled at my epiphany. Melanie would be proud.

I grabbed both sides of my shirt and pulled. Buttons went flying across the tile.

He laughed. "I can see I'm going to need to buy stock in the company that makes those tops you like."

"Or just find a good tailor to replace the buttons." I let the shirt drift over my shoulders and land on the floor.

He cupped my breasts through my bra, thumbing my nipples. They hardened under his touch, poking through the cotton fabric. Then, no longer gentle, he grasped the front of my bra and ripped it from my body.

"I'll have to buy a lingerie company too," he said.

I began to laugh but then moaned when he fingered my nipples and twisted them. Tingles raced along my skin—inward, inward—until the little tickle between my legs became unbearable. Ryan bent toward me and took my lips in a searing kiss, all the while playing tug of war on my nipples.

I opened for him completely, willingly, letting his tongue swirl around mine, taking me to another place, another time.

A place where only the two of us existed, where none of the horror of the past several weeks could touch us.

He swept me into his arms and walked swiftly toward his bedroom.

He laid me prone across the bed and tugged my jeans and undies down. I heard the swift zing of his zipper...and then he was inside me, thrusting, pushing, pumping...making me whole.

"God, Ruby. I love you so fucking much."

"I love you too, Ryan," I wailed into the comforter.

Tears welled in my eyes.

I loved him. Loved this man with my whole being. With everything I was.

And I would marry him.

I wouldn't be losing myself. I'd be finding something so much more fulfilling.

I'd be finding us.

With that revelation came the swift convulsions starting in the deepest core of me.

"God, yes," he groaned. "I feel you coming around me, baby. I can't... I'm going to– Ah!" He pushed hard into me, touching my innermost soul.

When he finally stopped convulsing inside my walls, he pulled out and then gently removed my shoes, jeans, and underwear. He turned me so I lay on my back, looking up at him. He was, of course, still fully clothed except that his jeans and boxer briefs were at his knees.

I smiled. "We've been in this situation before."

"So we have."

"I like this," I said shyly. "I like being naked before you, ready for whatever you want to do to me."

He lifted his eyebrows. "I like it too. Very much."

Time for the words. To tell the man I loved what I'd made him wait to hear.

"Ryan, I want to marry you."

He leaned over and kissed my lips. "Finally. You know I wasn't going to stop until you agreed."

"I thought a lot about you when I was taken to the island, especially when I was locked in that room with Juliet. I wanted to get back to you, and I knew you'd come to me. But I didn't want you to come. I knew you'd be walking into danger. I couldn't lose you. I just couldn't." I sighed. "I've been so afraid of losing something else by letting you in. Some part of me. But I was wrong. I'm gaining something. Something wonderful."

"We'll get married tomorrow," he said.

"Not yet. I don't want a courthouse wedding. Let's have something small and nice, like the wedding in Jamaica."

"You want to go back to Jamaica?"

"No. I don't want to go near the Caribbean for a while. But we can have something nice here. At your house."

He smiled. "Our house."

The thought didn't freak me out or give me pause. "At our house."

CHAPTER FORTY-SEVEN

Ryan

I stood and pulled up my jeans. Then I went to the top drawer of my dresser and removed a gray velvet box. I'd purchased the ring a while ago, after I'd given Ruby the sapphire bracelet that had belonged to my grandmother. I'd thought about asking my father about the bracelet, but I'd decided against it. If my mother had been lying and it hadn't belonged to my father's mother, I didn't want to know. The piece was so perfect for Ruby, and I didn't want it tainted by my mother's possible lies. For as long as the piece stayed in our family, it would be an heirloom from my grandmother. Perhaps one day Ruby would give it to our daughter.

God, a daughter.

Or a son.

Hopefully some of each.

Melanie would soon have Joe's first child. Talon and Jade most likely wouldn't be far behind, and neither would Ruby and I.

We hadn't talked about children, but Ruby was a natural mother. I'd seen the way she dealt with Dale and Donny. Even with Juliet. And the way she fussed over her new puppy. She was very nurturing and caring.

We'd talk about it all later. Right now, this amazing woman

had finally agreed to be my wife. She had sat up on the edge of the bed, her naked body gleaming, and I knelt before her and opened the box. "Ruby Lee, I love you with all my heart. Would you marry me?"

I picked up the sapphire ring set in platinum and placed it on her finger. I'd guessed at the size, but it fit perfectly and matched the bracelet.

She inhaled sharply. "It's so big! It's like Princess Diana's!"

"Princess Kate's now," I said.

"How in the world did you know that? You don't seem the type to keep up with the royals."

I chuckled. "Neither do you, actually. I have no idea how I know that. But it doesn't matter. This one belongs to Princess Ruby."

"I'm hardly a princess."

"Sure you are. A beautiful naked princess." I kissed her lips. "I hope you like it. It's not a diamond, but I thought—"

She cut me off with another kiss. "It's perfect. Perfectly beautiful."

"It matches your eyes. Except your eyes are even more dazzling."

"Never in my life..." She choked up.

"What is it, baby?"

"All those years, afraid of men. Keeping them at bay. None of it was a mistake because it all led me here. It led me to you. To a love I could never have imagined in my deepest dreams."

"I, for one, am glad it did."

She smiled, her eyes glassy. "I am too." She pressed her lips to mine.

I opened for her, and we kissed until my cock was hard and I couldn't wait to have her. I broke the kiss and inhaled deeply. "Baby. Please. I need you. I need your ass."

She tensed against me and stepped backward, fingering the ring on her left hand. "Ryan..."

"If you're not ready, I understand. I won't push you." Even as I said the words, I had to bite back the urge to command her.

But when her gaze met mine, I knew. Her eyes sparkled with more fire than the jewel on her finger.

"I trust you, Ryan. Take what you need from me." She lay down on the bed, facedown, grasping the sheets.

I walked slowly to my dresser, found a bottle of lube, and then returned to her, turning her over so she was supine. "I want to see your eyes when I take you."

She smiled. A little shakily, but it was a smile. I spread her legs, knelt between them, and drew my tongue across her swollen, wet folds, inhaling the scent of our combined juices. My cock throbbed for her, but I was determined to go slowly. Not just because she needed me to, but to savor this gift she was presenting me.

After the horrors we'd just witnessed, she was truly gifting me with something special.

I licked her and sucked on her clit until she was near orgasm, and then I squeezed a little lube onto my hand, warming it, before I spread it over her anus. "Relax, baby." I slid my tongue back over her clit as I breached her tight hole with my finger.

She inhaled, tensing.

"Shh," I said. "Easy. Let it feel good."

She closed her eyes, exhaling. "I'm all right."

"I won't hurt you. If you're uncomfortable at any time, just tell me. I'll stop."

"I know. I trust you."

I worked my finger in and out while I continued licking her pussy, bringing her to the edge again. "That's it. Come on. Come for me."

She moaned low in her throat, and her pussy quaked beneath my tongue. The walls of her ass pulsed against my finger, and I nearly lost it. While she was shuddering in climax, I added another finger.

"Ryan! God!"

I shoved my tongue into her pulsing cunt and continued to drill my fingers into her. When her orgasm began to subside, I withdrew the fingers and nudged the tip of my cock against her ass.

"Ready, baby?"

"God, yes. Please. Take me. All of me. I want to be yours."

I placed her legs upon my shoulders, closed my eyes, and slid into her quickly.

She cried out.

"Easy, baby. Tell me when."

Then she opened her blue eyes, and the fire within them scorched my soul.

"Now. Take me now."

I slid out and slid back in. Sweet, tight heaven. I didn't expect her to climax again, so when she started to finger her clit, all thought rushed away in a flash. Only feeling remained— such an amazing feeling of headiness and comfort. Of love.

When she flew into her climax, moaning my name, I thrust inside of her deeply and emptied everything into her— my heart, my soul, my life.

She was my life.

I stayed inside for a minute or two while we both came down from our euphoria. Then, I silently withdrew, walked to the bathroom, wet a wash cloth with warm water, and then returned and tended to my woman.

She smiled. "I can't believe I did that."

"Would you believe it was the first time for me too?" I'd engaged in anal play with others, but never had I actually performed the act itself.

"Why didn't you tell me?"

"I didn't want you to think I didn't know what I was doing." I laughed and lay down next to her.

"She propped her head on her hand and gazed at me with her gorgeous blue eyes. "That makes me happy."

"It does?"

"Yeah. In a way, now I've taken your virginity!" She chuckled and pressed a light kiss to my forehead. Then she cocked her head. "I hear Ernie whining on the deck."

"How can you possibly hear a puppy all the way in here? We're pretty far from the deck."

"Trust me." She stood, looking around. "My shirt is in the kitchen, and it has no buttons anyway." She laughed, walked to my closet, grabbed one of my shirts, and wrapped it over her naked form. "I'll be right back."

I couldn't keep my eyes off her as she walked toward the door and out of my bedroom. I didn't doubt for a minute that she'd heard the puppy. Again, I knew she'd be an amazing mother.

I began stripping off my clothes. I'd be ready to take my fiancée to bed when she returned to me after seeing to her fur baby. I looked around my bedroom. It was good sized, but we couldn't stay here forever. This was a guesthouse, not a real home. It was high time I built my own house on our land. Ruby and I would do it together.

I lay down naked, my cock already hardening again, and—
A scream—
Then, Ruby's voice. "What the hell are you doing here?"

CHAPTER FORTY-EIGHT

Ruby

Wendy Madigan stood in the entryway to the kitchen, dressed in baggy navy-blue sweatpants and a T-shirt. I held a squirming Ernie.

"Funny to run into you here. I just came from a visit with your father."

Before I could react, she continued, "That's an adorable puppy. May I hold him?"

"He needs to go back out," I said, knowing it might end with him whining at the back door again. But Wendy Madigan might very well be the kind of person to twist an innocent baby animal's head off if the spirit moved her. After all, she'd had a child tortured and raped out of vengeance. No way was I letting her near my puppy.

She didn't appear to be armed, but I backed away slowly, depositing Ernie back outside with Ricky. When I returned, I examined her closely.

I was wrong. Something protruded beneath the fabric near her right ankle.

She was armed.

Ryan came running in from the bedroom clad only in boxer briefs. "Ruby, are you all right?" Then he saw his mother. "What the fuck?"

"Watch your language, Ryan. And for goodness' sake, put some clothes on. You're clearly just like your father." Wendy nodded to me. "You too. It's the middle of the day."

"Spare me any information about my father's sex life, please. What are you doing out of psych?" Ryan demanded.

"Really? You think they can hold me there? I could have gotten out long ago, but it suited my purpose to be there."

Ryan slowly inched forward, placing himself between Wendy and me. "Then why are you here? What do you want?"

"I came to see your father, dear. I know he's home."

"How do you know that?"

"Do you really think your father makes a move without me knowing it?"

Ryan and I stayed silent. Brad Steel was smarter than any of us had given him credit for. He'd allowed Wendy to find out what he was doing. That way, she thought they had no secrets, and it gave him the chance to hide Daphne away without Wendy knowing.

I'll be damned.

"She's armed, Ryan," I said.

"No, I'm not."

"You are." My nerves jumped. "You're carrying on an ankle strap."

"I'm not. Where would I get a gun, coming right out of the loony bin?"

Good question. However, according to both my father and Ryan's, this woman could make just about anything happen. Ryan strode cautiously toward her, and my belly clenched. I didn't think she would harm her own son, but she was a madwoman.

He pushed up both legs of her sweatpants and found the

strap. He took what looked like a derringer and examined it. "Loaded too. Any explanation, Mother?"

"That's between your father and me."

"What do you want with him?" Ryan asked.

"Closure," she said. "This all ends today, Ryan."

"According to him, you broke a promise by telling me that you're my mother." Ryan said, seeming to enunciate his words more than usual. "You've been the cause of everything horrible that's happened to my family. My father won't see you."

"Oh, he'll see me."

"What makes you think he will?"

"You'll make sure of it."

"No I won't."

In a flash, she pulled another piece from inside her roomy waistband and pointed it straight at me. "You will. Because if you don't, I'll send your girlfriend here to hell."

Panic bubbled in my gut. She'd fooled me. The ankle derringer had been a decoy. The woman was good. Once I noticed the one she'd wanted me to notice, she knew I'd stop looking. Rookie mistake. I should have known better than to take anything about Wendy at face value.

She'd played me just like Brad had been playing her, letting her find out what he wanted her to find out, and then she didn't look any further to find Daphne.

"Don't you dare harm her, Mother," Ryan said through clenched teeth, his hands in front of him, "or I'll never speak to you again." He began inching backward toward me.

"I don't want to harm her, darling. But I need to see your father. So take me to him and make sure I get in to see him, and your girlfriend lives."

"Don't listen to her, Ryan," I said. "Don't unleash her on

your brothers and sister. They've been through enough. We can handle this right here and right now."

Martial arts moves rushed through my brain. I could easily take Wendy down before she could pull the trigger...if I could just get close enough. I needed her to focus somewhere else. On Ryan. I had to keep him talking.

"Give me the gun, Mother."

"I can't, my sweet son. I'm sorry."

"If you love me the way you say you do, please give me that gun."

"I do love you, Ryan. More than you'll ever know."

"Then take the gun off Ruby. This has nothing to do with her."

"Wrong," Wendy said. "This involves all of you as well as your father. And I can assure you this. Someone is going to die tonight. It's up to you, Ryan, who."

Up to him? I resisted the urge to wipe the sweat out of my eyes. Perspiration framed Ryan's face, and he held himself rigid. Surely Wendy could see how tense he was, how frightened.

"The only person who might die tonight is you, Mother. You will not hurt Ruby. Now hand that gun to me." He extended one hand to her.

"I might very well be the one to die tonight. And after I have the closure I seek, I will not hesitate to accept my fate. But to get to that point, I need to see your father. You will take me to the main house and get me in to see him. Now go get dressed, and bring her some pants."

"Hell, no. I'm not leaving her."

"Have it your way." She gestured to me. "We'll come along with you."

CHAPTER FORTY-NINE

R y a n

"I'm sorry," I said to my father and my siblings once we'd gotten into the main house. "I had no choice."

My esteemed mother was holding on to Ruby, the gun pressed into her side. Ruby was a trouper. She'd mouthed to me that she could overtake Wendy while we were walking to the main house, but I'd begged her with my eyes not to. She must have understood. I would not take a chance with Ruby's life.

I couldn't lose her. Not when happiness was finally within reach.

Ruby hadn't flinched once, and though I knew she was nervous, no one could tell by her demeanor. This was far from the first time she'd been held at gunpoint...although perhaps the first time by someone as psychotic as my biological mother.

"We understand," my father said, turning to Wendy. "How did you get out of lockup?"

"Come now, Brad," she said. "You know me better than that. You know I could have gotten out at any time."

My father nodded, clearing his throat. "Yes. I know."

"Look," I said. "I got you here. Now state your business. My family has been through enough these past several weeks. Let's just get this over with."

"I am part of your family too, Ryan," she said. "Or have you forgotten?"

How I wished I could forget. But I didn't voice the words. I couldn't risk setting her off, not when she still had Ruby at gunpoint.

"Your business is with me," my father said. "Let Ruby go."

"My business is with all of you," she said. "I came to finally get what's coming to me."

"You said you wanted closure," I reminded her.

"Yes," she said. "By the time I'm done here, we will all have closure."

My brothers and sister had been uncharacteristically silent throughout this. My father had called them all to the house, and now they stood together on one side of the large office, Jade holding tight onto Talon's hand. Thankfully, Melanie had gone to a doctor's appointment and wasn't available.

Joe's eyes betrayed his thoughts. He was getting ready to strike.

I shook my head slightly at him, hoping I was conveying my message for him to stand down. I couldn't risk Ruby being hurt. But I knew my big brother. Once he set his mind to something—

"Take that gun off my daughter, Wendy."

Marjorie gasped as we all turned our gazes to the doorway. Theodore Mathias stood there, gun in his hand, pointed at Wendy's head.

Wendy didn't turn around to face him. "I figured you'd show up, Theo. You're the one person who's better at covering his tracks than even I am."

"I learned from the best. Now get that gun off my daughter,

or I'll splatter your brains all over this room."

"You don't have the balls," Wendy said.

Was she kidding? This was the man who'd spent the better part of his lifetime stealing and torturing people, and she didn't think he had the balls to shoot her? According to what he'd told Ruby, she'd been the reason for his downfall. He should have been thrilled to do her in.

"You have something in place, don't you, Mother?" I said. "A failsafe. Something that will take my father and Mathias down if you die."

She smiled. "I always knew you were brilliant, darling."

Of course. That was why my father and the others hadn't blown her head off years ago.

I regarded my siblings. Talon's face had gone pale. Blankly pale. He'd come face-to-face with the last of the men who'd tortured and raped him all those years ago, and paralysis seemed to grip him. Jade snuggled into him, rubbing his shoulder, soothing him.

But no one was here to soothe Joe. His eyes were on fire, his jaw tensed.

Somehow, I had to stop him. Right now, a gun was still trained on the woman I loved, and I didn't trust the woman wielding it any more than I trusted the man threatening her.

"Mother," I said as calmly as I could. "If you love me as you say you do, please let Ruby go."

"My audience is with all of you," she said. "I will not."

"You will," Mathias said.

But before he could strike, Wendy moved with snakelike stealth.

I jumped at a gunshot.

A bullet from the gun previously pointed at Ruby had

shot into Theo's stomach. He fell backward in the doorway, blood gushing from his abdomen. The metallic and raw stench permeated the air.

Did the woman have eyes in the back of her head? He could have easily shot her first.

It dawned on me then. My mother hadn't been lying when she said she might be the one to die today.

She was ready to go, which made her even more dangerous.

I had to figure out what her angle was. She might be planning to take all of us with her.

Ruby fell to her father's side and checked his pulse. He muttered some words to her that I couldn't make out, and then he grabbed her other hand.

"It's weak," she said. "I don't think he's going to make it."

Then Joe struck. He swiftly walked forward and raised his foot.

"Joe!" I said.

He lowered his foot, staring at me.

"Let him," Ruby said, dropping her father's hand. "His pulse is barely there. He's as good as dead already."

But Joe backed off as Talon seemed to reanimate. He stepped forward as well. "You bastard!" he yelled. "You fucking bastard." He knelt down and pulled up Theo's left sleeve, showing the tattoo of the phoenix. "Fucking evil bastard." He curled his hand into a fist, ready to punch.

Joe got a grip then. He pulled Talon up. "He's gone, Tal. It's over."

Talon stood, nodding. "You're right. This isn't who I am anymore. Good riddance."

I kept one eye on my mother. She still had a gun in her hand, though she wasn't pointing it toward anyone at the moment.

Ruby sat, staring into nothingness. I knelt down to her. "Baby, are you okay?"

She nodded, gave a sniffle, but no tears came. "He saved my life."

"Maybe. I'm not sure Wendy was going to hurt you."

"I'm calling 9-1-1," my father said.

That jarred Wendy back into action. She pointed the gun right at him. "You're doing no such thing. Besides, he's already dead. I never miss."

He put the phone down. "All right. We'll do this your way, Wendy. What do you want?"

She closed her eyes for a second, still holding the gun, and then opened them. "I was always jealous. Even when I was a tiny child, before I even met you, Brad. Did you know that one of the symbols in alchemy for copper is what we know as the female symbol?"

"Wendy," my father said, "what are you—"

"Did you ever figure it out? The symbol on our rings?"

"The symbol was nonsense," Brad said. "Now put that gun down, and we'll talk about this."

"Even then I knew I was different. My parents didn't understand me. The future lawmakers never understood me. Only you, Brad. You knew exactly what I wanted and needed. Sometimes I dream about how you used to tie me—"

"Damn it, Wendy!"

"Our son was conceived in love." She glanced to me. "You do know that, don't you? I was bound for your father's pleasure when he planted the seed that became you."

"Wendy!"

She turned back toward my father's voice, laughing.

"Oh, you knew me, Brad. You destroyed me, and I let you. I coveted you. We were soul mates. But you never figured out the symbol."

"It's the symbol for evil," I said. "The devil." I pointed to Mathias's now motionless body, blood seeping all over the hardwood floor. "He figured it out. So did Larry Wade. And so did we."

"Of course you would, my brilliant son." She smiled—a sickeningly sweet smile, right out of a slasher flick. "I contorted it a little, but at its center was the symbol for female...and the symbol for evil. But it's also the symbol for copper. Do you know why that makes sense?"

No one spoke. I looked around. Jade was holding on to Talon. Joe's eyes moved back and forth. He was planning something. If I could take my mother down, get that gun away from—

"Copper is a soft metal, you know. Soft, like a female. Not hard like iron. Like a male."

I gathered my courage. My father might be shot in the process, but—

"And copper turns green. Green, the color of envy and jealousy." She smiled again. "I never was good at sharing. I always envied others who had what I wanted. So I took things. I made people do things to suit my purposes. But it was never enough. Never enough, Brad, because I never really had you. I could have forced you to be with me long ago. We both know that. But I didn't. I wanted you to come to me, to admit the truth about our connection. That we were always meant to be together." Her fingers tensed around the firearm. "I'm done waiting. Now I will finally have what is mine. You and I are going to be together, Brad. The two of us and our son. One way or the other."

Panic shredded through me. She truly was crazy. Not that I'd ever doubted that revelation. But then—

The memory...

Never. I'll never believe that. You'll pay for this, Brad. I swear to God you'll pay.

What she'd said after that emerged into my mind. I could hear her say the words in the voice I now knew as I pressed my ear to my bedroom door.

You and I are going to be together, Brad. The two of us and our son. One way or the other.

My father was no longer enough for her. She wanted us both.

I suppressed a shudder as my skin chilled around me like a cloak of ice.

She turned to me slightly, still holding the gun at my father. "It's your choice, my beautiful son. Either we're all together in this life...or the next. What will it be?"

"I'm not sure"—my voice cracked—"what you mean." In reality, I had an inkling of exactly what she meant. My heart thundered, and a wave of sickness traveled through me.

"Darling, you're not a simpleton. You're the son of two geniuses. You know very well what I mean. You choose. Do you and I and your father stay together here, without the rest of these people, or do the three of us go together into the next life?"

My blood pulsed in my head like a freight train. Was she truly asking me to choose whether my siblings or I lived?

No.

I'd just found happiness with Ruby.

But Talon was healing. Joe and Melanie were having a

baby. Marjorie was young, so young, only twenty-five years old.

My father was dying anyway, and Wendy's life wasn't worth anything to anyone.

But my life...

Damn it, I wanted my life! I wanted a life with Ruby, with our children, with my brothers and sister. My true siblings, even if I'd been borne to this lunatic.

"Wendy," my father interjected. "I will go with you into the next life. Our son deserves a life here. Don't put him through this."

"Why not? It's time to find out where his loyalty lies."

"You're asking him to choose between his own life and his siblings. It's not fair."

"What if the three of us go off somewhere together?" I said, the words coming out rapid and jumbled. "You don't have to kill my brothers and my sister. We can keep them away from us. You guys will leave us alone, right?"

"O-Of course," Marjorie stammered. "Won't we?"

My two brothers and Jade said nothing. Even Joe was speechless, his face pale and his eyes...something different about his eyes, something I'd never seen before. Fear. He was scared.

"No," Wendy said. "My mind is made up. I deserve closure, and this is how I aim to get it. I've waited long enough to have my family together, and I won't have anyone fucking it up for me."

I knew the answer in my heart before I voiced it. Talon, Joe, and I had recently had a conversation about the horror Talon had lived through. He'd told us that he'd have gone through it willingly if it meant saving us from the same fate. Joe and I had both agreed. We would do the same.

And I would do that now.

"I choose my siblings." My voice was strangely monotonous, but it didn't crack. "They will stay. We will go."

"No!" Ruby and Marjorie shouted together.

Ruby stood, leaving her father's lifeless body and running to my arms.

"Easy," I said, holding her tightly. "I love all of you."

Joe finally came out of his stupor. "We're not going to let this happen, Ry."

I eyed my mother, who still had the gun trained on our father. "It's okay. I'll be okay. May I please say something to each of them first?"

"Of course, dear."

"Joe." I looked to my big brother, trying to draw in his strength.

"Hey, you wait. This isn't going down like this," Joe said. "I'll fix it. Somehow."

Always the big brother. But he couldn't fix this. "We don't have a choice. You're having a baby. You need to live. You're the bravest and strongest of all of us, and you're going to be a hell of a father, Joe. Tell your child about me. Please."

I shifted my gaze to Talon, wise beyond his years mostly from losing his innocence at such a tender age. "And Tal, you'll always be my hero. Be happy. Please. Every minute."

"How can I be happy if I lose my little brother?"

"Because you have your wife. You have Joe and Marj. You'll have children someday."

"Ryan, please!" Ruby shouted.

"Baby. Try to understand."

She gulped back sobs, still holding on to me as I turned to my sister, who represented youth and joy. "Marj, you're so young, so full of life and energy. Find your life and live it. For me."

My baby sister said nothing, just bit on her lip, sobbing.

I turned to the woman I loved. She nodded slightly at me, and an understanding passed between us.

"I love you, baby," I said. "You've shown me things I didn't think were possible. I'll always love you."

My mother pointed her gun at my heart.

I pushed Ruby away as hard as I could, and she fell to the floor, sliding against her father's body.

I closed my eyes and absorbed every fear I'd known in my short life. What would it feel like to die?

"No." My father's voice. "You will not kill our son. Not before you kill me."

"Fine."

I opened my eyes. She pointed the gun back at my father. I breathed a sigh of relief without meaning to.

"You may have your last request, Brad. You know I could never deny you anything."

She fired the gun, and my father slumped over his desk. Screams echoed, as if they were being yelled from the top of Pikes Peak.

My mother turned to me.

And a shot rang out.

CHAPTER FIFTY

Ruby

The gun my father had held on Wendy fell from my hands and clattered to the floor. This was not my first kill, but taking a human life—even a human as psychotically deranged as Wendy Madigan, who was bent on shooting the man I loved—was never easy.

I had hesitated. For a split second I'd thought Wendy wouldn't harm Brad Steel, and I'd been so relieved that she'd taken the gun off Ryan. I hadn't been able to save Ryan's father, and I'd have to live with that.

I ran to Ryan and fell into his arms. "Are you all right?"

He didn't say anything, just held on to me and wept against the top of my head.

Marjorie had run to her father. I had no idea what the other two Steels and Jade were doing. All I could do was hold on to Ryan and never let go.

He sniffled. "You saved my life, baby."

"I'm sorry I couldn't save your father. I was so relieved when she took the gun off of you that I didn't act quickly enough. I'm so sorry."

"He's ill. He would have gone to prison. You saved him suffering through cancer while he was incarcerated."

That didn't make me feel any better. "I hoped you

understood that I was going for my father's gun. I should have taken it sooner, but when she pointed that thing at you..." I choked out a sob.

"It's okay."

"No, it's not. I'm sorry."

He kissed the top of my head. "You're here. I'm here. My brothers and sister are here. That's what matters right now." He pressed his lips to my forehead. "We both lost fathers today. Fathers who weren't anything close to what they should have been...but they both ended up saving our lives."

The truth in Ryan's words flowed through me.

I hadn't put any stock into my father's promise when he first uttered it, but he had fulfilled it.

I'm going to make sure she doesn't hurt you.

He had made sure Wendy didn't hurt me.

I wasn't sure how to feel about that.

The others buzzed around us, making calls, crying, hugging each other, but it was all white noise in a haze of relief and gratitude. I just held on to Ryan.

For a long, long time.

★ ★ ★

Both my father and Ryan's were cremated with no ceremonies. As far as the world was concerned, Brad Steel was dead already, and no one mourned Theodore Mathias. Not even Jade's mother, Brooke Bailey, who'd once fancied herself in love with him. Jade had told her the truth about Nico Kostas aka Theo Mathias, and though Brooke hadn't believed it at first, she finally did when Talon corroborated the story.

Wendy's failsafe had appeared in the form of ironclad

documentation linking my father, Tom Simpson, and Larry Wade to the human-trafficking operation—a moot point since they were all dead. Oddly, Brad Steel was not implicated in any way. Perhaps she had never planned to bring him down, despite her threats. In her own warped way, she had truly loved both him and Ryan.

Talon and Jonah had begun working on arrangements for their mother to come back to Colorado. Now that Wendy was no longer a threat, they could have their mother close by.

And who else had turned up? Trevor Mills and Johnny Johnson, the high-priced PIs who had disappeared in the middle of the Steel's investigation. It had been Wendy, not my father, who had kept them away with doctored documents accusing them of crimes. They'd gone underground and used their own know-how to prove that the items had been forged.

My father had told me something right before he died, something I shared with Ryan a few days later when we'd all recovered a bit from what had occurred.

Gina's dead. I'm sorry.

I hadn't been surprised. But at least she was at peace now. He'd also pushed a piece of paper into my palm. I'd pocketed it and forgotten about it until after both men had been cremated. It had been through a wash cycle, but thankfully I could still read it.

The paper had a name on it. Diamond Thornbush. My mother. And an address.

Ryan and I were headed there now.

My nerves were jumping.

We drove into a trailer park on the outskirts of Grand Junction. Would she be there? Was this one last hoax by my father?

I had no way of knowing, but I had to check it out.

We drove up in Ryan's pickup. The yard was well kept, and a plastic lawn chair sat outside. The stoop built of rickety wood creaked as I walked up to the door. I knocked once. Then again.

The door opened, and a woman stood there in capri pants and a worn T-shirt.

A woman I recognized, though her hair was silvery white now and a few lines marred her pretty face.

"Mom," was all I said.

Her blue eyes—the same color as my own—widened. "I think I'm seeing a ghost."

"It's me. It's Ruby."

"It can't be. He told me you were..."

"I'm here."

"Your father forced me to leave. He said he could give you a better life. He said... I didn't believe him, but he threatened both of our lives, and he meant it. I figured the best thing for me to do was disappear and make you a ward of the state. I thought they'd protect you. God, I've always regretted that day! How could I give up my baby?" She grabbed me into a hug.

I inhaled. She still smelled the same. Like honeydew melon.

"I'm sorry I didn't look for you. I was told you were dead."

"Sweetie, it's okay. Did they protect you? Did you have a good life?"

I couldn't bear to lie to her. At least not yet. "I've had a good life. And it's about to get better." I motioned to Ryan. "This is my fiancé, Ryan Steel."

"Ms. Thornbush," he said. "It's good to meet you."

"Honey, call me Diamond. Or Didi. Or Mom. Whatever you want."

"Mom sounds good." Ryan smiled that killer smile of his.

His words rang true. He'd call her Mom. One of his mothers was dead, and the other lived in a cloud of fantasy and wasn't really his at all. So he had an opening for a mother. I'd be happy to share mine.

"Well, come on in! It's not much, but it's mine."

"Mom," I said. "You don't have to stay here. We're going to take care of you now."

"You bet," Ryan agreed.

Finally, all the pieces of my life were coming together.

EPILOGUE

Ryan

My brothers stood beside me in the backyard of the main ranch house. I wore a black suit, no tie, and Talon and Joe both wore blue-gray. The weather had cooperated beautifully for November. The orange and gold colors of fall surrounded us, and the temperature was a balmy sixty-two. Ground had been broken for Ruby's and my house, and it would be ready by spring.

Today was Thanksgiving Day, and Ruby and I hadn't been able to think of a better day to exchange our vows and begin our life as husband and wife.

We had so much to be thankful for.

Next to Talon, having put on a little weight and wearing suits matching his and Joe's, were Dale and Donny Robertson, soon to be Dale and Donny Steel. Talon and Jade had begun the process of adopting the two brothers. Having a father who truly understood what they'd been through would be healing for all three of them. Melanie had started working with them, and she'd arranged for them to see a preeminent child psychologist in Denver twice a month. And they'd have another sibling soon. Jade had announced their good news at our rehearsal dinner the previous evening.

In chairs, waiting for the bridal party, were Ruby's mother,

Diamond Thornbush, who looked radiant in a soft-pink dress; Brooke Bailey, finally without a boot on her leg, wearing soft beige; and Bryce Simpson, Joe's best friend, holding his toddler, Henry. A few other close friends completed the scene.

The string quartet began playing, and Marjorie strode forward first, wearing light blue. Jade followed in a slightly darker hue, and then Melanie in darker yet, her baby bump apparent, as Ruby's matron of honor.

The quartet slowed, and those in chairs stood for the bride's entrance.

I was expecting a vision in white, but Ruby never failed to surprise me. She entered in a dark-blue silk dress, completing the graduation of color. Her skirt billowed in the soft breeze blowing through the leaves on the trees and scattering several to the ground in a colorful collage. Her nearly ebony hair had been curled and piled loosely on her head. On her arm sparkled the sapphire bracelet, and on her left ring finger, the engagement ring.

The red and gold leaves on our maple trees rustled. The crisp and cinnamony scent of autumn permeated the air.

And my love strode toward me, smiling.

The End of the Steel Brothers Saga

MESSAGE FROM HELEN HARDT

Dear Reader,

Thank you for reading *Unraveled*. If you want to find out about my current backlist and future releases, please like my Facebook page: **www.facebook.com/HelenHardt** and join my mailing list: **www.helenhardt.com/signup/**. I often do giveaways. If you're a fan and would like to join my street team to help spread the word about my books, you can do so here: **www.facebook.com/groups/hardtandsoul/**. I regularly do awesome giveaways for my street team members.

If you enjoyed the story, please take the time to leave a review on a site like Amazon or Goodreads. I welcome all feedback.

I wish you all the best!
Helen

ALSO BY HELEN HARDT

DISCUSSION QUESTIONS

1. The theme of a story is its central idea or ideas. How would you characterize the theme of *Unraveled*?

2. Discuss the following characters in depth. How have they grown throughout this nine-book series? Talon, Jonah, Ryan, Jade, Melanie, Ruby, Marjorie

3. What do you think of Brad Steel's decision to fake Daphne's death? How did this decision shape the events in the Steel Brothers Saga?

4. What about his decision to fake his own death? What might have been, had he stayed with his children?

5. What kind of life do you think Ryan and Ruby will have? Will Ruby ever return to detective work?

6. Compare and contrast Brad Steel and Theodore Mathias. Neither were model fathers, yet they both ended up saving their children in the end. Did they love their children? Did Mathias have any good qualities at all?

7. Do you believe Wendy truly loved Brad and Ryan? Was she capable of love? Discuss what might have led to her psychopathic illness. What might her parents have been like? How was she able to lead a life as a journalist? What might her psychiatric diagnosis be?

8. How did you feel about Talon's adoption of Dale and Donny Robertson? Will this make Talon's life more difficult? Why or why not?

9. Do you believe Theo loved Ruby? Was proud of her? Why or why not?

10. Discuss how Brad handled Wendy. What do you think his true feelings for her were?

11. Ryan applies the virtues of strength and wisdom to Jonah and Talon, respectively. Do you agree? What virtue would you apply to Ryan?

12. Discuss the antagonists of the saga. What role did each play? Theodore Mathias, Tom Simpson, Larry Wade, Wendy Madigan

13. Was Brad Steel an antagonist as well?

14. What might the future hold for all the Steels now? Will Marjorie find love? With whom?

ACKNOWLEDGEMENTS

The end has come! This was a difficult book to write, both intellectually and emotionally, as I had to tie up all the loose ends and bring ultimate happiness to the Steel family as they so deserved. I made myself cry more than once as I unraveled the remaining secrets. We said goodbye to some characters (and let's face it—we won't miss them) and hello to some new ones as Ruby and Ryan—and all the Steels—finally got their happily ever after. I'll miss the Steels, but I'm excited about my next series, which is already taking shape in my head.

A very special thank you to my husband, Dean, a PADI-certified SCUBA diver, who helped me with Ryan and Talon's diving scene. Thanks so much to my amazing editors, Celina Summers and Michele Hamner Moore. Your guidance and suggestions were, as always, invaluable. Thank you to my line editor, Scott Saunders, and my proofreaders, Jenny Rarden, Amy Grishman, and Chrissie Saunders. Thank you to all the great people at Waterhouse Press—Meredith, David, Kurt, Jon, Yvonne, Jeanne, Renee, Dave, and Robyn. Special thanks to Yvonne Ellis for the beautiful cover art for *Unraveled* and for the whole series.

Many thanks to my assistant, Amy Denim, for taking care of business so I can write. I couldn't do it without you!

Thank you to the members of my street team, Hardt and Soul. HS members got the first look at *Unraveled*, and I appreciate all your support, reviews, and general good vibes.

You all mean more to me than you can possibly know.

Thanks to my always supportive family and friends, and to my local writing groups, Colorado Romance Writers and Heart of Denver Romance Writers, for their love and support.

Most of all, thank you to the diehard Steel fans who have stuck with the saga through nine books. I hope you found the ending worth the wait!

ABOUT THE AUTHOR

#1 *New York Times*, #1 *USA Today*, and #1 *Wall Street Journal* bestselling author Helen Hardt's passion for the written word began with the books her mother read to her at bedtime. She wrote her first story at age six and hasn't stopped since. In addition to being an award-winning author of contemporary and historical romance and erotica, she's a mother, an attorney, a black belt in Taekwondo, a grammar geek, an appreciator of fine red wine, and a lover of Ben and Jerry's ice cream. She writes from her home in Colorado, where she lives with her family. Helen loves to hear from readers.

Visit her here:
www.facebook.com/HelenHardt

CHAPTER ONE

Heaven.

He had to have died at last, and somehow—*God only knew how*—ended up beyond the pearly gates.

Garrett Hawkins didn't bother questioning the admission details beyond that. No sense in tempting Saint Peter, or whoever the fuck was standing watch today, into checking notes and realizing a mistake had been made. Wouldn't do the guy any good. At this point, Garrett wasn't past blowing the balls off anyone who told him he had to leave.

The deal was, heaven was nothing like the scene they'd taught him in summer Bible school. No sugar-spun clouds. No bad haircuts. Not a single angel with a half-tuned harp.

Heaven was silk sheets, his tongue on the inside of Sage Weston's left thigh—and her sigh in response.

"Garrett! Damn it! Higher. Please...higher!"

He chuckled and sank a soft bite into her tawny flesh. "Is that any way to talk in heaven, sugar? Ssshhh. You're gonna get us tossed out."

He spoke the last of it as he crossed to her other thigh, making sure his mouth brushed over her glistening pussy in the process. Christ, how he wanted to stop there, and he thought about it as he watched new drops of arousal on her sweet pink folds, but there'd be time to return for all that sweet ambrosia and then some. In heaven, they finally had all the time they needed.

A shiver claimed the new skin that he began to suckle and lick. "Sergeant Hawkins, you're making me insane!"

"I hope so."

"Ohhhh! Bastard!"

"Mmmm. You taste like cream and honey."

"*Garrett!*"

He sighed and laughed again. "So impatient. So greedy." He trailed his lips toward her knee, inciting another protesting moan from the silk ribbons of her lips.

"Impatient? You've been teasing me like this forever!"

"And isn't it fun?"

"I hate you."

"No you don't."

"I'm leaving."

"No you aren't."

He was about to taunt the inside of her ankle when she really did yank it away from him. He raised his head in question, only to have the back of it bonked by her other foot as she swung that over the edge of the bed as well. "Sage! Hey!"

"Don't pull petulant on me, Garrett Hawkins. I invented it, and I do it way better than you."

He almost smiled. She'd been a ball of sass and fire since they'd met at that dive bar in Tacoma, and he loved her a little more every time she rekindled the attitude. It also helped him choose the next words out of his mouth, issued as a deep and heated growl.

"You're not going anywhere, Ms. Weston."

Her eyes widened, ablaze with bright peridot shock. She pushed out her chin and tacked on a smirk. "Is that so, Sergeant?" She stepped into a little white thong trimmed in sexy-as-hell pink lace and then tugged a white tank over the bra he hadn't gotten the chance to get off yet. "Why don't you watch me?"

He laughed, though the sound was made of anger, not mirth. Thanks to the countless sessions with Shrink Sally, as he'd affectionately come to call the poor woman assigned to "fix" him a year ago, he also recognized that the rage was directed at the guy in the mirror across the room, not the woman in front of him. That only tripled the resolve for his next action.

Without giving her any warning, Garrett hooked two fingers into the lace at her hip and pulled hard. The surge of her body returning to his side matched the rush of joy in his blood and the roar of arousal in his cock. This was where she belonged. This was so fucking right.

With a grunt, he twisted the panties tighter. The fabric gave way in his grip. It fell away, exposing her incredible golden hips. Sage gaped at him, though he took that from her too, ramming their lips together while he pulled her and flattened her to the bed again.

"I've got a better idea," he growled, rolling his hips so she felt every pounding inch of his erection. "Why don't *you* watch *me,* sugar?"

She did just that, jerking her brilliant green eyes wide as he jammed both her arms over her head and lashed them together using a bungee cord off his mission pack. For a second he wondered why his pack made it to heaven with him, but he was too grateful to question the issue for long. It was just as weird that her old bed had made it too, a wrought-iron thing he'd never liked much, thanks to its headboard full of fancy curlicues that tangled with each other like a damn tumbleweed. But right now he was really grateful for the thing.

The two bungee hooks fit perfectly around a couple of whorls in the headboard.

With a frustrated whimper, Sage wrenched her arms. "Wh-What are you doing?" She craned her neck, exposing the nervous drum of her carotid artery. "Garrett, why—"

"I told you." He stated it with steeled calm. "I'm not letting you leave. It was a mistake to do that the first time. It was a mistake not to go after you. So now I'm keeping you right here, safe with me. Just trust me, my heart. You're going to be very happy." Without preamble, he tore her tank top down the middle. "And very satisfied."

Her breath caught on a sexy-as-hell hitch. "My hero." The sigh changed her voice, too. Her tone transformed from incensed to breathless but climbed into a strained cry when he took care of her front bra clasp with one deft snap. "Oh... mmmm!" she moaned, arching into the fingers he trailed around her dark berry nipples, pushing her puckered fruit up at him. He gave into the craving to sample one with deeper intent, pinching the nub and then pulling. Hard.

"Shit! Ohhh, Garrett!"

Damn. Her startled cry made him want to try it on the other nipple, and he did. Both her areolas were red and irritated now, their tiny bumps standing in attention around the distended peaks at their centers.

To his perplexity—to his shame—he got painfully hard.

That didn't stop him from getting greedy. With both his hands on her tits now, he couldn't resist tugging on both her beautiful nipples at the same time.

"Damn it!" she screamed. "Garrett, th-that hurts! Oh God! Oh...mmmmm..."

She fell into an enraptured moan as he made up for the

man-pig behavior, soothing each breast with long, tender licks. That wasn't a huge help to his aching body. His cock had gotten harder and hotter, throbbing between their stomachs. He shifted a little so he could dip his hand between her thighs, intending to continue his gratitude by giving her pussy a nice little rubdown—but what he discovered had him grinning in delighted shock. Her tunnel was gushing, warm, and creamy for him. She took one finger, then two, then three, her walls secreting more tangy juices all over his skin. Her arousal revved his mouth again. He pulled his tongue back from her nipple and bit into the stiff nub.

Her whole body bucked off the mattress. "Garrett! Hell! Why are you doing that?"

"Because you like it," he said while working a fourth finger into her. With one of his thighs, he shoved hard on the knee he'd just been worshipping, opening her legs wider. "Because the pain makes you wet for me."

He dragged his mouth against hers again, but this time she didn't let him into her wet heat. She opened her lips only enough to get her teeth into his bottom lip.

"Damn you to Hades," she whispered, her teeth still anchored in his flesh. He yanked back, licking at the flesh she'd torn open, though he did it on a dark smile.

"Too late, sugar. I think my passport's already got that stamp."

She looked adorable as she rolled her eyes. "Which is why you're in heaven with me?"

Before he answered that, he did kiss her. He did it thoroughly and desperately, possessing her tongue in bold sweeps, permanently tangling his essence with hers.

"We've always lived on borrowed time, my heart. We

both know it." He gripped her leg, hooking her knee around his shoulder. "Which is why I'm going to fuck you hard now. Which is why you're going to let me. Which is why you're going to love it."

Her eyes shimmered with tears. Her lips lifted in a misty smile. "Okay."

His penis surged against his fingers as he guided himself to her tight, glistening entrance. "Tell me you want it."

"I want it, baby." Her obedience didn't land him in heaven again. It made his whole heart and soul turn into paradise. "I want your hot cock, Garrett. Please. Now. Deep inside me."

"Yeah." He swirled the searing precome around his bulging head and then pushed himself into the first inch of her channel. "Oh yeah, sugar."

"Garrett." Her strident gasp filled him. "Garrett... Garrett..."

"Soon, my heart. Soon."

"Garrett! Fuck, man. Open the door!"

What the hell?

His fiancée suddenly sounded like his best friend. Correction—his demanding, door-pounding, subtle-as-a-linebacker *ex*-best friend.

"Hawkins! Get your ass out of bed and answer the door!"

Garrett slammed his eyes open. Squeezed them shut again. "No." His voice was a croak, absorbed by the grimy walls of the room in this no-name Bangkok hotel he'd checked into last night. He looked down, trying to piece together this new truth. The precome was real. One of his hands was still wet with the stuff. His fingers were also really wrapped around his aching boner as he lay beneath a mound of cheap, cloying sheets.

Sage was nowhere to be found.

Of course not.

Because she was dead. For a year, two months, sixteen days, and almost twenty-four hours now.

The knives of grief, all ten million of them, reburied in his chest. As he gulped through the resulting dearth of air, he raised his clean hand to his chest, scrabbling for his dog tags. More accurately, he searched for the gold band that hung on the chain between them.

Though his head ordered him not to do it, he slipped his ring finger back through the band. For one wonderful extra moment, the knives went away, and he relived the day he and Sage had picked out the jewelry... The day when he'd thought it would soon become a part of his wardrobe for good.

He remembered every detail of how beautiful she'd looked. It had been a brilliant late-spring day. Her hair was a cascade of light-brown sugar that earned her his favorite nickname, falling against the freckled shoulders that peeked from her pink sundress. But her smile... Ah, he remembered that the best. Her lips had glistened with her joyous tears and quavered with her soft whisper.

I can't wait until you get to wear it for good. I can't wait until you're all mine.

A month later, he'd gotten the phone call from Heidi Weston that upended his world forever. The woman who was preparing to become his mother-in-law stammered that he needed to come over right away. He'd actually packed a bag, thinking Sage had been hurt, maybe badly, judging by the sound of Heidi's voice. He was prepared to stay long enough to get as much info as he could about her condition and then head for the base to force himself onto whatever flight was headed anywhere near Botswana. When he'd walked in to see the Casualty Notifications Officer and the Chaplain sitting there, on either side of a sobbing Heidi, his knees hit the floor along with his pack. Only half their words had reached his brain through his roaring senses. *Tribal warfare...region unexpectedly unstable...van sidetracked off the main road... likely rebels...found burned out...nothing but ashes found...*

He swallowed hard and pulled his finger back out of the ring. As expected, his brain crowed while his heart screamed on the torture rack of memory. He waited, breathing hard, for the agony to end. He begged the wounds to bleed hard and fast, letting the anger get here and turn the pain into a scab. After that, he'd be able to move again. To function again.

"Hawk! Damn you, man!"

Anger moved in on the grief. Thank fuck. Fortunately, nothing got him more pissed off than Zeke's mommy-hen act. After rolling from the bed, he tugged on his briefs and then stumbled across the room. The dirty light and sound of traffic beyond the thin shutters told him it was about midday. Or maybe his growling stomach did.

"Okay, why are your panties in a wad?" He glanced at Zeke after opening the door, the last of his grogginess obliterated by the lime green and banana yellow print of his friend's tacky tourist ensemble. Z's khaki shorts were baggy on his timber-log legs, which marched him into the room before Garrett could even think about reclosing the portal. "Don't tell me you're bored, with all of Bangkok out there for the taking. We don't roll on this mission until nightfall. That gives you at least five hours to work your flogging arm and your kinky cock through a lot of cheap tail, my friend. I'll bet the girls at Club Subjugate are missing you something fierce, Sir Zekie."

"Sir Zekie. Aw. That's cute, honey." The guy kicked the door shut behind him. Zeke's six-foot-six frame was only a couple of inches taller than Garrett's, but the man's mountainous build intensified the effect of his stature, especially in this room seemingly designed for people half his size. "As much as Chelsea and Chyna like my side-by-side spanking special, shit like that gets boring by myself. You tried the fun-filled dungeon field trip once. Think you want to sign up this time?"

Garrett snorted and flopped on the bed again. His friend wasted his breath with the memory. Yeah, he'd gone. Yeah, he'd tried it. Z had gotten him in a weak spot around the six-month mark after Sage's death. He'd been desperate to forget the pain for a while, hoping "the magic of BDSM," as Z called it, would help. More urgently, he'd been hoping to figure out the kinky-minded demon that had been crawling in the back of his imagination since...well, he knew since when. The secret would go with him to his grave. An occasion, God willing, that would come sooner than later.

Needless to say, he'd scratched the itch just fine that night. Or, as truth would have it, hadn't scratched. That part wasn't such a state secret, and it justified the response he tossed at his friend.

"You really think that offer's relevant?"

Z shrugged. "Lots of water has passed under your bridge, dude. Maybe commanding a sweet little subbie will fire your rockets this time around."

"No," Garrett snapped, "it won't."

"Right. Because you'd rather stay here and just beat off after your wet dreams about Sage."

"Fuck off."

"It's been over a year, Hawk."

"Fuck *off*."

"Fine." Z pulled the faded Yankees cap off his head, revealing the miniature broadcasting station literally sewn inside it, before scrubbing a hand through his tumbling dark-brown hair. "Turns out free time just got drastically cut, anyhow. That's why I'm here collecting your sorry ass."

He'd just cracked open a lukewarm soda and was about to take his first guzzle. He stopped the can halfway to his lips and shot a quizzical look across the room. "What do you mean, 'cut'?"

Zeke dropped into the room's sole chair and shrugged. "CENTCOMM received a line of new intel. Seems we're gonna be more effective going in to rescue these girls as the badass uniformed machines we've been trained to be instead of a bunch of American dorkgasms looking for some girl-next-door-type pussy." He stretched his tree trunk legs out, crossing them at the ankle on the foot of the bed. "So as soon as you get your ass dressed, we're buggin' back to the embassy. They're gonna let us change and get haircuts and shaves." He scratched the scruff on his jaw. "Thank all that's holy."

Garrett cracked a dry smirk. "You sure it's not just because you blew our cover with that shirt? Maybe somebody with half a brain looked at you and realized no normal person, even a dorkgasm, would willingly dress in that."

Z looked at his getup with a frown. "What's wrong with the shirt?"

"Oh c'mon. It's hideous. It's not yours, is it? Central gave it to you, right?"

"Yeah, uhhh, right."

Zeke followed up his hasty answer by cracking one of the shutters and feigning interest in the activity outside. Garrett rose, shoved into jeans and a plain white T-shirt, and listened to the scene that his friend beheld. Scooters zoomed, taxi drivers argued, bicycle bells dinged, and food sizzled. All in all, it was a typical day in Bangkok—probably the same kind of day that ten American aid workers had been enjoying just six weeks ago, prior to boarding a plane for their mission in Myanmar.

The five men and five women had never arrived for their flight. Two days later, the men had been returned unharmed, spelling out the abductors' purpose with more clarity than a Soi Cowboy titty-bar sign. Undercover CIA agents had been rapidly inserted on the case, and sure enough, after ample questions were asked and money was tossed around, they were invited in on the newest trend for discerning American businessmen looking for a good time in East Asia—American girls who would do everything a native girl would, at exactly the same price.

Tonight, the assholes running the racket were going to find a new surprise waiting for their sorry dicks. Garrett's blood surged with the anticipation of delivering that surprise. He hoisted his pack, slipped into his "lazy American tourist" loafers, and then cocked his head at Zeke.

"You gonna sit there moping because I called your shirt a fashion disaster? Come on, Fashion Sparkle Barbie. Let's depart this fair establishment."

To his perplexity, Zeke didn't budge. He closed the shutter with unnerving calm. "Just another sec, Hawk."

The gnat of suspicion in his senses morphed into a mosquito. "What is it?"

"Sit down. There's one more thing we gotta discuss."

The mosquito started biting. "No," Garrett snapped,

"there isn't."

Without looking back at Z, he went for the door and had his hand on the knob as his friend's rejoinder hit the air.

"You don't get to load up for the op unless we drill down on this."

Garrett watched his fingers go white around the knob. Officially he and Zeke were equal rank, but his friend's tone clearly pulled a top dog on him. That only meant one thing.

"Franzen put you up to this, didn't he?"

Z lowered his legs and then balanced his elbows on his knees. When he lifted his head, deep assessment defined his stare. Garrett almost rolled his eyes in return, but he caught sight of himself in the dusty mirror over the bureau. His hair, a nice gold when it was clean but the color of a worn dishrag now, was as rumpled and long as Zeke's brown waves. His eyes also looked like rags—blue ones that'd been used on muddy boots. His skin was sallow. He hadn't slept well in over a year, and it showed in every wrinkled, grungy inch of him.

He scowled. If he was Franz, he'd likely have a few concerns about adding his name to the mission roster too. It didn't matter that he'd proved himself on over three dozen ops in the last year. He knew the concern was for *this* trip. He didn't have to be told why. But he'd put up with the formality anyway.

"Yeah, okay," Zeke conceded. "The captain and I had a brief talk about your involvement on this one. You're a key piece of the team, Hawk. We could really use you. Even though you look like crap, your reflexes are still the best on the squad. You're able to make smart snap judgments even if the shit gets thick and the op goes sideways."

Garrett dropped his pack and leaned against the door. "Are you planning that much on this one taking a detour?"

"No. Hell, no." Like the protest about the shirt, his friend's answer flew out suspiciously fast. "It's just—we're gonna be deep in the forest on this one, G. I wouldn't be surprised if we come across fucking Jurassic Park or something."

"You know Jurassic Park is technically off the coast of Costa Rica and not Thailand, right?"

"It's sick that you know that."

"It's pathetic that you don't read."

His buddy's stubbled chin gave way to a grin. "And it's nice to see you getting pissy about something." In a murmur, he added, "Maybe there's hope for your humanity after all, Hawkins."

"Shut up and get to your point."

Zeke let the smile fall. "Okey dokey, Prince Charming." He rose and crossed his arms. "To be frank, the captain and I are concerned about your focus on this one."

A needle of irritation joined the knives in his chest. "That's never been an issue before."

"We've never been called to retrieve hostages before."

Garrett snorted. "Yeah, what about that? The Rangers and Delta getting their nails done or something?"

"You think I know or care? The op is what it is. More importantly, the hostages are what they are. American women, many with fair hair and eyes." Z leaned forward, intensifying his gaze. "I need to know you can keep the emo lockbox down on this, G. Complete objectivity. These girls will be terrified and traumatized, but our main objective is to get them to safety using any means necessary. The conditions will be shitty and the time frame will be worse. I need to know you can do that. I need to *know* you're gonna maintain your edge."

Garrett pushed off the door in order to take a determined

stance. He bolted his stare into Zeke's, unwavering in his purpose, unblinking in his concentration.

"You think I'm gonna go cookie crumbs on you because some girl *looks* like her?" He shot out a bitter laugh. "You think that alone would do it? You really don't remember what Sage and I had, do you?"

"Why do I need to? You're doing the job to stellar perfection for me and half the world."

"And?"

Zeke's eyes slid shut and his mouth tightened, his version of contrition for the accusing words. "You haven't let go of her. You still got that goddamn ring hiding between your tags, which should be secured to your bootlaces, assface, *not* your sorry neck. I can write you up faster than—"

Garrett cut him off with a derisive laugh. "Oh, that would be entertaining."

"I've got genuine concerns here, Garrett."

"Got it, Oprah. Can I get you a tampon for that now?"

Zeke closed the space between them in one wide step. His jaw went harder beneath his stubble. "What you can do, damn it, is look me in the eye and swear to me that you're squared with the personal shit and are solid to go on this op."

Garrett notched back his shoulders and set his own jaw. He confronted the stare of his friend again. He'd seen those hazels oiled with booze, gunned with adrenaline, bleary with exhaustion, afire with exhilaration, and likely a thousand other things. But this was one look he always treated with respect. This was a stare of the guy who would be at his side out there in Jurassic Land, holding the gun that could save Garrett's life. He'd be counting on Garrett to do the exact same.

"I'm solid," he said. "And you know I'd tell you otherwise,

Z." The last shrouds of his dream fell away from his mind, dissolved by the salvation of mental mission prep. "Let me help you get these dick lickers."

Zeke didn't answer at first. He subjected Garrett to another minute of silent scrutiny. That was all right. He'd been through it before. What he couldn't handle were the daggers Z kept trying to add to the others in his chest, to open up new parts of him so he could "move on" and "live again." That wasn't going to happen. Not today, not tonight, not anytime soon. The knives were his. The pain was his. As long as both were still there, he still had some part of her with him.

Finally, Zeke cracked a lopsided grin and chuckled. "All right, you charmer. Let's get the hell out of here. You need a shower, dude. Bad."

"Says the chump who smells like ass."

Zeke knuckled him in the shoulder. "You sure you got everything in that pack? Did you get your Jane Austen novel off the back of the toilet?"

"I've got your Jane Austen at the end of my dick."

"Hawkins, your dick is probably as blue as your balls by now." Z snapped his fingers. "Hey! Maybe that's where you should secure your tags, yeah?"

Garrett rolled his eyes, scooped up his pack again, and discreetly adjusted the body parts his friend had insulted with screaming accuracy. His cock was still doing its best to relax, though his balls throbbed in frustration, sending shots of erotic what-the-fucks at him. They were supposed to be enjoying some post-jackoff serenity right now, and the bastards were hitting the target damn well at reminding him of that every two seconds.

Get used to it, guys. He sent the dismal promise as he and

Zeke made their way out into the sultry Bangkok afternoon.
Life isn't going to change anytime soon.

This story continues in Saved: Honor Bound Book One!